GW00838375

UNCONQUERED WARRIOR

UNCONQUERED WARRIOR

THE WOMARA SERIES
BOOK ONE

J. L. NICELY

Copyright © 2018 J. L. Nicely

All rights reserved. No part of this publication may be reproduced, distributed, or transmitted in any form or by any means, including photocopying, recording, digital scanning, or other electronic or mechanical methods, without the prior written permission of the publisher, except in the case of brief quotations embodied in critical reviews and certain other noncommercial uses permitted by copyright law. For information address JLNicely.com

For permissions address:

Braintree Press

830 Park Row #825

Salinas, CA 93901-2406

Published July 11, 2018

Printed in the United States of America

ISBN: 978-1-7321010-0-5 pbk

ISBN: 978-1-7321010-1-2 ebk

Library of Congress Control Number: 2018948801

Cover Art by Godfrey Escota

This is a work of fiction. Names, characters, places, and incidents either are the product of the author's imagination or are used fictitiously. Any resemblance to actual persons, living or dead, is entirely coincidental.

Within every woman lies a warrior and, with the call to change, a voice of courage.

CONTENTS

1

THE BEGINNING

Her name was Rowan, but no one ever spoke it after that spring morning when she and a small group of women and young girls, baskets in hand, left the village early. Walking into the surrounding forest, they wandered leisurely among the trees, searching for the first of the mushrooms on the forest floor. The children following them ran among the foliage, squealing in delight as they played hide-and-seek. Rowan's steps were light, and she smiled to herself as she walked arm in arm with her favorite aunt.

"Did I not see you in the pasture yesterday with the boy who tends the goats?" Her aunt squeezed her arm and smiled.

Rowan felt her face flush bright pink at her aunt's question. She smiled shyly as the other women exchanged glances and grinned at each other.

I know why you tease me. How self-assured was I only recently with my bold words about how little value boys have—yet today he looks completely different to me. How did I not see before how deep brown his eyes are?

Rowan had barely seen the passing of thirteen summers, but her aunt beamed at her blossoming womanhood and the first flush of infatuation.

The group continued along the well-worn paths that bordered the marshes, watching the morning mists dissipate as the sunlight penetrated them. As the women drew closer to the banks, lurking, dark forms rose from hiding places among the reeds. The pack of men, their bodies covered in animal skins and adorned with helmets of winged feathers or animal horns, appeared as ghostly images in the retreating fog.

The women froze in shock, staring at the half-dozen raiders advancing toward them. A chill of terror ran through Rowan's body as she realized that her group's escape was blocked, before she regained her senses enough to yell, "Run!"

The smaller children still playing in the trees scattered into the woods, and the men watched them escape as they scrambled to close the distance between the women, falling upon them and knocking them forcefully to the ground.

Rowan was rooted in fear at first but then forced herself to spring for an opening as the raiders restrained the older women. Attempting to get to her feet, her aunt screamed as a raider forced her back down to the ground. Turning away from her escape, Rowan reached for a large rock at her feet and threw it her aunt's assailant, striking him. His malevolent look immobilized her in fear as he lunged to grab her by her hair, pulling her close to him. The smell of wet animal skins filled her nostrils before his blow knocked her several feet, driving the breath out of her body. Crawling on her hands and knees, she gasped as the men bound the hands of those they had captured and the women began to wail while straining against their binds.

"Stay quiet." A raider held a long knife to the throat of a young girl. "Cry out, and she dies," he snapped, as the girl's mother whimpered her compliance.

As Rowan, too, was bound and pulled roughly to her feet, her mind raced while she frantically scanned the woods for any rescuers.

No! No! Where are our people?

The men herded her into the group of women and young girls all roped together, then jerked the binds to force them to start walking. Rowan fell to her knees and was dragged briefly. As she struggled to regain her footing, she drew the men's attention. "Watch out for that one," a raider said, pointing her out. "She's a fighter."

The men moved them quickly toward the inland waterways. Loading their captives, they paddled swiftly and silently to waiting longboats, hidden in a remote part of the bay, and then hastily set sail for the open sea. Rowan watched the horizon, seeing her lands diminish in the distance, until there was only the empty plane of the ocean. Sick with anguish, she doubled over and retched.

Once she righted herself, she moved closer to her aunt, huddling against the crying and moaning women who clung together on the decks, and whispered, "We must escape. Will our kin come? How will they find us?" Her aunt did not answer; she merely gave her niece a look of utter resignation that filled Rowan with more despair.

When they were far out to sea, the men turned their attention to the women. The leader spoke aloud, startling them: "You are destined for the slave markets, but that does not mean we cannot enjoy you until we reach the ports."

For a brief moment, Rowan stared at him, not understanding

his meaning. The women instinctively tightened their circle as the older women, including her aunt, were torn from the group, hauled screaming to the center of the deck, and assaulted before her eyes.

Rowan watched in shock, witnessing the darkest side of men's brutality for the first time in her young life. She tried to cover her ears against the women's awful cries as she desperately surveyed the boat for an escape route.

The men turned their attention to the remaining girls, now cowering behind Rowan, while the mothers begged for mercy for their daughters. As the men advanced, Rowan ordered the girls, "Stop crying and stand up behind me." Her commanding tone halted the men in their tracks, and they looked questioningly at each other.

"We are virgins," Rowan said directly to the leader. "Will we not draw a higher price if we are untouched?"

He eyed her and nodded to his men with a smirk on his face. "She's right, and isn't she the clever one, too? Leave these alone," he ordered his men.

Rowan drew a breath of relief when the men turned away, but the blood drained from her face when the leader then turned back to her and added, "You may have delayed the fate of the others, but I will take personal pleasure in breaking that strong will of yours, even if you fetch a lower price."

The men laughed as he dragged her from the clinging girls and stripped her naked before them. Her aunt turned away, sobbing uncontrollably. Rowan bit her tongue to prevent herself from crying out when he pushed her onto her stomach over a large barrel. Tears streamed down her cheeks and she clenched her fists against the searing pain as he raped her, but still she did not make a sound.

When he had finished with her, he strode away without giving her another look.

Rowan slid to the deck, hunched in pain. She could feel blood trickling down her legs as she collapsed in a ball against the barrel. Her aunt's expression was wild as Rowan watched her being dragged to her feet, about to be passed to another man. The boat rocked on a large wave, and, in a brief moment of distraction, her aunt broke free of the men's grasp and ran to the side of the boat. She locked eyes with Rowan for a moment, then turned away, looking out to sea.

Rowan's shout of protest froze in her throat as her aunt climbed over the rail and flung herself into the water, sinking below the waves. Rowan rose painfully to her feet, only to receive a sharp slap to her face that knocked her back down as the men panicked to contain the women.

Rowan would have jumped with her aunt if she could have, but now she could only keep repeating in her mind, *I must survive.*

They arrived in a large port several days later and moored in a great harbor. Broken in spirit and body, the women and girls were unloaded and forced to stand before a crowd of jeering men on the docks. Most stood trembling, heads lowered, unable to meet the piercing stares of the crowd, but Rowan stared defiantly into the sea of faces.

The younger girls were sold first, to the local pleasure house, where men would pay the highest price on their first night. The men judged and haggled over the other women as they were sold like prized cattle, one by one.

Then Rowan was pushed to the front. "This one's got spirit—and she's strong, too," the auctioneer announced.

A man assessing her lewdly bought her quickly. As he was leading her away, Rowan glanced back over her shoulder to take a last look at her kinswomen, her eyes tearing.

I fear we will never see each other again.

Tied to the back of an open cart, Rowan watched the strange landscape pass by as they traveled many miles away from the seaport town to her master's village. Upon their arrival, she was put to work. Every day she labored under the burden of the daily tasks of fetching water, gathering wood, washing, and cleaning. Her only constant was a gnawing hunger as she lived off the leftover scraps from the family meals and whatever she could scavenge. She was beaten severely several times for what her master deemed her defiant attitude.

One day, passing her master's wife mirror, she caught her reflection and gasped. She hardly recognized herself. Her body was gaunt and soiled, her red hair was dull and matted against her head, and her eyes, which once had sparkled, were now sunken above dark circles.

At night she fell exhausted onto her bed, a makeshift pile of hay in the pens that held the animals. She had fought hard when her master had first assaulted her, but she no longer resisted his nightly visits; she lay stiff and unmoving, staring numbly at the ceiling, as he took his pleasure.

She forced herself to focus on her lost family, always thinking of escape and avenging her dead aunt, and was comforted by the promise she had made to her master: *There will come a time when I will make you and your family suffer as I have.*

2

A NEW DAWN

Two and a half years passed. Rowan was a young woman of almost sixteen, but she felt old beyond her years as she stood gazing out to sea, waiting for her master to finish retrieving his goods from the trade boat. This land was not her home, but its closeness to the ocean and her knowledge that her lands lay across the great expanse of water gave her a small degree of comfort. These factors also renewed her memories of grief surrounding her first arrival to the seaport, and her thoughts turned to all she had lost.

One day I will escape this land and return home, or death will set me free trying.

She watched her master in the distance, talking with an elderly man, and as they looked in her direction, they exchanged coin. Her heart pounded as they advanced toward her.

"This is your new owner," her master announced while Rowan looked at him, stricken with panic.

Stepping toward her master, she begged, "Have I have not served you well? Please, please do not send me away."

"I have already kept you too long. You are barren and have no value to me if I cannot increase my holdings with children," he answered disdainfully.

I might not have been barren once, she thought, *but how could this starving body now ever bear a child?*

Rowan flushed and could not hold back her words: "I thank the gods there are no children born to man such as you and this slavery."

"Hold your tongue, you red-haired bitch." Her master moved to strike her but held his hand when he eyed the man beside him casting a critical stare. "You are fortunate that your new master cares little for any additional mouths to feed beyond his immediate family and wants only a slave for his elderly mother."

They departed immediately, and Rowan fought back the bile rising in her mouth as they journeyed toward the great mountain range and farther from the sea. They traveled inland for days to the home of her new owner and finally arrived in a strange new village. Rowan's stomach churned as she gazed around at the remoteness of the region and the fringes of the wild forests beyond.

The same endless duties of cleaning and fetching filled her days under the watchful eye and constant grumbling of her master's mother. Her master had no interest in her sexually but used her for barter with the men of the village. She stood with fists clenched in anger, waiting as he offered her body as a bargaining piece.

She experienced brief moments of solitude when, not under the indiscriminate demands of her master's mother, she was allowed to roam unconstrained to gather the old woman's favorite berries or herbs along the edges of the forest. In those moments, she used her time wisely, scouting her surroundings under the guise of completing the tasks.

One morning began as usual, with a barking command from the sullen grandmother. "Girl! I am hungry. Fetch me some berries near the river."

Rowan rushed to comply. She wandered into the forest and spied the first of the spring mushrooms emerging through the bed of pine needles at the base of the trees. Dropping to her knees to pick one, she drew it to her nostrils, breathing deeply the familiar scent of earth and musk, which spurred memories of home and family. As she let the mushroom drop from her fingertips, her shoulders sagged, but she could not cry, feeling beyond tears with a heart hardened from years of hard work and abuse.

Shouts in the distance pierced the silence of the still forest, causing Rowan to leap to her feet as she ran to the edge of the clearing. A spiral cloud of black smoke rose like a beacon in the sky. She gasped. The village was under attack.

Dropping back into the forest for cover, she waited anxiously for a long time before moving silently along the edge of the trees toward the village. Most of the huts were ablaze, and the dead lay where they had been struck down, many in their own homes, caught in the surprise attack of a rival clan seeking vengeance. Small children were crying and wandering among the fallen, searching for mothers who had hidden them in a pile of skins or inside baskets of food. All the men were dead, and the women who had escaped to the woods wandered dazed, staring in disbelief or sitting in shock beside a dead master, husband, or child.

Rowan walked slowly among the devastation and stopped before the ruins of her own hut. Inside, she looked down dispassionately at her master, his wife, and his mother, crumpled in a heap where they had been felled. She startled when her master stirred, groaning as he lifted his head toward her, pleading, "Help me."

She drew back, turning to view the chaos of the burning village, and realized that none was alive who could challenge her freedom—none except he. She weighed her options: *Will I wait to be claimed by another and enslaved again, or will I escape now?*

She clenched her jaw as she moved to hover over him. His eyes went wide when she drew his knife. She hesitated a moment; then hatred filled her, and she drove her blade into his neck, feeling it strike bone. She staggered backward, momentarily horrified at her gruesome act, as blood pulsed from the wound. But then, remembering the terror he had inflicted upon her, she spat on his dead body.

As she retreated from the hut, she thought, *So, this is what I have become: a murderer. My fate is now cast, for I have killed, and from this day forward, I cannot look back. I must flee, for I would rather live in the wild, among the beasts, than live another day in bondage.*

A chill ran down her spine at these thoughts, but her resolve to escape overpowered her fear as she moved swiftly to gather whatever supplies she could. The remaining survivors watched numbly, following her movements with dazed expressions. Rowan stared back, momentarily moved to compassion for those remaining, some of whom had shown her kindness in the past.

Her gaze traveled to the mountains and the unknown interiors of the great forest that stretched beyond. Knowing the outcome that would befall the women and children who remained here, she called out, "To stay here is to die, and I will not surrender to death! You must make your own choice, but those who wish to live may come with me."

No one spoke; no one asked where they would go. They silently rose, gathered what they could carry, and followed her out of the burning remains of the village.

The journey took almost a week. The small band, consisting of thirty-four women and children, moved closer to the mountains along a great valley, scavenging what they could eat along the way. For the most part, they walked in silence, but Rowan often contemplated the magnitude of her words when she turned to survey her bedraggled companions.

I see the dread in their faces, and they turn to me for answers. Can I even fend for myself, let alone this entire group? And how will we survive? Those dark crests in the distance, growing closer with every mile, may make my blood run cold, but I will not let them see my fear.

When they finally stood before the immense woods, which provided a natural barrier against the valley and the mountain range beyond, the women trembled.

"These woods are said to be haunted by the spirits of the dead," one woman cried aloud. "We cannot go in there."

"We will," Rowan answered forcefully. "And we will ask the spirits for their protection. For we are shadows of our former selves, and I hope they will welcome us."

Survival was the single-minded purpose of the escaped band in those first years as they penetrated deep within the old-growth forest. In the times that followed, Rowan would think often of their first night, of cowering around a single, small fire while the descending night deepened the looming shadows surrounding them.

The women learned to build their shelters next to large fallen limbs or the exposed roots of trees. They lashed together long branches, covering them with boughs and leaves to purposely blend them into the vegetation. Everyone foraged for food on the ground and in the trees, which provided a rich supply of insects, worms, grubs, edible wild plants, and birds' eggs. The small dams they built in the streams and pools of water trapped crayfish and small fish. With nets made of cloth, they scooped snails and frogs from the banks while handmade snares caught a variety of small animals and wild birds.

Women grew small gardens in patches where the light penetrated the tree canopy. One of them became the healer for the group. Some tended the fires and cooked, while others wove baskets or cured the skins of animals. Rowan and a few women practiced with bows and arrows, or small, sharpened tree limbs made into spears, to become proficient in hunting the larger forest animals. Even the children had a role in the daily tasks of living by shooting game with slingshots, or by gathering fallen acorns, plants, or wood for cooking.

Fear of the deep forest turned to reverence at the beauty and tranquility of their new world. Their phantoms became the spirits of the trees, who whispered to them in hushed voices through the rustling leaves upon the wind as their gods' faces emerged from the twisted bark of trees. They created their own spiritual life, honoring the ancient practices of those nature gods, and called upon the forest and animal spirits who lived within, believing that all things of nature possessed a living essence that watched over them.

They shaped their world while huddled around communal fires in the evenings, preparing their meals together and sharing the stories of the places they had once lived. Most of the women had stories similar to Rowan's: captured from their homes and taken as slaves. Pain still etched their faces when they spoke of lost loved ones and beloved lands.

One night, Asha, a woman with skin the color of brown earth and amber eyes, and one who rarely spoke, told her tale.

"I come from a great land of open plains and hills where the most fearsome beasts live. There are animals as high as mountains that trumpet their warning cries with long trunks, and a great cat is the king of all beasts," she exclaimed, as the women's eyes grew wide. "I was the daughter of our tribal shaman. As I was traveling to the village where I was to be married to the leader's elder son, the slave traders abducted me and I was sold at the slave markets along the coast. It has been many years since my capture, and each time I was sold, I was moved farther and farther from my homeland. I know I will never see my family again." She turned away for a moment, eyes glistening with tears in the firelight.

Then she turned back to look at Rowan. "You will be my family now."

Rowan nodded back to her, resolved to an unfamiliar but growing emotion as she looked into Asha's eyes and around at the faces of the women, filled at last with hope.

This forest is our home! I care about these women. We belong together.

Almost a year had passed before Rowan and a few chosen women ventured from the forest to make the week-long journey to trade along the fringes of the closest villages and townships. Baskets woven from pine needles, bird feathers for adornment, and the skins of river otters provided their wares for barter. Rowan felt a small measure of security in her new world but shivered again with renewed panic as she approached the towns of men. At the outer perimeters, she stopped as she glanced with momentary trepidation at the women beside her, before turning away to steel her nerves, telling herself, *I will not show them my fear.*

Her dread soon seemed unfounded, however, as the people of the township paid no particular mind to a few nameless female visitors to their markets. The women's sidelong glances reassured each other as they secured the first of the trades. Rowan breathed a sigh of relief as they departed unimpeded and carrying desperately needed provisions.

On future trips, they always returned with essential supplies, and often with other women. The displaced and abandoned found their way to the growing settlement within the forest. Many were widows living a bare existence after the loss of a husband; others were abandoned slaves or castoffs of their clans and not missed. They came alone or with their children and what few possessions they had. No woman in need of sanctuary was turned away.

The group accepted that the outsiders started naming them the Womara, the women who live without men. Those early survivors would not know that they had resurrected an order of women with dominion over their own lives, and generations later, with thousands strong, they would be a warrior clan that none of the men in the surrounding regions would dare to challenge.

3

BEYOND THE MOUNTAINS

Seanna stood with her fellow scouts at the edge of the Womara valley. "Which way will you travel?" Thea asked her, already knowing Seanna's answer as she turned to view the gray mountains rising in the distance.

"To the mountains again? There is nothing there but old animal trails," the other scout teased her.

"Maybe so," Seanna answered, "but that is the way I go." She mounted her horse and added, "I will return by the new moon," then waved her farewell.

She had to ride for several hours to reach the mountains from the far eastern border of her valley. The high peaks that rose up in front of her formed an impenetrable barrier to the continent to the north. The looming crests always drew her back to explore when she patrolled the far perimeters of their territories.

In truth, she had made that her quest, following a common belief among her people that what lay beyond those mountains was a vast, uninhabited region, and beyond that the great port cities of a far northern continent accessible only by sea.

To Seanna, the peaks presented an obstacle to conquer. She tolerated her fellow scouts' teasing, but she was driven by a certainty in a tale of her people from a hundred years ago, and in the words of her great-great-grandmother Rowan, that one from the other side of the mountains had lived among her clan.

"Let's go." She nudged her horse forward and stared up at the ascent as the mare climbed sure-footedly, accustomed to the narrow, stony animal trails. A light wind blew loose wisps of Seanna's hair around her face as she felt the cooler air sweep across her cheeks. The only sounds she heard were the echoing clip of her horse's hooves on the path as she reached out to run her hand over the rough surface of the great granite rocks.

She took a long inhale of the pristine air into her lungs, feeling as if she could breathe more deeply in these higher places. It was the reason she often camped for days on a rocky ledge in the crags that provided a place to look down upon her world. As a scout, first for her clan and now also for the newly formed alliance warriors of the neighboring clans of men, she pursued her adventuresome yearning to explore the unknown outside her valley. Although she traveled through a wide range of territories beyond, something deep within her called her back to the mountains time and time again.

Seanna's searches did not uncover much. What life she found was scarce and clung precariously to the rock ledges: low-lying shrubs, birds that fluttered to their high nests, a few snakes, rabbits, and an occasional mountain goat, but not much more.

She explored for most of the day and camped on a wide ledge overnight. In the fading light, she built a small fire and sat watching the moon rise over the pinnacles as the nighthawks called in the distance. She leaned back against the granite wall, thinking, *This high place gives me solace and freedom from the demands of duty. Here, I am alone where no one can find me.*

Seanna's mother had insisted upon placing her in service to Lord Arden and his alliance warriors, believing it an opportunity to know their kind better. *Not such an easy task, Mother, when I must so often face the judging stares and whispered slurs of men from the outside clans. Perhaps our good relations with the nearest clans falsely bolster us. We must remember that not all men are so welcoming.*

In the morning, she rose stiffly from the hard rock and stretched her body, gazing upward at the higher points, bathed in the pink-and-gold light of a mountain sunrise. The changing hues moved across the mountainside, when something caught her eye: a shadow cast in the distance by one rock face upon another appeared distorted. It looked like a ridge that she had not noticed in the flat, gray light of the prior overcast day.

What is that?

She moved to another vantage point, keeping one hand grounded on the rock wall as she leaned out, away from the ledge, she saw that the rock face appeared to have depth. The distortion was a thousand feet above and would be a hard climb, but her heartbeat quickened at the expectation of a closer examination.

Seanna carefully traversed the path along a narrow ledge, leading with soft words her skittish horse, who sensed her excitement.

The massive granite face appeared completely flat as she climbed closer. *My eyes must have deceived me,* she thought.

The rock continued to expose nothing until she drew within the last hundred yards and the clouds opened to cast more morning light, revealing a chasm that had created the shadow she had seen from below. She ran her hand along the crevice, her heart beating wildly as she stepped into a narrow opening. She was able to walk upright through a gap of very high walls just large enough for a person and horse to pass. She climbed upward, toward a narrow shaft of light that grew stronger until she emerged through the passage. Standing at the crest, she looked across the other side of the slope and caught her breath at the sight that lay before her.

"By the souls of my ancestors," she said aloud.

Descending the mountainside, more granite outcroppings were scattered among the steep inclines, which eventually lessened and opened into miles of a vast, desolate-looking plain. In the distance, Seanna could see a long alpine valley and the great expanse of a river fringed with dark green forest that snaked along as far as the eye could see. She gazed in wonder at the vista. Myth became reality as the long-lost pass and the lands beyond, previously known only in the tales of Seanna's ancestors, spread out before her.

She spent most of the day exploring the upper summit and detected no visible signs of habitation except for animal trails. That night, she camped again among the high crags, but this time with no fire. Gazing up at the brilliant stars in the night sky, she pulled her cloak tightly around her shoulders, not to ward off the chill but to contain a tingling sensation that made her shiver. She had spent many nights of solitude in the wilds as a scout and had never really been lonely, but tonight she could not quiet her excitement and wished that some of her clan were here to share her discovery.

In the morning, I will explore farther down the mountain, before returning home.

The following day's exploration was uneventful as she traversed several miles down the steep slopes. The grades lessened into a more level plain but were still strewn with the same sharp boulders, forced up through the ground by the movement of the great glacier and covered with sparse grasses.

"Time to turn back," she said aloud to her mare. She was leading the horse around to ascend back up the slope, when her eye caught a disturbance in the grass. Moving closer, she froze when she saw the footprints of what appeared to have been many men moving among the rocks. The tracks were days old but easy to follow, leading to a grim sight.

A dozen men lay dead within a camp. Seanna stiffened, placing her hand upon her sword as she stood silently. There was no movement, save for the stirring of the wind rustling the dry grasses and heightening her guard. She surveyed the camp, then moved silently to the fallen. The tracks told a story. The men appeared to have been trapped in an ambush by some band that had approached from a single direction overland.

She searched among them for possible survivors, but their waxen, sunken faces and the rigid angles of their bodies confirmed that all were dead. A small cluster of them had died encircling another man, who Seanna assumed was important. Their clothes and appearances denoted that they were all of the same race, with light skin and mostly black hair worn long, some in braids held with gold and silver clasps. Their weapons, still clutched in the stiffened grasps of the dead, displayed fine artistry, with intricate inlays of valuable metals and precious stones.

Robbers would have taken all of these things, Seanna speculated. *Who are these men? Who attacked them? And what were they all doing in this remote place?*

Seanna widened her search as she scanned a larger range of shrubs and bushes, searching for more signs. She stopped abruptly and her pulse quickened as her eye traced the path of something that had dragged itself into the brush. Its tracks disappeared into a large bush. The wind rustled again through the shrub branches, and her nerves stood at attention.

Drawing her bow, she moved forward slowly. A foot lay partially exposed underneath. It moved as she approached, and Seanna stood ready.

"Reveal yourself!" she demanded.

"I cannot. I have a broken leg," a male voice answered.

"Let me see you," she ordered, stepping closer, bow drawn taut.

Slowly, the shrubs parted, and Seanna stared into the face of a young man not much older than she. It was apparent that he was of the same clan as the murdered men, for he had the same long black hair and similar dress. His eyes were dull with pain.

"Who are you?" he asked in amazement.

"That is not important. Throw out your weapons," Seanna demanded.

The young man pushed a long sword forward.

"Now, pull yourself out so I can see you."

Seanna kept him in her bow sight as he stared at her in apprehension but followed her command, pushing himself slowly forward and dragging his legs behind him. Seanna lowered her bow and dragged him roughly into the open, searching his clothing for

weapons as he moaned in pain. Satisfied that he posed no immediate threat, she let him lie there for a moment, still scrutinizing
him, as he continued to gape at her.

Stepping forward, she drew her knife and his eyes went wide
with fear.

"Let me see that leg," she ordered, but the man did not move.
"You will have to trust me so I can help you. If I were here to kill
you, I would have done so already."

She dropped to her knees and began cutting away his pant
leg to reveal the extent of the wound. She lightly touched his
lower shin, causing him to gasp in pain. Though the bone had not
broken through the skin, it was still a serious fracture. She quickly
gathered bush and built a fire, moving him closer to it as carefully
as possible. He shivered uncontrollably before the warmth started
to penetrate his body. From her pack, Seanna opened a rolled
skin of herbs and brewed a tea to dull the pain. She offered him
dried meat, but he would not eat. Instead, she placed it in water to
simmer for a broth.

His eyes followed her every move. "What is your name?" she
asked.

"James," he stammered. "I am called James."

"My name is Seanna, James. I have training in the healing arts.
I will need to set that broken bone. You must prepare yourself."
His eyes widened again.

"Drink more tea," she instructed. Once James had drunk the
contents of the cup, Seanna handed a stick to him. "Place this
between your teeth, and try to lie still. It will be over soon."

James bit down into the wood and cried out involuntarily
while Seanna swiftly set the bone. She bound his leg between
pieces of wood, then wrapped it with torn lengths of cloth to

stabilize it. When she finished, James was pale and sweating. She made him as comfortable as possible, wrapping him in his cloak and offering him the broth she had been steeping. Within a short time, his color returned and he looked much improved.

Seanna watched him resist, for as long as possible, the dulling properties of the tea, but eventually he closed his eyes and fell into a deep, exhausted sleep. She leaned back against a large log, watching his body shudder. In the quiet, she gathered her thoughts, wondering once again, *What have I stumbled upon here?*

Her many questions of him would have to wait until the morning. For the time being, she gazed at his sleeping form in astonishment, listening to his breathing, studying his features. His face had a symmetry that she found pleasing: a straight nose with defined nostrils, full lips. His unmarked, youthful complexion was shadowed with stubble, not yet a full beard. He had dark hair like most of his men and, under his closed lids, blue eyes. His clothes denoted wealth and privilege and did not disguise his lean, muscular body. His hands had held a sword but were unaccustomed to hard labor. He moaned in his sleep, shifting uncomfortably, his high forehead etched with lines of pain.

He will need to rest another day or two to regain his strength, but then what?

At first light, roused by the chilled morning air, James struggled back to consciousness. He had been dreaming that he was in a great ocean, attempting to rise from its dark depths, unable to breathe and desperately reaching toward the surface, where shafts of light cast the only illumination. All around him, his kin sank deeper. He reached for his father, who vanished into the black with his arms outstretched toward his son.

Upon waking, he felt the dull throbbing of his leg and the stiff brace that bound it. When he opened his eyes, he knew what he would see. The woman had seated herself near the fire and was wrapped in her cloak, staring back at him. His body lurched to attention as he managed to lift himself up and looked into her penetrating green eyes.

How long has she been watching me? James wondered, reddening at the thought.

"How is the pain?" she asked, as she rose to tend the fire.

"Bearable," he answered, attempting to sit more upright.

He watched her movements as she brewed some sort of drink. In the shock of the previous day's events, it had been enough to allow Seanna to tend to his injuries before he had passed into exhaustion. This day, he had awoken with his grief and with questions.

"Where do you come from?" he asked abruptly. He had seen fair-haired women who looked like her in the slave markets of the northern realms that still traded in human flesh.

"I will answer your questions with time," Seanna replied, "but first I need to know what happened here. Are we in danger of another ambush?"

Uncertainty spread across James's face. "I don't know if we are safe. But by now, the men who are waiting for me and my party in the lower valley will be wondering where we are. We are overdue to return, and they will begin making their way here." James watched Seanna's body stiffen at his revelation, and he assumed that the possibility of more men coming sobered her expression. Would she now have thoughts of abandoning him?

James took the hot broth that she handed him, studying Seanna with curiosity over the bowl while he sipped the contents. He noted her clothing and especially her weaponry. She was dressed for the outdoors, in men's clothes, and carried the weapons of a soldier.

Before he could ask more questions, she rose and filled his bowl again. "We will need to move our camp if someone is coming back," she offered, by way of warning.

James's face darkened with renewed grief as he glanced toward the location of his fallen comrades. "My father is among the dead. I cannot leave him."

"Show me his body, and I will bury him," she offered. "I can conceal him so that no one will find him. When you heal, you can return to take him home."

He nodded halfheartedly, thinking, *The loyalty of the men who are coming to find me will determine whether I depart from this place or join my father in death.*

With Seanna's help, he painstakingly covered the distance back to his men and pointed out his father among the dead guards. Seanna nodded knowingly and began to search the crevices located within a small canyon filled with rocks and bush.

"This will be a perfect hiding place," she called to him. "I will need my horse and ropes to move him."

James nodded sadly. "I want a moment with him." His expression was stricken with anguish as Seanna helped him to his father's body. Seanna watched as he spoke in hushed words to the dead man.

"Father, my king, I am not ready to take your place! But I promise you this: I will not contain my grief and rage at this betrayal until I have avenged you. This oath, I pledge upon your grave."

He leaned in closer over his father's frozen visage, placing his hand upon the king's chest. He removed a chain with a gold medallion from his father's neck and placed it inside his tunic. His tears betrayed his grief as he dragged himself away from the corpse and turned to signal Seanna that he was ready.

She wrapped his father tightly in his robes, a makeshift shroud, before dragging him as gently as possible to the rocks and interring him in his wilderness tomb.

"The rest of the slain bodies will have to remain where they lie. I will protect them as best I can with rocks," Seanna stated, "and I can conceal some pieces of jewelry and weapons in another rock alcove."

James agreed reluctantly. He hated to leave them as they had died, but he had no choice. He made the same vow silently to the dead men that he had made to his father and grimaced in pain as Seanna helped him onto the back of her horse.

They rode higher into the mountains along the trail that she already had explored, making a new camp with a greater vantage point. James trembled as she helped him down, and watched numbly as she started a fire. Seanna checked his leg again while he tried to make himself more comfortable, and offered him the now-familiar warm herb tea.

"I will see if I can hunt something to eat," she announced, leaving him by the fire.

Alone in their camp, James gathered his thoughts and surveyed his surroundings, scanning the bleak landscape that only days before had been the site of an exciting, uncharted exploration with his father.

A sense of helplessness overwhelmed him as he realized, *I am miles from the valley floor, and the descent down through these rocky slopes is barely passable even on two good legs. I will need a horse to get down. My fate is tied to this unknown woman, and I will not survive without her help!*

They remained in their makeshift camp for another day, and James's condition began to improve. The swelling in his leg subsided, and he was relieved when Seanna proclaimed that no infection had set in and the limb would heal well. Once James was out of danger for the time being, she left him several times to check different vantage points for any signs of the movement of more men, but all was still.

As twilight descended on the next night in their new camp, Seanna tended the fire and finished preparing their meal. James watched her every movement with curiosity. She was tall and slender. Her clothes were all soft greens, the color of leaves and of her eyes, which were riveting. His very soul felt examined when she looked at him. Her tawny hair was tousled, its contrasting strands of ash and light browns unable to be contained in the long braid down her back. Beneath the dirt smudges, James noted fine bone structure and clear skin. She was probably even pretty when properly dressed. Her only adornment was a single, thin braid hanging from her left temple, clasped with an ornate silver bead.

She appeared completely at ease in this foreboding place. She had the suppleness of youth, but also something much more. There was a prowess behind her movements, and she moved with the stealth and grace of a wild animal. She was well-armed beyond what a mere hunter would require, and he speculated that she was skilled in defense. How else could a woman possibly be alone here?

They sat wrapped against the chill, facing each other across the fire. Seanna shifted and stared silently at the flames. She had told him little, if anything, about herself, leaving them poised in a calculated game of chess, waiting to see who would make the first move. James weighed his judgments about her and whether he could trust her. He had already resigned himself to the fact that he would need her help in returning to the lower valley, but what would she demand in exchange for such a service? Now that his strength was returning, he wanted to go home more than anything, and to begin to fulfill his burning desire for revenge on those responsible for his father's death.

"You said you would tell me where you came from," James said, breaking the quiet.

Seanna turned from the fire to look at him with her penetrating gaze, pausing a long moment before answering him. "I will, but first I want to know where you have traveled from and if you know who ambushed your party."

James thought for a moment, before nodding in agreement. "I come from the great seaport city of Bathemor."

"How far is your city from this place?" Seanna pressed.

"It is a four-day ride from here to where my boat waits. We traveled down the river for two days before we reached this valley," James replied.

"The men who ambushed your party were waiting for you. They came not ahead of you but from a different direction. They must have known of your plans to lie in wait in this remote place. They were no mere bandits—they intended to kill, not rob," Seanna said.

James's expression darkened. "There are those who would use the death of my father for political gain."

He stopped, wrestling with his anguish and reluctance to

continue, before he blurted out, "It was my fault that we are here in this vulnerable place! I was the one who implored my father to explore this valley and the mountains. He relented, indulging my desire for adventure and to appease me; we arranged a hunting trip. I wanted to venture farther. I always want to go farther . . . ." James lowered his head for a moment, resting it upon his folded arms to hide his emotion.

"It was a bold ambush for a mere hunting party," Seanna said.

James raised his head. "We were ambushed because my father is the king and some wish another on the throne."

Seanna's expression changed. Her brows knitted in concern at his confession, which, he guessed, had shifted the stakes dramatically and now placed her at great risk.

"Who wants your father killed?" She leaned in.

"I don't know, but I will pledge my life to finding them. I suspect my cousin is taking a rare opportunity to eliminate two impediments to his ascension to the throne: my father and me," he stated coldly. "Men loyal to my father have been waiting at the river encampment and will now be searching for us. I need to get down the mountain to meet them and return to my people, and then those responsible will pay with their lives."

"Are you certain of the loyalty of the men who wait for you?"

James nodded, for they were some of his most trusted, including Cedmon, his bodyguard, who had protected him since childhood.

James diverted her queries with a question of his own: "Where are your people? Do you come from across the seas to the north?"

Seanna shook her head slowly. "I come from a land to the south of this realm."

"Then you traveled up the coast to this place?" he pressed.

He watched her hesitate, before she answered, "No." She turned and pointed toward the summit. "I came across the mountains."

James's eyes widened. "From across the mountains? Then you have found a way through?"

"You know of the pass?" she asked, startled.

"Only from the stories of my people," he replied, "but those have always been considered simply the musings of old men. The notion of a true passage between the mountains has never been taken seriously. I know something of the lands beyond our borders, and that there are many clans of men in your region, but I have little knowledge of them. How is it that you are in this wild place alone?"

"I am a scout for my people and for a proposed new alliance of those clans you speak of," she stated.

What kind of alliance? James thought. *And a woman scout?* "What is this new alliance of clans?" he asked.

"A union seeking to achieve a common objective of building ports and expanding trade along our coastlines."

"You are the wife of another scout? You became separated searching for new routes?"

"No," Seanna answered sternly. "I came alone, and as the daughter of my clan's leader, I will represent our interests in a vote for inclusion in this alliance when the time comes."

James was puzzled—*What father would send his daughter into this solitary place unaccompanied?*—but resisted further inquiry, reminding himself, *Such questions are not as important as her help.*

"I need your aid to return to my men. I will reward you handsomely," he added, though he sensed his offer lacked real merit if he did not regain the throne, or if the wrong men found them.

A log dropped into the embers, and the crackle of the fire was the only sound in the still night as James continued to watch her face in anticipation. He suspected that she was measuring the man for whom she could be risking her life, but he was unable to judge her thoughts beneath her fixed expression. However, as much as her character was unknown to him, he felt a degree of certainty that she would not have tended his wounds and nursed him back from certain death merely to leave him here in this wilderness.

Finally, he spoke up: "You are weighing your fate if you should help me, and I would feel the same if I were in your place. Might I offer more value to you by giving this new alliance an opportunity to discuss trading rights in my city?"

Seanna's gaze did not change as she spoke. "Our peoples are unknown to one another, and I do not know whether you are friend or foe, but the protection of my clan is more important than any one man's life."

James's heart sank at her words. His death would assure the secrecy of the newly discovered pass.

She continued, "But you are a prince, and even if you were a common man, I could do no less that to deliver you to safety. Your offer of reward means nothing to me if I do not return to my people. I will take you down the mountain to the river encampment, where we will see if your men are waiting, but I will go no farther. One day I may call upon your gratitude and the merit of your words, but for now I ask only for your pledge that I will have your leave to return to my home."

James released an inward sigh of relief, his hopes renewed. "I give you my word," he answered solemnly.

"Get some rest, then; we leave at first light. Tomorrow we have a long trek that will test your strength," Seanna ordered.

As James stretched out beside the fire, he could not contain his excitement about the next day's journey and a hopeful reunion with his men. As he stared out into the night, his thoughts raced. *I wonder why Seanna has asked for so little. Could there be more demands later? Is her story true or just a clever decoy for some greater deception? How is it possible that these clans of men have accepted a female scout?*

He tried to calm his mind as he surrendered to the obvious.

I must trust Seanna, even though I don't fully understand why.

He drifted into sleep knowing that his life was in her hands, and in those of whatever fate awaited them at the bottom of the mountain.

At first light, they broke camp. James grimaced as Seanna rebound his leg, then helped him stand and mount her horse. He tried to ignore the throbbing limb, impatient to begin their journey and willing to bear anything to return home.

They made their way cautiously down the steep mountain incline. Every time Seanna's horse stumbled, James winced in pain. He was exhausted and drained when they finally stopped to make camp in the late afternoon.

Seanna had spoken little to him that day, concentrating on negotiating the difficult trail. He sat absorbing the warmth of the fire, drinking hot broth and beginning to recover. He gazed back at the mountains and the path they had taken. "Do you think we made good progress today?" he asked.

"Considering the remaining distance, I judge that we should reach the lower valley by tomorrow," she answered.

James sat back, encouraged, taking a deep breath to relax, but his stomach knotted with the anticipation of reaching the valley and finding his men. He stared off into the descending twilight of the mountain sky as darkness closed around him like a heavy curtain. The silence, broken occasionally by the calls of a distance hawk, was penetrating.

How truly desolate this place is! I find it such a curious thing that the presence of this woman brings me a certain degree of calm.

Never before had he spent such an extended amount of time with a stranger—and especially a female, aside from his mother. The sensation of receiving well-being from anyone but his trusted guard was foreign to him.

How could I be at ease with someone about whom I know so little?

If they reached the forest the next day, this might be their last evening together, and there was much about this woman he still did not know. She had offered up little additional information about herself. James sensed not so much a withholding on her part as a keen instinct for observation and evaluation. Intuitively, he believed that she did come from the mountain pass and proved the old myths true.

There is more I want to know about the clans and her people, but mainly I want to learn more about her.

His curiosity overcame his prudence not to press her goodwill. "The mountains of this region have always been a mystery for my people, and, it seems, for your people as well. You are a scout for your clan, but why have you come to this place alone? Where are your clansmen? Do they wait for you on the other side of the mountain?"

"There are many clans beyond these mountains, as you may already know. My clan is called the Womara," Seanna replied.

"The Womara?"

"Yes. It means *women who live without men*."

James eyes widened, and he could not hide his astonishment. "A clan of only women! The old stories have spoken of a clan of fighting warrior women. Are you a living descendant?"

"Yes, I am," she answered, her voice full of pride.

"Tell me about your people." James implored.

She gave him a slight smile, pulling her cloak more tightly around her shoulders. "This is a story of my ancestors' time and how we came to know of this pass between the mountains."

4

THE MAKING OF A
WARRIOR

Several years had passed, during which Rowan's new tribe of women thrived. Now, she stood surveying their unique village with pride. Clusters of huts stretched out before her along the forest floor. Lean-to shelters, once built from limbs, leaves, and bark, had been replaced by larger structures, covered with thatched roofs or animal skins, blending with the foliage. Well-worn paths led to the river and gardens in the open spaces, where more sunlight penetrated. Pens held small herds of goats and sheep, and the horses were corralled a short distance away. Many chickens roamed freely, searching for insects. At the center of the community, a large circle of stones marked a communal fire area. Children played among the trees while mothers paused in their tasks to smile at their laughter.

Rowan was their leader, in the beginning by default and later by the group's choice, as a testament to her unfaltering commitment to their survival, which had earned her the women's continued respect. She watched as the scouts returned from a township with a few more newcomers. Arriving in their new surroundings, the women walked slowly, heads lowered or staring in amazement.

Rowan clenched her fists against her side. *I still must fight back my anger when I see beaten and abused women, their wills broken at the hands of men.*

Over the years, women seeking sanctuary began to seek out the Womara as they traded in the towns. Destitute or desperate, willing to forgo their former lives in order to have a chance at an existence of something more than abuse or deprivation for themselves and for their children, they left quietly from their villages or waited by the road at the outskirts of the township, bundles in hand, until the scouts appeared.

The Womara's numbers had grown to almost a hundred, and so far no men from the outer clans had come forth to challenge the band's right to exist. The group had been fortunate so far, but this fact gave Rowan no peace. When Asha related an incident in town upon her return, Rowan's heart skipped a beat.

"What happened?" she asked.

"A slave challenged her master today when he refused her release to go with us," Asha reported. "He had told her years ago that one day she could gain her freedom by selling eggs from the one chicken he had allowed her to keep. When she presented the payment amount today, he balked, challenging that it was now not enough."

A familiar chill ran down Rowan's spine, before Asha continued, "Can you imagine how long it took her to save the pennies she raised for her freedom? The woman became distraught, and only upon intervention by some of the town's elders was the man forced to honor the agreement. We departed immediately, but not without the scrutiny of a gathering crowd of men."

"We will not trade there for a while, and we must be more cautious not to draw so much attention," Rowan advised, as she swallowed the lump in her throat.

That evening, Rowan could not shake her sense of foreboding as she listened to the women chatter around the fire while they prepared their evening meals. She caught Asha watching her closely. "Your heart is heavy this night, my friend," Asha said.

Rowan nodded, sitting next to her.

"What troubles you?"

"I look around at this tranquil scene, but I cannot be at peace," Rowan answered. "Can we ever be truly safe? I know we are vulnerable."

"All people can be vulnerable," Asha replied.

Rowan nodded. "But at least men will fight to protect what is theirs. We must also learn to defend ourselves and what is ours," she said forcefully, as the women stopped their tasks to listen more closely.

"We cannot be taken again against our wills if we learn to fight for ourselves. We must use the bows we have for more than shooting squirrels," Rowan added, raising her voice.

"Learn the use of weapons?" a woman protested. "We live in peace here. No one bothers us. The other clans leave us alone."

"Do you think that this provides us with safety?" She made a sweeping gesture in the air with her hand as she looked around the forest. "If any man or clan wanted what we have forged here, or us, they would take it. It is only that until now, they have deemed us as holding no value."

The women began to seat themselves silently around the ebbing fire.

"But when they come, and I think they will," Rowan continued, "I would prefer to die defending what I believe is my right to live as I choose. I would fight for my freedom."

"How can we fight?" one woman asked.

"We will learn," Rowan answered. "I have carried a silent vow in my heart for all these years, but now I will speak it out loud." She rose to her feet and said, "I will never let anyone return me to slavery again. Who will join me in that pledge?"

"I am not sure what you ask of us," Asha asked, "or how we might defend ourselves." The women murmured among themselves in agreement. Asha stood as well now, looking intently at Rowan. "But what I do know is that I will not go back to the life I lived before. So I will pledge with you."

Rowan watched as the other women glanced at each other and then, one by one, stood, touched their hands to their hearts, and bowed their heads.

Rowan touched her own heart. "We pledge to live our lives as free women with dominion over our destiny."

The women all repeated the same vow in unison, their eyes shining brightly in the light of the fire. Rowan stood tall before them. "From this day forward, we will become warriors and this oath will be our guiding creed."

Rowan and a few women were the first to begin fostering their fighting skills, learning to master the bow beyond their basic hunting needs. They practiced for hours every day, until their accuracy became deadly, learning the distances that it took to kill beast or man. Gradually, all the women trained in some form of weaponry: slings, bows and arrows, and, in time, short and long swords.

Also, understanding that the women would need to use their intuition to judge their foes' weaknesses, they developed proficiencies in outwitting much larger opponents by using agility, speed, and the cover the forest provided. The emerging female warriors grew to know the surrounding terrain intimately while they honed their abilities, spending weeks at a time in the wilderness and becoming one with the forest.

The transformation that Rowan felt within herself was more distinct, tapping into a spirit that had lain dormant. *It is such a small thing to hold this bow in my hand, yet I feel something different now. To fight is my choice, and that is everything.*

Rowan walked to an open clearing to practice her bow shots and paused to smell the crispness in the air; soon a change of seasons would be upon them. Long before the leaves changed color, the Womara would fill their winter caches and prepare for the colder days. She lowered her bow in curiosity as other woman scouts arrived across the clearing, dragging a makeshift carrier that appeared to have a body upon it. When the scouts lowered the carrier in front of her, she stared down in shock at an incoherent man.

"We found him near death in the rock outcropping at the base of the mountain. He must have been crawling for days with a broken leg. He keeps mumbling about the rocky peaks and descending from the mountaintops," the scout reported.

"That's impossible," Rowan snapped back, looking at the distant line of impenetrable mountains that bordered their valley. "Why did you bring him here?"

The women stood in silence, heads bowed, before the lead scout stepped forward. "He has perpetrated no misdeed against us. We have not lost our capacity for compassion, and why would we not help someone in need? If not, then we will be no better than the beasts we hunt. We could not leave him there to die," she challenged.

Rowan scrutinized the man as he lay unconscious. He was the first outsider among them, about her age and strongly built, with light brown hair and a close-cropped beard. He wore clothes that were not of the local clans. He carried weapons: a knife, short and long swords, and a quill with arrows but no bow, which she assumed was lost. His face was handsome but drawn and pale. He moaned and grimaced in pain and with fever.

Rowan felt the heavy weight of judgment and the penetrating stares of the women as she looked down at his still form, holding his life or death in her hands.

"Take him to the healers," she commanded, and walked away.

It was several days before the man regained consciousness. Stirring slowly, he gazed in confusion around the hut and at the faces of the unknown women who attended him.

"Where am I?" he asked.

"You are in the valley of the Womara. Our scouts found you at the base of the mountains and brought you here."

He struggled to sit, but the healer restrained him.

"What are you called?" she asked.

"I am Landon. You are from the other side of the mountain?" he asked with amazement.

The healer looked at him with a questioning look. "Do not tire yourself. Rest. You are safe here," she answered.

Landon closed his eyes and fell back into a deep sleep.

For the next several weeks, he was tended by two women, who told him the break was serious and his recovery would be slow. He was aware enough to gauge that so far no males had come to judge his condition and that he appeared to be among a community of women only. The healers answered all his questions briefly but asked many more of him. Where did he live? Had he traveled alone? They relayed any information they gathered from him back to a tall, dark woman who waited outside the hut. He guarded his answers, giving himself time to assess his surroundings and his perplexing circumstances.

One morning, Landon stirred from his sleep to the rustling of one of his healers building a small fire to soak her herbs. She was young, maybe a few years older than he, dark and exotic-looking. He had seen many of her race in the slave markets of his city. She grinned as she watched him rub the sleep from his eyes.

"Let me see your leg," she ordered, drawing down the loose leggings, lightly touching his cloth-wrapped thigh.

Landon felt the involuntary stirring of his groin and flushed.

"More than just your leg is healing," she said, smiling at him suggestively. She glanced at the entrance of the hut, before placing her hand enticingly upon his thigh.

"I can satisfy that need if you desire," she stated matter-of-factly.

Landon felt his face redden at the boldness of her words.

"W-w-where are your men?" he stammered.

"There are no men here," she answered, as she stroked his leg. "You are the only one."

"Why are there no men here?" he pressed.

Before she could answer, the skin to the enclosure was opened and she quickly withdrew her hand as the other healer entered the hut. Landon glanced away sheepishly as the woman looked at her suspiciously.

"I think it is time he exercised that leg," the other woman ordered.

When Landon emerged from the hut with their assistance, they beamed with pleasure at his initial faltering, assisted movements as if they were observing the first steps of a small child.

Every day, he ventured a little farther, chatting as he walked, playing with the children. He also spent long periods of time at rest, observing the comings and goings of the community surrounding him. *Everyone seems to have a united purpose here. The lack of men does not appear to have hindered the prosperity of the community. In truth, the diversity of cultures seems only to add to the overall strengths of the group. I have never seen anything like it.*

He learned that the tall, silent woman who had never approached him was their leader, and that her name was Rowan. She continued to watch him from a distance, aloof, arms crossed across her chest. She often stood with the dark-skinned woman at her side, their heads bent in private conversation. He did not consider approaching her unsolicited, knowing instinctively that his accommodations depended on her acceptance and his compliance, but he enjoyed watching her movements.

She is beautiful, with her long red hair, and there is a wildness behind those green eyes.

Landon observed that most of the women and adolescents carried some form of arms. All children had slingshots or small bows with arrows, practicing within the games they played as a daily ritual. Those who shot the bow did so remarkably well, and in the absence of men, he surmised, they trained not for mere game hunting but also for defense. His swords had never been taken from him and still lay within his hut. He sensed that these women feared neither him nor his weapons.

One day, Landon felt Rowan watching him keenly as he went out to play among the children. They followed his slow movements around the camp with their wooden mock swords, laughing with delight as he feigned fright and retreat. Even with his damaged leg, he still displayed the grace and technique of a seasoned fighter. This day, he had retrieved his sword for the pleasure of the children, letting them hold it. The older ones possessing greater strength sliced and thrust at an imaginary foe and were delighted to be holding a real weapon.

Landon was standing among a group of these children as Rowan advanced toward him across the clearing. He crouched awkwardly and placed his sword on the ground as she drew closer.

She stopped before him, looking directly into his eyes. "You are a soldier?"

"Yes, I was," he answered.

"You must earn your keep here. In exchange for your shelter, you will teach me in the skills of the sword."

Her request was simple and direct, a command. Up close, Landon noted that her green eyes were alive with flecks of gold and amber. Her expression was serious, and he sensed that refusal was not a choice. *There could be worse ways to pass the winter*, he thought. But Rowan's stern countenance soon sobered his musings.

"How can I refuse such a request from such a generous host? It is my pleasure to offer my service in any way that could be of value," Landon answered formally, suddenly feeling self-conscious.

"We will meet tomorrow in the meadow," she replied, brushing aside his flattery, and departed without a backward glance.

Rowan and several other women began to meet with Landon each midmorning for several hours of instruction. Landon was not surprised that Rowan proved to be an able and talented student, one who approached their lessons with an obsessive focus. He started at the beginning, with the basic footwork and holds of the short sword. As the women's hand grip and arm strength grew, they advanced to the longer sword. He would observe Rowan later, practicing for hours in the distant meadow, repeating his teachings. He wondered what drove her relentlessly beyond a mere desire for mastery of a weapon, as she always pressed him for more advanced techniques and fighting strategies.

These daily lessons soon attracted the attention of others. Small groups of women and some older children began to join them, and every day Landon found himself at the center of a most unusual training camp of fledgling soldiers. When not practicing under the tutelage of weapons, his students spent hours sitting and discussing fighting tactics, and learning how to use the ground and the natural cover of the forest to their best advantage.

Landon knew Rowan deferred to him as the teacher, but he always kept a certain distance, never speaking of personal things beyond what was necessary to her training. She reminded him of a wild animal, always on guard, and he knew never to press the intimacy of their encounters. When he moved his body close to her to demonstrate a strike, he felt her stiffen at his proximity. From what little information he had gathered from the women's stories, she had been a slave and treated very badly. She did not talk about where she came from or how she had come to be in these lands, but her words were not necessary, for she carried her pain in those amazing eyes.

Landon grew to admire and respect his most gifted student. Rowan had a keen mind and was an intuitive leader, whose primary concerns were the welfare and safety of the group. He would never know that what they shaped together in their training would become, several generations later, the foundation of a warrior society that clansmen in these regions would not challenge.

He achieved a certain degree of acceptance from the women. They never pressed him about his origins; his healers, at least, seemed to believe his explanation of traveling from the northern coast. He had been hoping for a softening in Rowan's vigilant nature, too, when one day she asked him a more personal question: "I have been told that you come from the coastline. How did you get so far inland? Why did you travel alone?" she asked.

Landon hesitated, realizing that her question was more strategic than personal and that lying could cost him his life, or at the least, all the trust he felt he had built with the women over these months.

"I do come from the northern realm beyond your mountains, from a city on the coast that is a great seaport," he answered.

"Then you traveled down the coast? It is very dangerous. What was your purpose?" she demanded.

"No, I did not travel by sea; I came over the mountains. I found a way through the highest point."

Rowan stared in disbelief. "There is a way through?"

Landon nodded.

"You will show us this pass," she said.

Landon shook his head. "I am not sure I could find it again," he answered truthfully. "My leg is not strong enough yet, and it will be a hard climb." He turned to smell the air. "The snows will begin soon. There is a risk of being trapped in the mountains. If you allow me to stay through the winter, I will take you in the spring and we will search together."

5

THE DESCENT

When Seanna paused for a moment in her recounting of the Womara history, James shifted his posture to make his bound leg more comfortable, realizing that he had not moved a muscle throughout the telling of the tale. She had woven a narrative that was beyond anything he could have imagined as he listened, fascinated by the story of the origin of her clan and the women who had lived there.

"Today we are thousands strong," Seanna stated proudly, "and a people seeking change and a place among a new alliance of clans, as I told you."

James watched her face come alive as she described the aspirations of the alliance and its purpose.

"When the gathering of the clans is called to meet in the months to come, the Womara will seek inclusion in this new, progressive order," she concluded.

At that, he noted a slight change in her voice and a subtle shift in her confidence, and asked, "Why must you seek inclusion when this union of the clans seems a surety?"

"There will be opposition," Seanna stated matter-of-factly. "There will be clans that do not want to allow any female influence."

He nodded in understanding and thought of his own father's advisory king's council, which seemed rigidly opposed to accepting changing attitudes, repressed its curiosity for new possibilities, and placed itself in a cage of intellectual isolation. He sensed a great gulf between his world and the lands outside its boundaries, and his existence felt much smaller.

"I am most intrigued by this tale," he said. "I have heard stories of a similar clan before. My grandfather spoke of lands that lay beyond the barrier of our mountains, and of a tribe of women. He told of a bold invasion by sea, in which men and women fought side by side to drive back the hordes and save their lands. These accounts passed to him from his grandfather, but they were believed to be a mere exaggeration of a traveler's tale. You say you are thousands strong now, but did your ancestors fight back this invasion?" he asked.

Seanna nodded with pride.

James continued, "We have our own stories of war, and the threat of invasion has been in our history, too. Invaders have battered our lands for a century. The assault that you spoke of probably would have reached our shores eventually, had your people not stopped those invaders. If they had gained a foothold in the lands to the south, in time they would have swept up our coastline and into the interior. But it is events like this, in times of war, that create myth."

"We are not mythical," Seanna replied.

James was silent for a moment. "Myth or a seed of truth? Even so, my grandfather would always add, in his prudence, 'A tale may be true or false. Take care not to believe or dismiss it too easily and allow the real world to catch you unawares.' What became of the one who crossed the mountain?" he asked.

"That is not fully known," Seanna answered. "Only that he returned to his people."

"What is the structure of your clan?" James asked.

Seanna scrutinized James's expression from across the fire, seeming to evaluate the sincerity of his question. She looked to the mountains and then back to him. "Our clan lives on the other side of these peaks, across a great valley. Our heart and center is the interior of a vast woodland, with a township that radiates out like the spokes of a great wheel throughout the forest and surrounding lands. Our core leadership is all female, but in the outlying farm areas, men and women may live together. Parents raise their children in the ways of the Womara, but boys born into the clan live among us until puberty, then leave to dwell outside, among the clans of men. They may return in time if they wish, after they have experienced the outside world."

James wrinkled his brow as he pondered her simple explanation, then asked, "How is it, then, that men and women come together? There are children, as you said, but it seems that traditional marriage does not exist."

Seanna nodded, surmising the underlying curiosity that his gentility and decorum masked.

"Yes, it is different for us," she replied, searching for an adequate answer while James waited. Finally, she explained, "Our gods live among us as the spirits in nature, and all life is sacred. We worship the cycles of the natural world and honor those life forces at our sacred fire. At each full moon, we have a gathering and a celebration of life. It is a time of renewal. We come together as families, old friends meet, and new friendships are forged. All people are welcome, and those who wish to participate celebrate with the dance of life around the fire. Any woman of age who may desire a child, a mate, or merely a companion for the night will attend. A man who desires the same will also be there."

James felt his eyes go wide with surprise at the full comprehension of her words. "Women are free to choose whatever man they want? I have never heard of such a thing."

Seanna took a deep breath, before answering, "This is often a difficult aspect of our order for an outsider to accept, and creates the greatest misunderstanding. There is no simple answer to your question, except that we are not property or objects to control. It is a woman's prerogative to choose freely. Just as a man would."

James remained silent, staring at her.

"We have free will and a belief in the right to choose how we live our lives. We can love, mate, give birth, and live with men if we wish, or not. The core of our society remains female. It does so because we believe that by living in freedom, we maintain dominion over our lives."

"I have never considered that a woman might want her own life, separate from a man," James answered, shaking his head in puzzlement.

"That is because you were born with the right to determine your destiny and you have never faced a woman's limitations," Seanna stated icily, catching a familiar flush of resentment when explaining the Womara's opinion of equality.

"Then you choose your way of life because you dislike men?" James asked, realizing that his knitted brow must convey his disquiet.

"No," Seanna stated. "As I told you, many men live among us, but the authority of our leadership remains female."

"Why would women want to live like this?" he protested.

"Because we believe that women are endowed with free will, just as men are, and that how we choose to exercise that free will is what defines our life. We have built our world on that simple truth. It is the right of every man and every woman that none should have sovereignty over another's destiny," Seanna challenged.

James felt his expression cloud, but he did not stop her. "Go on," he said.

"Have you thought about what it would be like to live an entire lifetime that was not your own?" she asked. "You could be loved and cherished, but everything could taken from you. A man having dominion over you could cast you out, enslave, rape, or kill you as if you were a mere possession. That you might have a mind and intellect to be developed is not considered. In other clans, a woman is deemed too inferior to be allowed rule over her own life."

"But the physical differences alone between a man and woman create inequality. Do you think your physical strength equal to that of a man?" James asked.

Seanna eyed him. "It is a valid question, and we do not underestimate the limitations of our physical abilities against men, but we possess other attributes that balance those inequalities."

"What kinds of attributes?"

"As a Womara scout, I am proficient in many weapons. I am also smaller and lighter than a man, and I use that inequality that you spoke of to my advantage. You would find our fighting techniques unconventional," Seanna answered, with a slight smile.

"Is that why you would venture into the wilds alone, unconcerned for your safety?" he pressed.

"I did not say I was unconcerned for my safety. Any one person can face that threat, for that is the way of our world. But we choose not to let fear limit our freedom."

"Just the very fact that you are a woman compromises your words!" James argued.

"Yes," Seanna responded, "that is an unfortunate truth. Some men believe that they have the right to do violence to my body and take from me that which I do not wish to give merely because I am alone. The difference is that I will fight to protect myself, as would you."

James leaned in toward her. "So you are suggesting that it is your prowess with weapons that is the determining factor. But weapons can be taken away," he challenged.

"True again, as it would be for any fighter," Seanna countered, seemingly enjoying the banter. "But it is the fighting spirit that makes us who we are, and a fight to the death, no matter how long it may take to exact revenge, makes the men of my realm think twice about any assault."

James frowned. The fire ebbed, and Seanna threw another log into the coals, watching the embers rise into the night sky. She looked back at him.

"You are destined to be king, are you not?"

"Yes," he replied warily.

"You have had the finest of tutors for your education. They have cultivated your intellect and encouraged your imagination, opening your mind to the wonders of the world."

James nodded again.

"You have freedoms that allow you to contemplate your life with all its possibilities." She allowed for a pointed pause, then went on: "Now, take that desire for knowledge and your passion

---

for life, with all its possibilities, and place those feelings in a female body."

James looked up, shocked.

An edge crept into her voice. "Now, all those aspirations have changed just because you have had the misfortune of being born female. You may feel all those hopes and desires, but your gender discounts them. If you are a woman blessed with the intelligence to understand this inequality, you suffer the anguish of knowing that you are living only part of a life."

She did not take her eyes from his. "What you have can come only from freedom of choice. That is why we fight to protect what some would take from us. We fight to remain who we are."

As Seanna looked across the fire and into James's eyes, she sat more upright, keeping her gaze unwavering and unapologetic. She felt no need to speak in defiance or to say words to provoke him. *I want him to understand*, she thought, *but I will not seek his validation, either.*

James sat silently, his expression reflecting confusion. She anticipated his announcement of his refusal to accept such a premise, but that statement never came. The man who sat before her in the firelight did not look away from her in dismissal. Rather, the personal nature of his next question caught her off guard.

"You have danced at these fires?"

Seanna flushed at her remembrance of her first time at the fires. She had attended only after being teased relentlessly by her friends, who by then had danced at the fires more than once. The inviting stares of men across the flames had made her feel more awkward than aroused, and she had finally retreated to the solitude of her room, listening to the drumming and laughter from a distance. Her duties as a scout kept her away from her clan for months at a time, and she had not returned to the fires for any purpose other than to share in the communal gathering.

"I-I am sorry," James stammered. "I should not have asked that."

Seanna said nothing. She merely wrapped herself in her cloak, turned her back to him, and drew close to the fire to sleep, indicating that their conversation was over. James did not move for several minutes, but she sensed his gaze on her. It caused her body to shiver before he finally lay down.

The following day, they broke camp quickly, moving with the determination of reaching the lower valley by the day's end. Neither spoke as they settled into the journey before them, and James appreciated the quiet. He still regretted the inappropriateness of his bold question to her the night before. *She is a warrior in every sense but appears untested in the arena of love, and I have overstepped the boundaries of propriety.*

With each descending mile, the terrain changed, until they finally reached the fringes of the forest. James was relieved to be down the mountain slopes as they stood concealed in the upper tree line, viewing the winding river in the distance. Miles away, the dark outline of a line of men traveling in single file was ascending toward the mountain peaks, and he felt a leap of hope at the sight of them. He turned to Seanna, who showed no emotion but watched the advancing group intently.

As the men drew closer, James and Seanna moved to the edge

of the forest, positioned themselves within the trees, and waited. James's heartbeat quickened as Seanna stood steady, her bow readied at her side. The men crested a rise and made their way into the clearing, now within full view. James grinned broadly in recognition.

"Seanna, wait here until I signal," he commanded, as he urged her horse forward, into the open.

When he emerged from the trees, a shout of recognition came from the group as they spurred their horses toward him. The riders reined in from a full gallop and jumped from their saddles, surrounding their prince. Reaching up to support him, they lowered James from his horse to the ground, expressing their joy at finding him.

James' watched his guard and trusted confidant, Cedmon, view the unfamiliar horse and turn to survey the tree line. He held James by his shoulders and examined him from top to bottom, noting the bound leg, assessing the severity of his injuries and the well-dressed broken bones with a questioning look.

"My prince, we were concerned when you did not return at the agreed time. What happened here? Were you sent ahead because you are injured? Where are the others? Where is your father?" he asked.

James lowered his eyes for a moment, trying to control his anguish, before looking back up at Cedmon and replying, "We were betrayed and ambushed by men waiting for us. All are dead except me."

The men cried out in shock, as James pulled Cedmon aside and spoke in a hushed voice. "They knew we were coming. Keep your thoughts and words to yourself, for there might be one among us who is a traitor. I will tell you everything soon."

Cedmon nodded and ordered his men to action. "We will rest briefly, and then we leave."

"Wait—there is more," James said, then turned to the forest and signaled.

Seanna emerged slowly from the trees to reveal herself. The men turned and stared in astonishment at the strange woman advancing toward them with her bow drawn. They placed their hands upon their sword hilts to pull their blades.

"Lower your weapons," James commanded. "This is Seanna, of the Womara clan. She found our ambushed party, and she saved my life."

Seanna acknowledged his words, holding her ground while the men scrutinized her.

"This woman has my protection!" James raised his voice.

The men relaxed their stances but continued to gawk as Seanna lowered her bow.

"Leave us for a moment," James ordered.

The men snapped back to attention and stepped away. James struggled toward Seanna, dragging his bound leg. She moved to meet him, keeping watch on the men.

"It appears that all is well for you," she spoke. "I will take my leave now."

"You will depart so soon?" James answered.

"I am overdue to return to my clan and have a long climb back," she said, eyeing the peaks. "I am glad that your men are here. I wish you triumph in your trials ahead."

James stepped closer. "It seems as if there is more to be said." He paused, searching her face. "I have had many hours to contemplate my fate and my future as we journeyed down the mountain. I will have my vengeance upon those who killed my father and kin.

My life and lands are at great risk, and I must return immediately to take the throne, but I shall hunt down those who are responsible for these deaths, reinforce our alliances, and settle these scores."

He gazed back up to the mountains. "I realize that gratitude is not enough for my life, and I owe you a great debt. I also owe you something more—you have helped me to see things with new eyes and opened my mind to a different world."

Seanna smiled. "You were a captive and an attentive listener."

James reached out to touch her arm. "We can part here, and you can return home, as I have pledged, but I hope our time together is not over. I wish to ask something more of you: a pact between you and me, held in secret."

Seanna's look questioned him. "What more would you ask, milord?"

"I will be king"—James stood taller—"and I ask that you return to this place at the next summer solstice, so that together we may climb the mountain again. Only you and I will know this pledge to retrieve my father from his rocky grave and return him to the tomb of my ancestors."

James lowered his head for a moment, before speaking again. "It causes me great pain to leave him, but I think he will rest safely until that time when you and I may return. And in the time that passes, I will want to know what has become of your aspirations regarding the alliance that you seek."

Seanna stood silently before him, and James could see that his request for them to return had stunned her. "Do you have an oath of honor as a warrior for your clan?" he asked.

"Yes," she answered.

"We also have an oath of honor," James replied, "which I value above all else. I offer you that oath now for safe passage back to your home, but I would ask for your oath in return, and that you come back to this place. For now, I can ask only for your belief in the conviction of my words, strengthened by the pledge of a future king."

Seanna examined his face, staring unflinchingly into his eyes, and then slowly extended her hand. "I will pledge my oath to you, but in return, I ask one thing: The pass must remain my secret for now. It cannot be revealed or exploited as a way between our regions. It will place my clan at great risk."

James took her arm in his. They stood, forearm to forearm, as he stared into her eyes. "You have my oath on the grave of my father and my ancestors before him."

He called to his men, "Give her food and water."

Turning back to Seanna, he spoke quietly. "If you do not return, I will not seek the passage. But it is my sincere desire that I will see you here again in the year to come, at the highest day of the summer solstice."

Seanna bowed her head, placed her hand over her heart, and took the offered food and water. Then she grabbed the reins and mounted her horse.

James moved closer and held the reins to steady himself. "One year will be a long time, Seanna, but I will not forget what you have done for me."

She smiled down at him as he watched her turn her horse and move up the rise. At the edge of the tree line, she paused, turning to look over her shoulder, and raised her hand in a final salute, before disappearing into the trees.

6

THE PROPHECY OF ROWAN

Rowan sat upon a fallen tree limb, waiting for Landon to arrive. Today they would practice alone, reinforcing the lessons she now knew by heart. The air had changed recently, turning crisp and carrying the scent of the coming winter.

Her thoughts turned to Landon, though she wanted to brush them aside.

He should have gone—there is nothing more he can teach me—but I have promised him shelter through the winter so that I may learn the location of the pass.

She closed her eyes, turning her face up to enjoy the feeling of warmth from the pale sun on her skin. *I have had to dispel many of my harsh criticisms about him over the last months. The women have always spoken well of him, saying he possesses an amiable and quiet nature and conveys an appreciation for their tending.*

She opened her eyes and gazed across the meadow. *But I cannot change my feelings that Landon will be like all other men and still deserves no special accommodation. If they wish, let men be a part of the lives of women who regularly venture to the townships, but no man should be a part of our world within the boundaries of this forest.*

The grasses had turned brown, and the leaves on the trees were turning to golden yellows and reds, reminding her that it was once her favorite change of seasons. A deep sigh escaped her lips as the sound of her beloved aunt's laughter flooded back to her in vivid memory.

Rowan, Rowan, my love, come walk with me, her aunt called.

Rowan felt a tightening in her chest at the remembrance of her beloved relative's voice. Her aunt had also loved the changing colors of the trees, describing them as living things with spirits and feeling, their essence in everything that surrounded them.

They had often walked through the forest together, hand in hand, her aunt telling her the stories of these spirits. Rowan loved the tale of the spring, when the trees gave birth to their children from buds that burst forth with new leaves.

"Can you not feel their joy as their branches sway with the wind?" her aunt had asked on one such walk, smiling. "These beautiful, changing colors of the leaves are a last tribute to life before they wither and drop. They fall from the branches, their mothers' fingertips, and flutter to their death, one by one, at her feet, as she waits in silent patience for the spring, when all renews again. It is the circle of life, and we are not separate but a part of every living thing."

The image of her aunt's smiling face in the fall light, so full of joy, stabbed at her heart. Rowan's eyes welled with tears. She could not hold them back as they flowed down her cheeks, hot and stinging. Bowing her head, she felt empty, consumed with the deep anger that had long raged inside her, along with an ocean of grief.

Landon came upon Rowan as she sat, shoulders hunched, head down upon her crossed arms, sobbing softly. He had never seen her in distress, and he stood silently, watching her for a moment, unwilling to disturb her privacy. When he moved slowly to make her aware of his presence, she stood up and turned to him but did not attempt to wipe the tears from her face.

"What is it?" he asked. "Is something wrong?" But Rowan did not speak.

He paused for a moment. "Maybe it is something that no words can express?"

He moved closer, and she stood silently before him, her face streaked with moisture, still not moving. He cautiously put a hand on her shoulder and drew her slowly into his embrace, cradling her against his chest.

"Hush. Hush, now." He stroked her hair and held her close, wishing to absorb her pain with his own body, as he felt her stiff form surrender against his and heard her muffled sobs slowly wane.

Rowan drew back and looked into his eyes for a long moment, never uttering a word. She turned to walk from the meadow but paused to look back at him as he watched her go.

That night, Landon lay in his hut, staring at the ceiling. He could not forget the feel of Rowan's body pressed against his. His passion transcended mere desire.

I have never known a woman with whom I have grown to respect her strength first and then felt her vulnerability. My feelings have not been diminished by today's experience; they have only grown stronger.

Someone approached his hut, stopping outside and revealing her presence with a low cough. Tonight, he did not welcome the tending of a healer. He did not wish to be distracted from his thoughts of Rowan and the remembrance of those vibrant green eyes.

"I do not want to be disturbed," he announced. He was startled when the hide that covered the opening drew aside and the figure of a woman, crouching low, entered uninvited.

"I want to be alone. I need no tending."

The woman stood up and turned toward the firelight. He was stunned, for there before him stood Rowan.

"Are you all right?" he asked, rising from his bed.

"Yes," she replied. "It is just that . . . I need to express my gratitude for your comfort today."

"It is not necessary," Landon began, but stopped, seeing her look of uncertainty.

"I don't know why I am here . . ." She faltered, looking away.

Landon smiled reassuringly and extended his palm toward her. She stared at it for a moment and then slowly placed her hand in his as he enveloped her in his arms for the second time that day. Rowan did not resist, but she was trembling. He softly kissed her shoulders and stroked her hair.

"No man has ever touched me the way that you did today," Rowan shared.

Landon gently lifted her chin as his lips brushed her cheeks. He looked into her eyes and then gently kissed her lips.

"I don't know if I can—"

Landon touched her lips with his fingertips. "There is no need. Come here and sit beside me. I will hold you, if you would prefer."

Rowan nodded as he drew her down to his bed. He touched

her face, his eyes sparkling in the firelight. "You are beautiful," he said.

She searched his eyes for a moment and then reached up to touch his face, before leaning slowly toward him, kissing him. Landon remained still as her lips touched his and she moved closer to him. He pulled her on top of him, pressing her body to his as he began to move slowly, letting her feel him.

Rowan sat upright above him and pushed the robe from her shoulders, allowing it to gather at her waist, her naked skin glowing in the light. She leaned forward and kissed him again as he caressed her shoulders. Reaching for Landon's hands, she placed them on her breasts. Landon gently cupped them as he lightly stroked her nipples with his thumbs, feeling them harden under his touch.

Rowan gasped, then leaned back and lifted her robe. Straddling his manhood, she slowly lowered herself onto him. Landon moaned softly, opening his mouth to speak, but she placed a finger upon his lips to silence him. Staring down at him and breathing deeply, she began to rock in small, rhythmic movements. Landon ran his hands along her thighs, his eyes never leaving her face. Her motions became quicker, and her breath came in short gasps as she continued to move. Only when she cried out in pleasure did Landon release with a loud groan, unable to contain himself any longer.

Rowan continued to stare down at him in wonder as her eyes welled with tears. He pulled her to him and held her close.

"I am not sad," she whispered. "I just never thought that such a thing was possible between a man and a woman."

"I know," he answered, kissing her tears. "Sleep now." And she closed her eyes.

Through the months of winter, Rowan shared not only the intimacy of his bed but a growing opening of her heart, and in the
quiet of the night, they exchanged stories of their distant worlds.

Landon spoke of a great land beyond the mountains. He had
found a way through the peaks, but horse and man had fallen on
a narrow cliff ledge. He had dragged himself with broken bones
for days to the green below, where the clan women had found him.

"My city is an ancient one built of stone along a beautiful
coastline. It controls most of the trade for prominent sea routes
to the continents beyond," he boasted. "There is nothing in the
known world that has not passed through the great port. I have
seen amazing things and all races of men."

Rowan's eyes shone when he spoke of the places beyond the
sea. "I know where your lands are." He ran his finger gently along
her jawline, tracing the outline of her face. "I will take you home.
When spring comes, we will secure passage along the coast and
return by boat to my city. Then we can make the journey north
and across the sea to your lands."

"I was taken many years ago," Rowan replied. "I fear I would
not know any of my remaining kin. The women here are my family
now."

"I have hoped that I will be your family," Landon answered.
"We will go if you wish to your lands, but when we reach my home,
if you love my city as I do, I will ask that you remain there with
me as my wife."

Rowan lifted her head in surprise. His words did not bring her
comfort. The tight vise upon her heart had begun to loosen, and

her moments of joy with him had been heartfelt, but her loyalties were conflicted. Unable to answer him, she laid her head back down upon his chest, listening to his beating heart. *What would my life be like with Landon in his world? How can I leave these women, when we have forged so much together?*

Landon stroked her hair. "There is time for you to consider my words," he offered, as if reading her thoughts.

When the first signs of spring arrived, Landon asked Rowan the question that she had been avoiding: "If we are to leave, we must begin to prepare for the journey soon. What are your feelings, Rowan? There is no more time for doubt," he urged her.

Rowan's stomach knotted with uncertainty. "It is not an easy answer," she replied, as she watched Landon's expression darken.

"It is easy if you love me," he said. "Tell me what is in your heart."

"I have two hearts: one that beats for you, and one that beats for these women, whose lives are under my protection. Give me leave for a while. I will walk to the meadow for some solitude. When I return, I will give you my answer."

When she rose and left the hut, she was suddenly light-headed and nauseous. She staggered to the nearest tree and retched, leaning her head against the trunk to steady herself. She sought the healer, who only smiled after Rowan explained her ills. She placed her hands on Rowan's stomach and then her breasts. "You are with child."

Rowan stared at the woman, momentarily shocked. "It cannot be possible! I am barren," she stammered. "I was . . . I was so badly used when I was young. I thought that I would never be able to bear a child."

The healer felt the hardness of her stomach again, confirming her judgment. "Your baby will be born near the summer solstice," she answered.

Stunned, Rowan emerged from the hut and into the radiance of the morning. Her senses seemed altered, and the colors around her appeared more vibrant in the streaming sunlight. The astonishment that she carried a new life within her made her body tingle. This child had been conceived in the closest thing to love that Rowan would ever know, and the emotion brought her to tears as tenderness for the father rose in her heart.

She walked to the meadow and lowered herself against the trunk of her favorite tree, wrapping her hands around her stomach.

How can I leave now? I must protect this precious gift. Landon wishes to return home, but would he insist I go, no matter what my decision is, if he knew a child was coming?

A low, warm wind blew across the grasses, and she shivered. She took a deep breath to calm herself, looking down at her stomach and imagining everything she wished for her baby. Then the remembrance of a long-forgotten childhood memory—a tale her grandmother had told around their family fires at night—made her gasp.

Rowan had watched the light dance across her grandmother's weathered features, her eyes blazing with excitement as she spoke in hushed tones of the ancient ones, the great mother and the spirits of the earth. She had whispered the stories of the ancestors, clans of women who rode the plains on horseback, a great nomadic tribe who fought alongside their men as warriors.

Facing the threat of enslavement by conquering tribes, the ancient ones scattered like the wind, passing into myth. Their history was told in song and passed from mother to daughter so that they could always remember that women had once lived and roamed free. Her grandmother had always seemed a little sad in the telling of the tale, and Rowan had sensed a great loss of something wild, and of a way of life that was no more.

Her grandmother had often cast the ancient rune stones, carved with ancient symbols, reading their secrets. One night, she tossed the runes and stared silently for a long time, before she spoke somberly to Rowan.

"You are destined for great things, my granddaughter. From your seed, the old ways will be reborn. The signs are there," she said, pointing to the stones.

Rowan, sitting with her knees drawn to her chest, stared wide-eyed at the runes. She was only a child at the time and did not understand her grandmother's meaning, but would never have questioned her words.

"The past is not lost, Rowan." She moved closer and placed her wrinkled hand upon Rowan's heart. "You feel it here. It is a remembering, then a calling. We once roamed the lands in freedom before we lost our way, becoming docile and dull as cattle. That wild heart still beats, waiting, for I have seen into your soul and it will call upon you one day, my granddaughter."

"Who will call, Grandmother?" Rowan asked, but her grandmother would say no more.

Chills ran down Rowan's body again as the meaning of her grandmother's words resonated within her and a sense of great peace washed over her.

I will never leave this place that has become my home. The children born here, and especially our daughters, will be born to a different world, one that I and the other women will help forge.

She rose slowly, understanding that Landon would make his journey alone. When Rowan returned from the meadow, she declared, "I cannot leave. My place is here."

"Then you do not love me?" he asked.

Her heartache renewed at his wounded expression. "You know that is not true. But I will not leave this place or the women who have entrusted their lives to me." She answered in half-truths, unwilling to reveal the existence of their unborn child.

In the days that followed, Rowan remained steadfast in her decision not to leave.

"You have changed these last days," Landon told her. "I feel that you must distance yourself to remain true to your intent. But I am now reconciled that you will remain, and I will honor your wishes," he added sadly. "Will you still accompany me to the coast so that we may say our final farewells together?" he asked.

"Of course I will," she answered.

They would depart together for the coastline a day later, whereupon Landon could secure passage to the north, and Rowan would return home alone. They spent a last few nights under the open sky and around the fire, sharing the last stories that would sustain them for the rest of their lives.

On their final night together, Rowan stared at him for a long time, wanting to memorize every feature of his face.

"I have a gift for you," she offered. In her hand, she held a clear stone with a hole carefully chiseled in one end. Through it, she had passed a small, braided string. "It is called a moonstone. Its hue changes with the light of day. I hope it will be a pleasant remembrance of me." She placed it around his neck while looking deeply into his eyes.

He touched the beautiful stone fondly, and his eyes glistened with love and sorrow.

"I have nothing to give to you," he apologized, but Rowan stopped him by placing her hand on his chest. "You have given me something priceless," she paused. Landon looked puzzled before she continued. "You have given me an understanding of what it can be like between a man and a woman, and I am changed forever."

He smiled and drew her to him.

On their last morning, she stood upon the rocky coast, staring at the open sea, and watched his boat fade into the coastal fog. Landon stood rigid and grim-faced at the bow, one hand raised in farewell. She faltered, suddenly longing to call him back, but the words of her grandmother resonated once again: *You will be free, Rowan.*

Landon's face faded into the fog as she looked down to cradle her stomach and her unborn life.

I am certain my child will be a girl, born into a new freedom— and she will be a warrior!

Upon arriving home, Rowan dismounted and walked her horse along the trail that led to the forest center, where she knew the women would be preparing the evening meal. They greeted her with well-wishes at her safe return, none of them knowing her distress. Only Asha was aware of her inner turmoil, though not of her secret.

"Landon is on his way?" Asha asked.

Rowan nodded. "It was a difficult parting," she shared quietly.

"How could you let him go?" one woman blurted out.

Rowan acknowledged her words. "As I stood upon that shore, watching him leave, I faltered," she answered honestly. "I know my decision was difficult for many of you to understand, but he could not stay. Going with him would have meant my leaving this place and the people who are so close to my heart now."

The woman nodded to each other, smiling at the shared sentiment.

"There is something else," Rowan hesitated, glancing at Asha, who eyed her questioningly. "A child is coming." Many women gasped in delight and moved to encircle Rowan, touching her lightly and lovingly on her stomach.

Asha stood, shaking her head, before smiling broadly. "The gods have indeed blessed you."

Rowan flushed. "I do not know how to express my feeling about how my world has changed. Nor can I contain the joy I feel about the coming of this new life."

The women glanced at one another, their eyes shining. One young woman, with hair as pale as moonlight and large blue eyes, gushed, "I am so happy for you, Rowan. I have secretly longed for a child myself. It is my heart's only desire."

Her expression of delight dimmed for a moment, and sadness passed across her face, before her eyes brightened again. "Can I have the child without the husband?" She smiled, and all the women laughed.

Studying the earnest face of the young woman, Rowan paused to consider the truth underlying the innocent question. Why was this woman not entitled to such happiness, too? How could Rowan experience such joy while other women were denied it?

They had sworn that no outsiders would live among them, but Landon's presence had reminded the women of an element missing from their lives. Their trips to the outlying townships satisfied some of their need for comfort and male contact, but children were another consideration.

All the women stood in silence before her, and, as if reading her thoughts, one blurted out, "We have never questioned the presence of men among us until your Landon."

Rowan turned sharply toward her. "I understand, but he was not most men," she challenged. "When we allow them into our world, we risk changing the freedoms that we have all vowed to protect. Do we sacrifice this way of life, which has been of our choosing?"

In the awkward silence that followed, the women stood with eyes downcast and no answers. Only Asha stood tall, her arms crossed over her chest. "I do not need men. I agreed with Rowan that they could not live among us; it would change what we have." She moved to stand beside Rowan and affectionately touched Rowan's stomach. "But they—and this child—are part of life, undeniable in its expression. We will be judged harshly if we bring men into our world and adopt their ways. How we can balance this, keep it our own?" she asked.

The women's expressions were hopeful as Rowan looked around the circle. "What is it that you suggest?" she asked of Asha.

"Let them come. Let the outsiders see our world. We cannot continue in this isolation forever, and each woman will choose what she wants because we are all free to do so."

The women's faces brightened at her words.

"But this act cannot violate the sacredness of our unity. Their coming must be a part of our worship and purified by fire," Asha continued.

Rowan stood, shaking her head, knitting her brow, torn

between her uncertainty and the wisdom of Asha's words, while the women awaited her decree.

"So be it, then," she surrendered. "At the next full moon, bring your men."

7

THE CLAN SUMMONS

Seanna turned to look over her shoulder and viewed the mountain range behind her in the distance, before urging her horse forward into the shade of the woods. She dismounted to stretch muscles stiff from the day's ride and inhaled the faint scent of pine and musk. The air in the shadows felt cool against her skin. Shafts of light penetrated the tree canopy and fell upon the forest floor, clover covered the ground in a soft green blanket, insects hummed lazily among the foliage, and birdsong echoed through the trees.

Seanna's eye followed the panorama of the distant hills, which changed in color from soft blues to grays. Woman and horse stood quietly as one for a moment, resting in the shade.

"You will have a well-deserved rest soon," she stated softly, as she affectionately patted the mare's chestnut neck.

Although she savored the quiet surrounding her, she could not calm her churning thoughts. *I know full well what the clans' summons to the gathering means for the future of my people. My journey to the peaks has cost me time. Did I need the assurance that the pass still existed? It has been almost a year since my discovery and my chance meeting with James. The summer solstice is soon. Will he even remember my oath?*

Her horse reared its head and snorted excitedly as the birch leaves, rustled by the wind, and sparkling in the late afternoon sun, drew her attention. Beyond the forest lay a vast, open meadow and the trail leading to her final destination: the fortress of Lord Arden, clan lord of the largest of the northern territories.

By now, the clan lords of every region have arrived. A great concession has been granted to me to stand before the clansmen at the vote. Have I been too bold in my claims to my mother, of victory for the Womara and of the vote for inclusion in the alliance? My confidence cannot fail me now.

She remounted and nudged her horse into the clearing, taking no pleasure in the thought of the impending bustle of the township and fortress. She picked up the trail to the settlement on the far side of the meadow, which led to the first sentry outpost at the far boundary of Lord Arden's territory.

"Identify yourself!" the sentry ordered, as she stopped before the gateway.

"I am Seanna, of the Womara clan," she answered, pushing back the hood of her cloak to expose her face.

Three of the four men turned their heads sharply toward her in curiosity. The fourth man touched his hand to his heart and then his forehead, in her people's gesture of greeting and respect, and as a signal that he had been born among the Womara. She returned the greeting, then spurred her horse on, moving through the barrier and toward the township.

Lord Arden sat in his high-backed chair, motionless except for the impatient tapping of a single finger on the ornately carved arm. Rows of wooden benches and chairs stood empty of the clan lords who had been arriving over the last fortnight. Arden stared ahead at the barrenness of the large hall and a room that should have been silent. A chill filled the room, not because the evening fires were unlit but because of the animosity of the two men who faced each other.

Lord Warin, the head of the largest clan of the southern region, paced restlessly in front of Arden, speaking loudly. He waved his arms around in dramatic gestures, stopping to point his finger in Arden's direction.

"I am not questioning your vision for a governing body of men under your proposed alliance, and for a council that will unite our regions," Warin said, as Arden watched him. He was an unattractive man, with a squat body and thick muscles. He wore the full beard and long hair of his clan and always appeared disheveled. In his actions was a wildness that reminded Arden of a small, captive brown bear he had seen in his youth. The beast had padded endlessly from one end of the cage to the other in its misery. When Arden had approached the animal, it had stared at him, and he had seen no light behind its eyes—only the dull determination of a predator ready to kill. Warin had this same look, and Arden knew the man could not be trusted.

Lord Warin's voice rose again. "The logic to develop a seaport on the eastern coast, merging with the trade routes to the north, is sound and would herald a new era of expansion for our realms. I might agree that Lord Edmond's fortress is the best choice for that port, within his natural sea inlet. But the division of the northern and southern regions into two governing bodies with separate clan lords heading the council, and the development of an additional port on the southwest coast, makes for just as strong a proposal."

Arden stared ahead, remaining motionless.

"Are you listening to me?" Warin demanded.

"I am," Arden answered. "But the will of the clans will be what decides the outcome of the alliance and the formation of the council, not a covert agreement made between us for a division of regions."

Warin glared at Arden. "Does your proposed council still include the clan of women? I want to hear you speak it out loud."

"I have made no secret of my support for the inclusion of the Womara, and I will stand by that pledge."

"Your willingness to include all the clans in the alliance makes your position weak," Warin snapped. "That pledge will be your undoing," he added, before turning abruptly to leave.

Arden leaned back against the rigid chair, feeling the strain of the last several days. There was no place for two leaders in an alliance, especially with Lord Warin heading the southern clans, but did the other clansmen mistrust Warin as much as Arden did?

He sighed at the thought. These lands, ruled for centuries by feuding clans, had little need of allegiance to a greater whole, only to their own kind and their own territory. The only time of great unity had been during his forebearer's rule, when the clans had joined forces against a massive invasion by thousands of raiders who had attacked by land and by sea. They had barely saved their realm from being conquered.

Arden rubbed his brow in fatigue. *We are a common people*

with a common language, descended from an ancient blood, but we are a people divided.

His summons to the leadership of each region had set in motion years of painstaking planning to build a united coalition. He would honor the clans' vote regarding the alliance and its governing council, but he was concerned for the fate of the Womara if they were not included. With that, glancing toward the fading light in the open doorway, Arden realized that Seanna had not arrived yet.

Day had moved into dusk by the time Seanna reached the last outpost and passed through the gates without question. The outer grounds were a colorful canopy of tents and flags, each delineating a clan's separate territory. Groups of men sat around small cooking fires, sharing the evening meal. Seanna made her way toward the meeting hall and watched them stop midsentence as she approached, then heard them resume their conversations in low tones once she had passed.

She acknowledged some of the familiar faces, while others sat rigid. She knew that talk of the Womara's inclusion in any alliance divided men deeply along lines of acceptance, misconception, and outright prejudice. The clans in the vicinity of the Womara were more accepting of their ways, and trade provided a link between them—and for those men who visited the Womara's communal fires, there were be additional bonds, those of relations and offspring.

Seanna knew that some clansmen would recognize her as one of Lord Arden's scouts, a clandestine band of elite fighters—selected for their skill with weapons, fighting, and tracking, and for their knowledge of the wilderness terrain—who had sworn allegiance to him. The group roamed the forests, mountain ranges, and coastal areas to watch the remote and outlying territories of all regions and would ultimately report to a council for the alliance. Seanna was the only woman who had earned a place among these fighters.

Dismounting in front of the hall, she handed the reins to a young boy on duty. She removed her bow and quiver and her long sword, placing them outside the entrance. The youth stared at the knives still at her side and at the dagger secured in the belt behind her back.

"See that my horse gets good bedding," she ordered, and he jumped to attention before she strode into the hall. The soft glow of the lanterns enhanced the waning light of the day as all eyes turned toward her.

Lord Arden was in the company of his senior guards and several of her fellow scouts. She closed the distance between them, pausing for a moment to meet his eyes before dropping to one knee, her head bowed slightly and her hand on her heart. This gesture of respect and service from a Womara, who usually knelt to no man, signaled to the men that Arden possessed both from her.

"My lord," Seanna said as she stood.

"You were delayed?" Arden asked.

"I was. I hope that I have not postponed any urgent matters," she answered.

"No. The last of the clan lords has arrived today."

Arden's men stared openly at her, some with dark looks. She knew that her presence as a scout was contentious among some of them, but she stood erect, meeting their gaze unwaveringly.

Seanna returned her attention to Lord Arden and studied his

face thoughtfully, looking directly into his eyes again, a trait of her people, and examining the nuances of his features. It had been almost a year since she had seen him last.

He has aged. Has this dedication to his grand vision begun to take a toll?

Deep lines etched his forehead, and his beard and shoulder-length dark hair were salted with more gray now, but his eyes, his most noble feature, had not changed. They were still the same penetrating blue.

Seanna knew that his strongest qualities, fairness and good judgment, would be needed to unite the men of the surrounding clans. His generous nature, which endeared him to his people, was the very quality that some cited as working against him, reasoning that he lacked a hard enough hand to unite the outlying regions.

Turning to the men, he gestured. "Give me leave to speak with Seanna alone."

The men excused themselves. Among them was Gareth, a fellow alliance scout, who nodded his welcome to Seanna when their eyes met.

Watching the last man depart, Arden gestured to Seanna to sit beside him. "When you were overdue, I was concerned."

"Yes," she replied. "I scouted the mountain area before leaving my valley, delaying my journey." She offered no further explanation.

"Was something wrong?" Lord Arden pressed.

"No." She hesitated. "There is something I must discuss with you, but I will wait until the clan vote is over."

She saw Arden's curious expression as he studied her face. He leaned forward and offered her wine, but she declined. She reached into her tunic, withdrawing a scroll that she extended to him.

"It is a message from my leader. She sends her greetings."

Arden read slowly and then looked up at Seanna. "Do you know the contents of her message?" he asked.

"My mother has made the final decision that we will proceed with the petition for inclusion in the alliance," she answered.

Arden looked down at the scroll again. "I agreed with her that now is the time. You could delay to see whether the clansmen can form a united body, but I think you must be a part of the alliance council from its inception."

"The Womara council agrees with your conclusions," Seanna answered. "It is our wish that the new alliance will provide a forum for men to know us better."

"These next days will be challenging for you. It is Lord Warin who still poses the greatest opposition to the Womara's inclusion in the alliance and a place at the council. We cannot underestimate his influence, nor his ambition to sway the discussions unfavorably against your clan," Arden added.

"That is no surprise to me. His opposition has been a concern to our clan," Seanna answered. "He is a feared lord, ruling with intolerance and a ruthless hand, and demanding respect, instead of earning the hearts of his people."

"You will need to keep those words to yourself in the next several days. Warin's opposition will be a test of diplomacy, not the stronger will," Arden cautioned.

"The Womara's petition to join the alliance and council must stand on its own merit, or what hope do we have against a man as narrow-minded as Lord Warin, who advocates for our exclusion merely because we are women?" Seanna replied. "Was this not the greater purpose of my inclusion into the scouts that would serve the alliance—to live among them, to let them discover my character, and in that proximity to come to know that we share a common objective?"

"It was sound reasoning," Arden answered.

"I have also served some of these lords as bodyguard to their children, and I have spent the last several years protecting these lands for all clansmen. I believe that I have formed friendships founded in respect. My sword has been my word, and I have never failed in that duty."

"True enough, but are you confident in the worth of that duty?" asked Arden. "Warin has a black heart, and he is unmoved by such sentiments."

Her stomach constricted, betraying her misgivings. "Our lands are secured by treaty given long ago, but I know that the memory of man is short, and that loyalties once earned could be replaced by ambition or gain. This is a changing world, and the ways of man need to adapt with it. How will the Womara continue to live in peace or prosper if we are surrounded by a stronger coalition of clans, one that does not accept us into a new order? Sometimes a new vision must be forced upon those who refuse to see."

The sternness of her words made Arden sit more erect. "I understand your vexation, but again I caution temperance. I, too, do not wish to squander the years of sacrifice that you have made in service to this cause. Your mother has placed high hopes in that service as well. Do not think that all has been in vain. The opportunity for real change benefits all clans," he answered.

Seanna hesitated. "If I may speak my truth . . . I fear that I have failed to do enough to foster that change. The Womara have been complacent in our seclusion. We have relied on the goodwill of our allies to support our cause. We need to offer more."

"We will see," Arden answered. "But there is no need for any more talk tonight. Get food and some rest. We will speak more tomorrow." He nodded to dismiss her.

She rose, hand on her heart, and turned to leave, noting that he still held Dian's directive tightly in his hand.

Emerging into the cool night air, Seanna made her way toward the encampments. She found Gareth seated beside the fire at their camp; glancing up, he gestured with a tilt of his head for her to sit.

As he handed her a plate of food, he gave her a sideways grin. "I thought you would arrive before me."

"I know," she agreed.

"We have not missed anything but a day of this spectacle," he added.

For a few moments, they ate in a comfortable silence, having spent many hours in the wilds just like this, sitting around a fire and listening to the evening sounds.

"I do not envy Lord Arden in this undertaking. The minds of men are hard to change, and giving control to an alliance will be difficult," Gareth speculated.

Seanna continued to eat silently.

"Did you journey home after we parted last?" he asked.

"I had a brief visit. I spent some time along the mountain ranges before traveling here," Seanna answered.

"That was out of your way, was it not?"

"Yes, but I needed to go." She shrugged.

"What drew you there?" he asked.

"Strength in solitude," she answered, smirking.

"You will need that for the trials that lie ahead, my friend," Gareth answered, more seriously.

Seanna smiled. "I like that you call me 'friend.' I think that I will have few among the men here."

Gareth eyed her. "You have alluded to strength in mirth, but you will need to be strong. You have the allegiance of the clans that border your lands. Lord Edmond and his son, Stuart, along with Lord Arden, are your most powerful allies. You know the hearts of your fellow scouts."

"That brings me more comfort than you may know," she answered.

Gareth reached out to touch her arm. "I will vouch for you any day, and I would not have been able to argue the value of a Womara among us as scouts before you came. Your service has brought balance to our faction. This proposed new alliance would benefit from that perspective."

She turned to him. "I thank you for your words, and I hope that you are right, but we alliance scouts are few among the many clans here. Some men do not share that view. But there are those who have come to know me better, and that is why I will be the one to represent the Womara at the clan vote."

"Why are you alone?" Gareth asked.

"I asked for the privilege. And there will be something revealed about me in the coming days that I could not share. I wanted to, but I could not," Seanna stated. With that, she rose, turning her back to the warmth of the fire. "I need some rest. It has been a hard ride."

Gareth nodded his good night as Seanna departed for her tent. Now was not the time to press her. He was accustomed to her quiet and inward ways, and often few words. The fact that she did not converse in idle gossip and that he had never known her to speak an untruth had gained her his hard-earned respect and deepened their unique friendship. Once, he had shared with her that he liked her because she avoided the frivolous and unnecessary conversation he often associated with women. The comment had made her laugh.

Settling back, he kicked the logs, watching the embers spark. *I have sensed for a while that something greater at play is troubling her. What did her words mean?*

In a rare confidence, she had shared with him that her inclusion in the warrior scouts had accustomed her to the ways of men, and that she had accepted the challenge for the benefit of her clan, but that it was not by her choice alone that she served.

Is her service coming to an end? he wondered.

As scouts, they often wandered the wilds together, sometimes for weeks at a time. From what he had observed of her, she feared neither man nor beast. Gareth knew why, having been one of the men selected to judge her fighting skills and having voted in her favor to include a woman in the scouts.

He thought back to the day she had arrived, while the men stood together in the fighting area of Lord Arden's compound, watching her enter.

"What is she doing here?" another scout had asked him, but Gareth had been just as puzzled by her arrival.

Another man joined them. "She is a Womara," he declared. "She was the bodyguard of Stuart, the son of Lord Edmond." He leaned closer to the men. "It is rumored that she killed her first man at age fourteen. Lord Arden himself invited her."

The men continued to stare at her while she watched them from across the grounds.

"It is an insult that she is here. She cannot possibly compete with us, and I wager she is out in the first round," one man boasted.

Gareth declined to bet, but the rest of the men exchanged wagers with great enthusiasm. They had all stood humbled at the end of the trials after she had been rigorously tested in the bow and with swords. She had prevailed. And any man who had witnessed the trials would now have thought twice before challenging her.

Gareth had faced his own humiliation when he lost a mock fight to her. Seanna used several of her opening signature moves, which he now knew well but which at the time were effective on an unsuspecting opponent. He had been outfought and faced her in the circle as the other men stood in uncomfortable silence. He expected a haughty attitude from her, chin raised and eyes gloating at having beaten a man, but she surprised him.

"Good fight." She stepped toward him with a hand extended. "You almost had me." She smiled.

Gareth stared at the extended hand for a moment as his men watched in anticipation, before laughing out loud. "I won't be so easy next time."

Months later, after her inclusion in the alliance warriors and on a day Gareth would never forget, she proved herself worthy to them beyond any lingering doubts. He owed her a debt he might not ever be able to repay.

He, Seanna, and two other fellow scouts were on patrol and had been traveling the northern regions for several days. He had sent Seanna, the best tracker in the group, ahead of them that morning.

"I will scout the upper forest trails and rejoin you before sunset" were her parting words.

"Catch us some rabbits along the way for dinner!" another scout shouted.

"Only if you cook them, for once!" Seanna yelled back over her shoulder, causing the men to laugh.

"Let's move," Gareth admonished. "We need to make the coastal territory border by nightfall."

The men passed an uneventful day and moved off the trail to water their horses at a marsh. Dismounting and moving toward the water, Gareth paused, sensing an unnatural silence. There were no bird noises.

He glanced at his comrades, who were talking and stretching themselves, unaware of the quiet. Gareth was standing still, listening intently, when he detected the first movement of men who were camouflaged among the reeds, waiting for them.

The raiders rose from their hiding place along the bank. The front three men had bows drawn and arrows pointed directly at the men's hearts. Three remaining raiders revealed themselves next, stepping behind the bowmen with swords in hand.

"Stand where you are. The first one who moves is a dead man," one hulking figure snapped.

The scouts froze, glancing at each other, knowing that they were trapped and outnumbered.

"Take their weapons, tie their hands, and lash them together," the lead man ordered.

The raiders with the bows shifted forward, relaxing their stance only when all the men were bound and hobbled. Standing back, the man examined his captives, assessing their value, while the other raiders searched their belongings. Standing directly in front of Gareth, the headman lifted his chin with a knife to stare at him.

"They are strong and will fetch good prices as workers at the slave markets for the salt mines," he sneered.

Another raider spoke up. "We have enough men to sell for the mines waiting at the boats. These look like too much trouble. They are well-armed scouts or soldiers. Let us take their belongings and the horses and be gone."

Gareth surmised that they would die if they were deemed worthless. The leader stepped back and spoke in whispers to the man at his side, measuring each of Gareth's men in turn. When he turned away toward their horses, Gareth sensed the grim answer: it would be death. He strained against his ropes, feeling helpless as he stared into his comrades' eyes, knowing that each man knew their shared fate.

Out of the corner of his eye, Gareth caught a movement from the stand of trees to his left and froze. Seanna stood pressed against the side of a tree, hidden from the raiders' view, bow in hand and arrow ready. She slowly raised it to eye level, her focus fixed upon the forward archer. Gareth could see that to take her shot, she would have to step clear and expose herself. She would have the element of surprise and one chance to hit her mark.

The leader laughed and, with a sick smile, turned his back on them, walking behind the bowmen as he commanded, "Kill them. They will be too much trouble."

Suddenly, Seanna stepped from the side of the tree and shouted, "Stand down," startling everyone, including Gareth, but drawing the raiders' attention and shifting their bows toward her.

Her first arrow struck the closest one directly in the heart. Two more arrows followed in rapid succession, striking the chests of the remaining bowmen, whose startled grunts conveyed their bewilderment as they fell.

The remaining raiders looked in disbelief at their downed comrades, freezing for a moment, before one of them regained his senses and leaped toward Seanna. A knife thrown from her hand pierced his throat and stopped him short.

"Kill her!" the leader yelled, as he and the remaining man charged.

Seanna drew her sword. The captive men struggled against their bindings as the raiders fell upon her. She sidestepped her closest attacker and slashed his stomach, both hands gripping her long sword. He screamed in pain, falling to the ground and clutching his abdomen.

The leader charged toward her in rapid strides, raining down a high blow. Seanna could barely get her sword above her to ward off the strike. The force drove her to one knee and ripped the weapon from her hand.

Gareth continued to struggle, thinking that their brief moment of hope was over as the man pulled back for the death strike, but then Seanna jumped to her feet. Pulling her short knife from its hilt, in one swift, upward motion, she stuck the blade into his abdomen. He stared down in disbelief at the handle protruding from his stomach, then sank to his knees. Seanna jerked the knife free and met him with a slash across his throat. He fell forward, dead before he slumped to the ground.

Gareth gasped, releasing his held breath in disbelief, watching Seanna standing among the fallen men. She recovered her sword and moved to the fallen raiders, checking that each one was dead.

Advancing to the bound men, she cut their ties, stepping back and surveying them for injuries.

"I picked up their trail too late to warn you," she stated, almost apologetically. "They had backtracked, looking for a place to ambush."

The men rubbed the feeling back into their wrists and stared at the bodies lying before them.

"We were dead men," Gareth exclaimed.

"It was not your day to die but theirs." Seanna flashed him a rare grin as he watched her return to the bodies of the men and examine them closely. "We will take the horses, but nothing else. Leave them where they are," she commanded.

She drew her arrows from the bodies, then rolled the men's commander on his back and drove an arrow into his chest. "This is a warning to those who may pass that a Womara warrior killed these men."

From that day forward, Seanna's worthiness was never questioned, and word of her prowess grew, as did their friendship.

8

A REUNION OF OLD FRIENDS

Seanna slept hard and was roused from her deep sleep at mid-morning by the distant laughter of children playing in the camps. She rolled onto her side and listened to voices that were a pleasant reminder of home.

She slowly lifted herself upright, running her hands through her tangled hair, then walked to face the light that outlined her tent door and peered outside, judging the day.

Her stomach churned, and she judged the stirring to be a combination of hunger, nervous butterflies, and a slight sense of nausea.

I am not sure that I am ready to face the unfolding drama of events ahead. Staying civil will be a challenge. The outcome for the Womara in this future new alliance has created a feeling of loneliness greater than anything I have experienced in the solitude of the wild.

She took a long breath, steadying her senses.

First things first. I will find a bathing house so that I am presentable for the clan banquet tonight, and then a meal in the town square. Stuart must have arrived by now. My old friend will be a welcome sight.

She emerged from her tent into the bright sunlight and the activity of the encampment, making her way toward the marketplace. The streets buzzed with excitement. Folks were cheery at the arrival of so many people. The vendors carefully laid out their wares in their stalls for the best views, anticipating that their purses would soon be full.

Seanna's first stop was the laundry house, where the laundress was a large, rotund woman with cheeks bright red from years of exposure to steaming-hot water and harsh soaps.

"Hello, dearie. I see we are in need of a bath today," she noted, wrinkling her nose.

"Yes, and I will need my clothes laundered and this dress pressed," Seanna replied.

The laundress nodded and said, "Follow me," waddling toward a side room.

In the bathing area, the woman's constant prattling momentarily distracted Seanna from her pensive mood.

How can one person talk so continuously on an endless stream of topics? She has scarcely taken a breath between sentences.

Peace arrived when a young maid entered the room and whispered in the ear of the laundress, whose startled look, directed at Seanna, stopped all conversation.

Seanna smiled. *My reputation must be catching up with me.*

The women quickly exited, and she enjoyed the remainder of her bath in silence, emerging later in clean garments and with a pressed dress in hand for the banquet later that evening.

She ambled toward the market area, which was bustling with the movement and noise of people engaged in the commerce of the day. Braying donkeys and clucking chickens, mixed with vendors' calls to passersby to view their wares, added up to a discordant symphony. Stalls displayed a variety of fruits and vegetables, meats, fish, and breads. Barrels of nuts and grains were plentiful. The smell of spices and sweets tempted Seanna, who could no longer ignore her growling stomach.

The aroma of savory meats and vegetables cooking in a large iron pot over a fire at an outside tavern drew her attention. She purchased a bowl of stew with a slice of thick bread and sat upon an outdoor bench, eating leisurely, taking in the sights and sounds of the market. When her hunger was satisfied, her thoughts drifted back to the business of politics.

Lord Arden has been considerate not to summon me early. We have yet to discuss the impending votes and how to try to calculate the loyalties of the clan lords. Gareth is right. Those leaders extending their strongest support and allegiance to my clan are the ones from the lands that border the Womara's valley: Lords Arden and Edmond. Their combined support is a powerful advantage for us. Lord Edmond is elderly now, and I doubt that he has made the journey to the gathering, but I know Stuart will be the clan delegate.

Seanna and Stuart had known each other since their youth. She had been his bodyguard when they were children and had long called him a friend. Stuart had once been impetuous and headstrong, but he had grown into a thoughtful young man, chosen by his father to succeed him as clan leader. It had been several years since she had seen him last. It would be a welcome reunion to meet again, albeit under serious circumstances.

She paid the tavern owner for her meal and wandered among

the merchant stalls. A pale yellow silk flashed iridescent in the sunlight, catching her eye. She ran her fingertips over the exotic fabric, smiling. *This is beautiful and feels luscious.*

The merchant approached but, eyeing her men's garb, made no attempt to praise the value of the silk or waste flattering words that the color was sure to entice any man's eye.

Seanna smiled to herself. *He has wrongly assumed that the lure of the feminine is wasted on me, for I can imagine myself wrapped in this splendid fabric!*

She slowly turned away from the material, frowning, for its beauty had lost its luster as her thoughts turned again to politics.

It is hard to imagine the prospect of romance in a life so bound by duty and obligation. It has been almost a full year since I last attended the sacred fires, only to watch other men and women dance the flames. Am I resigned to a feeling that it is not my path to live as others do?

She was jolted from her thoughts when she heard her name called from across the market square and saw Stuart striding toward her.

"Seanna! Seanna!" He waved wildly, closing the distance between them as she waited to greet her old friend. He stopped before her, laughing out loud as they clasped forearms.

"Let me look at you! It has been too long. You are so grown-up," he teased, as he held her at arm's length, admiring her.

Seanna looked up into his beaming face. He was no longer the boy of her childhood but a man who towered over her. His light brown hair fell to his shoulders, and he bore the full beard of his clan. His face was handsome, with deep brown eyes that still twinkled with a touch of mischief. Seanna smiled warmly up at him, whom she had grown to love as one of her kin.

"You look well, my lord." She laughed.

"As do you," he replied. "We have so much to talk about, and you must tell me everything that has happened. How is your life as a scout? What kind of adventures have you had?" His eyes shone as he leaned closer to her, barely catching his breath.

Seanna grinned at his rapid questions. *He has not changed so much*, she thought. He still demanded to know everything with the impatience that had characterized him as a youth—the very same quality that had once almost cost them their lives.

"Let's find someplace to sit where we can speak in private," she said. "I want to know how your father is and hear the news from your home."

As they moved to leave the square, several of Lord Warin's men made their way into the market, drawing attention to themselves with their boisterous behavior. Stuart followed Seanna's gaze to watch them. Lord Warin and his clan were no favorites of Lord Edmond and his son; their mutual bitterness and mistrust had grown over many years of broken promises and unfinished agreements.

Stuart's face did not conceal his disdain. "There is trouble," he said under his breath. "I will be truthful. My men have endured taunting over the last several days for our perceived support of your clan, and it has tested all of our willpower to keep tongues civil."

Seanna nodded her agreement. The raucous men reminded her of an encounter the year before, when she and Gareth had stopped for a meal in the southern portion of Lord Warin's region. They had barely sat down to eat, when a group of four men at the adjoining table directed a slur at Seanna. Gareth rose from the bench, but Seanna pulled him back down. She would deal with the slight herself.

She rose and stepped to face the offending man. The instigator laughed out loud to his men as he loomed over her. Seanna moved in quickly with a powerful elbow to his diaphragm, dropping him to the floor and leaving him gasping for air. The men jumped to their feet as Seanna gripped her sword, sending a warning.

Silence hung in the air for a long minute while everyone stared, but then the entire tavern erupted with laughter at the humiliation of the fallen bully. Seanna relaxed, exhaling, as Warin's men glanced at the fallen man, who was struggling for breath on the floor, then dragged him from the tavern, allowing Gareth and Seanna to finish their meal in peace.

She turned to Stuart now, touching his forearm. "Ignore them. Let's not waste the time we have on the likes of them."

"I see that your tolerance for men's bravado has not increased," he teased her, as Seanna gave him a look of mock annoyance.

He turned serious then, as he asked, "How is Thea?"

"She is well and sends her greetings," Seanna answered. "She has asked me to invite you to return with me at the end of the gathering, before you journey home." Stuart's face brightened. "But set your joy aside for the moment and tell me of your father."

Stuart's smile faded, replaced with a look of concern. "In your time gone, he has changed much. Old age is upon him. His years as clan lord have taken a measurable toll. I wish nothing more for him than to enjoy his remaining years by sitting in the sun and watching his grandchildren play."

"What grandchildren? You had better get started," Seanna teased, giving him a sly look and bringing a smile back to his face.

"I fear I will be clan lord soon, and at times I feel great doubt about my readiness to be that man," he confessed.

"I know you will be a worthy lord," she replied. "You bring the future and the prospect of change for the benefit of your people."

Stuart stopped to look into her eyes. "I have always trusted the wisdom of your words, and I have missed your counsel, my old friend."

He paused. "But what of you, Seanna? Your trials have only just begun. Are you going to represent your clan alone?"

Seanna's heart constricted at his words, which touched the core of her fears and reminded her of the added burden of failure if the Womara did not gain acceptance into the alliance.

Leaning close to her, he lowered his voice. "Do you think that the presence of more of your clan, and especially your leader, would have made a stronger impression? Or was Dian afraid it would incite opposition?"

"It was at my request that I came alone. I have my reasons," Seanna answered, watching Stuart's eyes narrow at her comment.

"What do you mean?"

"Let's sit over there." Seanna pointed to a small stone bench. "I need your counsel," she added.

They sat upon the bench and settled against the cool stone wall, shaded by a hanging wisteria vine. Seanna glanced up at the sunlight filtering through the vine, admiring the beauty of the small purple flowers.

Stuart's expression entreated her to begin, but before she could speak, a servant of Lord Arden hastily approached them. "Forgive the intrusion, milady, but Lord Arden requests your presence," he announced.

She nodded to the servant and rose to follow, disappointed at the interruption. "I will see you at the banquet hall later," she told Stuart. "We will find more time to talk then."

Stuart leaned back against the wall, watching her go. Fondness for his old friend overwhelmed him.

My loyalty to Seanna is unquestionable, but I will receive more criticism among some clansmen for my support. How can others possibly understand the unbreakable bond between us formed so many years ago?

Stuart's hand strayed to the old wound in his thigh, and he remembered the first day he had met Seanna, as a young girl, tall for her age and barely older than his own sixteen years. She had stood in front of his father silently, with her unflinching gaze, as he had ranted against his father's decree that a Womara bodyguard would be his constant companion.

His father had admonished him in front of her, lecturing him, "Need I remind you of the Womara mandate that calls for all women to be raised with the ability to fight? Many are placed in highborn households to blend among the people they protect, and Seanna has been selected for ours because of those abilities. You should be proud to have such a protector."

Stuart knew that these child guards were the elite of their clan, and that, when older, they became the core of the warrior protectors. But none of this mattered to him then—only the humiliation he felt at the indignity of being shadowed by a female. Stuart glared at her and refused to believe that this girl standing before him, barely reaching to his shoulder, could act as any kind of deterrent to a would-be assailant.

Of course, his father's will was unquestionable. He loved his only son and heir and would leave no means unutilized for his son's protection. Stuart did not dare to openly defy his father's directive, but he vowed he would never tolerate Seanna.

A privilege of her service was that she would receive education alongside him. *What is the point of instructing a girl?* Stuart wondered. He watched her in their lessons. Her long braid could never quite contain the many wisps of thick hair that escaped it, giving her a look of wildness. But she was quiet and studious, focused intently on her writing, and when called upon recalled the answers. She spoke the ancient language and some of the dialects of the surrounding clans. Over time, Stuart could not deny that she had a keen mind, but he fumed with jealousy whenever his father invited her to play chess, a game that Stuart could not fathom anyone's wanting to learn. He would sulk, brooding in the distance, at their congratulatory laughter over a wise move.

The girls in the household shunned Seanna, and he often saw her sitting alone, book in hand, reading but always keeping a vigilant eye on him. Not once did he stop to consider how alone she was, and the toll that her service to his father exacted on her youth.

His wound had long ago healed, but the harrowing remembrance attached to it had not. He had returned to that terrible morning in his mind's eye over the years, reliving the encounter again and again and always judging himself harshly for his choices. He had become a man that day, but not because of his actions.

That morning, he had been insufferable in his restlessness, shut inside after days of rain, and unrelenting in his insistence to go riding with friends at the first break in the weather. His father had finally yielded and granted him leave for a short ride, weary of his son's dark mood. The small group of laughing boys, with Seanna following behind, galloped free of the village walls. Approaching the outer perimeter of the boundaries, Stuart spurred his horse on, taunting and eager to leave Seanna behind.

"Come on," he shouted over his shoulder to his friends. "Let's keep going. I want to see the coast. We can ride all the way and breathe in the salt air."

He glanced back again at Seanna, challenging her with his look not to follow, as the other boys reined in their horses. They would not venture beyond the protected perimeter of their lands to a coastline that always carried a degree of danger from marauding bands. Stuart felt Seanna's focus upon him as she tried to close the distance between them.

He rode wildly the remaining miles, trying to free himself from her.

She and my friends will not betray me to my father, and no one else will know of the risk. I will look upon the coast and then return quickly. She cannot stop me.

On a small, grassy knoll that faced the sea and a fringe of forest in the distance, he slowed his horse, finally conceding, unable to evade her pursuit. The wildness of the act had consumed him and dissipated his frustration as he dismounted to rest. He breathed the smell the sea, but the passion of the impulse was gone as quickly as his changing mood.

Seanna reined her horse to a halt a short distance away and scanned the horizon. Scowling at her, he turned slowly to remount, feeling spent. She dismounted and stood beside her horse, listening intently. All was quiet, save for the sound of the crashing waves and the cry of a solitary seagull circling above.

"Let's leave," Stuart ordered.

"Stand still," she commanded sharply. Her stricken expression made the hairs stand up on the back of his neck.

A second later, the whoosh of the arrow flew from the secluded edge of the tree line. Stuart screamed as the arrow passed through his thigh, and the searing pain dropped him to his knees. A second arrow pierced his horse in the neck, and it dropped, mortally wounded. He twisted in pain toward the direction of the flying arrows. Three men on horseback emerged from the grove of trees and charged at full gallop across the open knoll. Seanna had stepped away from her horse and stood rooted to the ground.

Stuart stared in horror. "Oh my God" escaped his lips.

The thought of the anguished face of his father flashed before him as he watched the young girl standing alone before the charging men, the only thing between Stuart and his fate.

Seanna's bow was out and an arrow in place, yet she did not move. Stuart wanted to cry out his warning, but he was frozen. An eternity seemed to pass while the raiders hurtled toward them. Stuart realized that it was just not courage that kept her waiting but the shorter distance her bow arm needed to find its mark. He held his breath, scarcely able to watch her stand her ground for so long, waiting for them to close the distance.

Seanna leveled her bow and released the first arrow. It pierced the first man through the heart, and he fell from his horse. She rapidly readied the bow again, shooting another arrow, slightly off center this time, but the second man fell, dead before he hit the ground. There was no time for a final draw as the remaining horseman bore down, knocking her to the ground. The raider reined the animal sharply around, glancing momentarily at Stuart, immobile in the grass. Stuart stiffened in fear as the man coldly assessed him as no threat, then returned his attention to the girl.

The man leaped from his horse, drawing his knife. Seanna struggled to get up but was knocked backward with a glancing blow across her shoulder. He grabbed her by the hair and yanked her head back, leaning in to slit her throat. The knife descended. Stuart winced, knowing it would surely find the mark.

In one swift movement, Seanna reached back to her quill, grabbing an arrow and driving it into her assailant's neck. He staggered back, clutching it, gagging and frothing blood from his lips, before he fell onto the grass, quivering in death.

Stuart watched in shock as Seanna briefly touched her shoulder, noting the gash. She ran to him, dropping before him and touching his thigh, assessing the wound as he winced in pain.

"The arrow has passed clean through the muscle," she said.

She stood quickly and placed her foot upon his leg, pulling the arrow through the flesh while he screamed in agony. Tearing her shirt, she wrapped it tightly around his wound as he moaned in pain again. She retrieved her horse, guided Stuart onto the back of her mare, then mounted behind him and spurred the animal to a gallop in the direction of the fortress.

Terrified for both of them, he shifted his body around to speak. "Seanna, I am so sorry . . . I am—"

She silenced him. Stuart could feel the rigidity of her body pressed against his as she spurred the horse faster. He realized that the spreading warmth on his clothing was not his blood but hers. His fear did not diminish even when he sighted the township's perimeter walls. Cries of alarm echoed throughout the inner compound as they galloped through the gates. Not until hands attached to unseen kinsmen helped him off her horse did he feel safe at last. He glanced at Seanna, pale and unmoving as she was lowered to the ground.

"Wait . . . wait." He struggled. "Is she alive?" he cried.

His father's face was before him, contorted with concern. It was his last remembrance before he sank into unconsciousness.

In the days that followed, Stuart hardly left Seanna's bedside. For a full day, he watched, looking down at her for any sign of recovery. When she finally opened her eyes, a sigh of relief escaped his lips.

"Thank the gods. You are awake, Seanna!"

She smiled weakly and returned to sleep. Stuart slumped against the chair, cradling his head in his hands, exhausted but filled with gratitude that she would live.

His father was astounded at the transformation in his son and his concern for Seanna's recovery. Stuart rarely left her side, and his father asked him later if this devotion was that of a young man in love.

"It is love bound by admiration and respect for a friend," was Stuart's only reply. He could not explain his feelings adequately to his father but knew that their brush with death would bond them from that day forward.

When she was able to travel, Seanna returned to her clan to heal. The day of their parting, Stuart fumbled for words, unable to express his gratitude for her service and his sadness at seeing her go.

He grasped her hand. "You and I have shared a rare moment, have we not? We will see each other again one day, my friend."

Seanna smiled back warmly as she departed with her kins-women. In her place, another Womara stayed: Thea, a fiery body-guard who would take none of his petulant behavior. He gave no protest, for he harbored no more doubt that no one would keep him safer than a woman of their clan.

9

STUART'S INVITATION

Stuart felt the familiar ache of the memories of that time, and he turned his reflections to more pleasant musings, his heart warming at his thoughts of Thea. Two years later, at the end of Thea's duty as Stuart's bodyguard, she knelt before his father, hand on heart and head bowed, as Lord Edmond released her from his service. Stuart watched her. He was a young man now, capable of defending himself, but he realized he would miss her presence. There had never been any question of impropriety between them—Thea would never have allowed it—but several times lately, she had caught his eye lingering upon her.

Lord Edmond stepped forward and placed his hands upon her shoulders, raising her to her feet. "Words cannot express the gratitude I feel to you and your clan for the protection of my son. Your people have earned my respect and a debt that I will not forget."

Thea bowed her head and turned to depart. Her eyes met Stuart's as she conveyed a silent farewell when she passed by him. He waited for a few moments, before excusing himself, mumbling something to his father about needing to send her off properly on her journey.

Thea glanced up from saddling her horse as he approached the stables.

"You must be ready to see your home and your family," Stuart said.

"I am," she replied. She paused for a moment. "But this has been my home, too. I will not forget it," she added.

Stuart nodded, looking into her eyes. "I feel there is something I must say that would also express my gratitude, beyond the words of my father," he fumbled.

"Your gratitude is appreciated, but I feel it is I who should thank you," she answered, as she mounted her horse. "And I would like to extend my gratitude with an invitation."

"What invitation?" Stuart asked.

"We have spent many hours talking together about our clans. You have always been most inquisitive about our ways, and your questions are insightful. We have built a bridge of understanding between our people."

"Yes, I would agree," he acknowledged.

"The next full moon is our celebration of life at the sacred fires. It would be our honor if you would visit as our guest," Thea said. She paused and then added, "Seanna would be pleased to see you again."

Stuart brightened at her words. Something in Thea's dark eyes gave him encouragement. He stepped forward and held the horse's bridle. "And what of you? Would you be pleased to see me again?" he asked.

"Yes, I would," she answered. She spurred her horse forward, leaving Stuart standing alone, smiling.

Weeks later, Stuart and his companions approached the far outer boundaries of the Womara lands. His father had granted him leave to serve as an emissary of sorts to extend the developing goodwill between their clans.

He felt a churning in his stomach and was not sure whether it was from the fact that he and his men were the first of his clan to have been invited as guests into the world of the women, or from his anticipation of seeing Thea again.

At the edge of a large, open meadow, he spotted Seanna waiting on horseback. When he and his men rode into the clearing, she galloped forward to welcome him. They both dismounted, smiling, and grasped each other's arms.

"You look well, my friend," Stuart said, squeezing her forearms tightly.

"I am well, and it is good to see you again. Too much time has passed between us. Your visit has been long awaited," Seanna answered.

Stuart nodded, his eyes reflecting his affection. "You are alone?" he asked, looking beyond the meadow.

Seanna smiled. "Thea would be here to greet you also, but she is on patrol. She will return tonight, and she asked me to convey to you her well wishes. She looks forward to welcoming you later."

Can Seanna see upon my face how eager I am for that reunion? Stuart wondered.

To conceal his thoughts, he moved aside. "Allow me to introduce my men." He gestured for them to step forward.

"You are all most welcome," Seanna offered. "My leader, Dian, awaits your arrival and is anxious to meet you."

They traveled the outer boundary along well-worn trails through more open meadows, making their way toward the forest and the center of the township within. A great mountain range loomed in the distance. Small farms with homes dotted the outer landscape, and men and women paused in their tasks to wave and shout their greetings.

It appears that we are under no more scrutiny here than the usual curiosity new strangers draw in any town, Stuart observed.

"As you can see, there are men who live among us," Seanna spoke, as if reading the men's thoughts.

"It is not difficult for the men who live here to be ruled by women?" Stuart asked.

"It appears not," Seanna answered, with a sweeping gesture of her hand. "We have the most productive farmlands in the region and a prosperous and thriving township. The men who live among us embrace our culture and contribute to that prosperity, and outsiders have chosen to marry or live with a Womara woman, start homes, and raise children," she added.

Seanna saw the men's exchange of raised eyebrows at the reference to children, and she turned to Stuart with an understanding smile. "But you will have many opportunities to ask all your questions of anyone who lives here, and you are free to form your own opinions."

Stuart smiled back. "We shall endeavor to keep an open mind."

The trails merged into the forest as they wound their way through paths among the towering trees, crossing over small bridges that forded the river, or the small ponds that bordered some of the wetlands. Side paths lined with rocks or logs led to homes nestled within the trees. Stuart marveled at the unique structure of the dwellings, the likes of which he had never seen before. Clusters of homes were built into the natural clearings of the forest floor, or interwoven among the trees.

"May I ask your thoughts?" Seanna asked, watching Stuart survey his surroundings.

"I am intrigued by your structures and that there is not a wall erected around a permanent settlement, but a people blending into the forest. It is strikingly different from the towns of men, who would have cut down all the living trees to build their walled forts."

"And what of defense, may I ask?" said another man.

Seanna directed Stuart and his men to gaze upward into the tree canopy. In the high tops of the trees, they could see platforms with small huts.

"The sentries above us are networked throughout the forest and outlying areas, signaling your presence long before you reached our boundaries."

"It is most interesting," the man replied.

"You will find that our defensive tactics for our terrain are not standard, either," Seanna said.

"Yes, but effective. As I have witnessed firsthand," Stuart added, with a knowing smile.

The forest opened into a large clearing, filled with the activity of any township. Stalls displaying the wares of artisans and crafts-women, a blacksmith's forge, a shop for leatherworks, bakeries, taverns, and many other places of commerce bustled with the day's business. Stuart and his men stopped at a blacksmith's stall to observe a woman forging a knife blade.

Seanna spoke proudly: "All the mercantile is managed by women. In our past, though, men were our primary teachers in all the trades. Now, we can boast some of the finest craftswomen and weavers in the region. These skills and wares are sought in the outlying territories and highly prized."

Most impressive, Stuart admitted to himself, as the looks of his men conveyed the same thoughts.

"This is the heart of our community," Seanna shared, pointing to a large circle of stones filled with logs. "It holds our sacred fire at the full-moon rites."

The large fire ring was the center of a radiating stone spiral, composed of seats carved from logs or tree branches and large stones with shapes natural for sitting. The surrounding trees displayed images of the women's nature gods carved into the bark, and the sound of soft chimes moved with the breeze.

Stuart and the men exchanged questioning glances, aware of the stories that surrounded the Womara fires. He had heard the rumors that it was a practice steeped in debauchery, as women freely chose men for an evening of pleasure.

As a man, I have to admit that the thought of such a spectacle excites me. But I am also repulsed by the idea of women being so free in their desires. How can I align myself with such decadent acts? And would that not demean the warrior qualities that I have witnessed in this clan?

The men stood silent for a moment, staring at the stones, before Seanna directed their attention to the far fringes of the fire circle, where a meeting hall stood.

"My leader awaits us for dinner. I will settle you in your quarters to refresh yourselves before we meet her."

Stuart observed his simple but comfortable accommodations,

then stepped outside for a moment, his eye drawn to a path that traveled deeper into the forest. He wandered slowly along the trail and stopped to sit upon a shaded log.

A small doe lifted its head from a thicket of ferns, eyeing him cautiously. He caught himself instinctively reaching for an absent bow—his first impulse to release a strike merely for the thrill of the kill. Instead, he suppressed the urge and sat unmoving, watching her. Deeper within the trees, a young buck revealed himself and beckoned silently to his mate.

The doe turned back to him for a moment, and Stuart's heartbeat quickened when their eyes met. A sense of connectedness with something sacred passed over him as he watched the lovely creatures moving slowly up a rise.

He rose and turned back, refreshed and filled with a sense of well-being.

Dian stood waiting for them before a central hall with large wood pillars decorated with more symbols of the Womara spirits. Stuart paused to take in the qualities of a female leader. She was a handsome woman, tall, like Seanna, and stood as regal as any queen. Her thick blond hair, laced with gray, was coiled and pinned up elegantly. Long strands that escaped the pins framed her face in soft curls. Her modest dress did not detract from her air of authority, and she looked at him with the same penetrating gaze as Seanna.

She smiled. "Welcome."

Stuart stepped forward, bowing at the waist before her.

"Lord Stuart. I have heard much about you and had the pleasure of meeting your father many years ago. He is well?"

"He is, and sends his greetings," Stuart answered.

"Those are good tidings. Come, gentlemen, let's begin our evening with a toast of wine to mark this most auspicious beginning," she said, as they stepped inside.

Dinner that evening was an informal affair, but insightful for Stuart. *Dian exudes the warmth of a gracious host, but this is a woman very comfortable in her command. I sense a keen political mind, and her pointed questions, interlaced with the pleasantries, seem to serve a larger, undisclosed aim.*

His instinct proved correct as Dian interrupted his thoughts: "I have heard talk that the clans are discussing the possibility of building a great port along your coast, Lord Stuart," she said.

"Yes, my lady. It is the great vision and design of Lord Arden. It appears that the prospect has developed real merit among the clans," he added.

"I have had the honor of meeting Lord Arden and have known of his quest," she said.

"And would the Womara seek a place in this new alliance?" Stuart asked.

"These objectives are years in the making, but why would we not? There is much we can offer to a new alliance. We thrive in commerce and would welcome the challenge of expanded trading beyond our territories. It is an opportunity to forge bonds that would contribute to strengthening a unity. That is why we have offered our service, to live among you. So you may know us better," she said, smiling.

"I agree that it has been an effective way for us to bridge perceived differences, but the mindset of men can be rigid," Stuart replied.

"Ever true, Lord Stuart. That is why I am encouraged that your

father has sent you here to observe our daily lives and our cus-
toms," she answered. "Our clans have a growing bond, and it is
your father's allegiance that we seek to earn.

"Now, let me pour you more wine." Dian smiled sweetly. "We
will have no more talk of politics tonight. I have several days of
your company. My purpose is to acquaint you with our ways and
make your visit enlightening."

Stuart tipped his glass to her and drank his wine.

She is charming, he thought. *But let me not forget that these
women are warriors, too.*

Stuart observed that Seanna sat quietly through most of the meal,
listening with keen interest to their conversations. She seemed
glad to leave the discussion of politics behind them when they
departed after dinner. The sun was setting as people began arriving at the town center for the lighting of the fire and the rising of
the full moon.

Stuart and Seanna, followed by his men, strolled in the warm,
inviting night air to the circle, where the adults talked and laughed
and children played among them. Stuart and Seanna stopped
often to speak with Seanna's acquaintances or to acknowledge,
with an introduction from her, a member of the Womara council.

As Stuart observed the gathering, sipping wine, Seanna
announced, "We are ready to begin," and the clan's priestess
stepped forward. She wore a long, simple brown dress, the color of
the earth, and her unbraided hair fell below her waist. Upon her
brow was a single tattoo of a crescent moon.

"Welcome, all," she said, with arms outstretched. "We come

together at the rising of the full moon to light this sacred fire, reminding us of the celebration of life and the divine that lives within us. The flames evoke the living spirit that brings us together in celebration and affirms our collective identity. Let us always remember our ancestors' lives, which forged what we have become today."

The priestess took a burning torch and lit the base of the logs. The smaller pieces of wood crackled, and soon the stack became a roaring blaze. People cheered as others approached, casting flowers, incense, and small parchments into the flames.

"It is our ritual to write our intentions or desires upon the parchments," Seanna explained. "The fire offers clarity for those who seek direction for their lives. When the fire consumes the parchments, those desires infuse the sacred fire. The smoke carries their hopes and aspirations into the heavens."

Stuart watched the parchments burn and small pieces of embers and smoke rise into the night sky.

"What might you wish for?" Seanna asked Stuart.

Before he could reply, the crowd cheered and clapped as the musicians arrived to play. Many people, young and old, began to dance around the flames together. Clusters of young men huddled in groups, nudging each other to approach a certain girl.

Seanna leaned closer and explained, "The young girls and women who wear the flowers in their hair are unattached, and the men who hold a flower in their hands are the same. They come to meet, to reunite, to dance, and more, if they choose."

"It is not what I expected," Stuart shared. He laughed as one of his men was approached by a young woman, who took his hands and drew him into the dance circle.

They sat, continuing to drink their wine, as Stuart watched with curiosity. There was no lewdness here, as he had conjured in his mind—no wanton dancing naked around a fire as men threw laughing women over their shoulders and carried them into the forest. What he was observing was the pleasure of any gathering of men and women dancing under a canopy of emerging stars in a rare outdoor ballroom.

Seanna pointed to a couple sitting and clapping their hands with the rhythms of the music. When Stuart turned to watch them, she said, "They have known each other for ten years now and come together only at the full moon. Many women chose to live within the clan, content with their solitude and with welcoming a lover only once per month. This couple's bond is just as strong as that of others who will stand before our clan leader to be granted a place among the community to raise their children. And for some, love is not a necessary element," she noted.

"And there are no judgments for any women's actions?" Stuart asked.

"It is the honoring of the choice that is the most relevant factor," she answered.

"It seems too idyllic," Stuart suggested.

Seanna nodded. "True, and I would be dishonest if I did not share that challenges arise. There are spurts of jealousy, competitions for affections, and men and women who wish to possess one another. We deal with those issues as they occur, and very few men have been forbidden to return to our fires."

Stuart smiled, relaxing into the evening, lulled by the wine, the music, and the laughter. "I think there is much that I can learn here," he added.

"I am glad you feel so." Seanna stood, helped him to his feet, took his arm, and guided him away from the center, toward a stand of trees.

There sat Thea, waiting for him upon a bench under the boughs. She wore a pale blue dress that matched her eyes, and her long, dark hair hung free around her shoulders. In her hair, she wore a white flower.

"You might want this." Seanna handed him a single flower.

He barely nodded, transfixed by the vision of Thea as he sat down next to her, looking into her eyes. He took her hand and drew it up to his lips, kissing it softly.

When Stuart departed five days later, he carried with him a much-altered perception of the female community and a changed heart.

I have witnessed a disciplined and thriving society where each person serves in a particular role, adding value to the whole. My own culture could benefit from the underutilized potential of women as a resource. Their ability to fight does not undermine the nurturing and healing qualities of their sex, and the warrior consciousness instilled in all of them from birth has not diminished their attributes as women to me, but only enhanced them. I know this to be true, because I have fallen in love with one among them.

Stuart returned his thoughts to the present and reluctantly rose from the bench, placing his hand upon his heart, rubbing more warmth into his chest, for the afternoon sun had paled.

There was no dividing line of loyalty for him or his father for the Womara, but he felt the weight of the conflict before him and the pending vote.

I feel like one man alone, standing against narrow-minded traditions. I fear that few of the clansmen voting will challenge the rigid conventions that must be lifted to secure the female clan a place in the alliance.

My concerns for Seanna are well-founded. She is unseasoned in her politics, and Dian must be very assured of an outcome. Have allegiances been discussed behind closed doors—allegiances that could determine the outcome for all?

10

THE VOTE OF THE CLANS

At the evening banquet, Lord Warin stood alone against a far wall, arms crossed against his chest, observing the clansmen talking among themselves. He silently assessed how he thought the vote would go the next day and congratulated himself.

For the clans in my region, I have demanded their loyalty to stand with me, assuring their vote. My opposing positions, voiced with the remaining clansmen over the last several days, have rekindled doubts about the soundness of Arden's judgment for even considering women's inclusion in the formation of an alliance. I have cast suspicion upon benefits gained by including women who believe they have the right to speak as they wish and who will obstruct our objectives with the sentiments of their weaker sex.

He had been pleased when his words had stirred heated debate, but annoyed when some men had argued that the Womara could add value beyond their fighting abilities. He sensed resistance from the neighboring clans to the north, as they cited the obvious success of the women's commerce and a willingness to consider their position.

Warin watched when Seanna entered the far side of the hall, pausing in the doorway. He caught his breath for a moment at the sight of her. She wore a light green dress, the color of forest ferns, fitted at the waist and falling in soft folds to the floor. The bodice did not cover her shoulders completely, revealing a hint of small, rounded breasts underneath. Her covered arms were long and elegant, and her unbound hair flowed below her shoulders.

The sight of Seanna stirred a painful memory from his youth; in her dress and unbound hair, she was the likeness of the only woman he had ever attempted to love—a flaxen-haired beauty from a neighboring village who had drawn the appreciative stares of men from miles around. Beguiling and flirtatious, she had shamelessly played man against man for her attention.

He had been intoxicated with her loveliness and had fallen hopelessly under her spell, fancying himself in love. He was the son of the clan lord of the largest clan region and judged himself an unquestioned attractive prospect for any woman. His chest tightened uncomfortably, remembering the day he approached her after spending all morning working up his courage to ask if he could escort her to a local gathering.

"I can have my choice of any man, and I will not consort with the likes of you," she mocked. "You are coarse and ugly," she added, as she stood with the other girls, laughing and staring with disdain while he retreated, red-faced and humiliated.

Several months later, her circumstances changed upon the unexpected death of her parents, and she was forced to temper her judgment, encouraged by her kin to accept his hand. They married, but her eyes could not conceal her suppressed contempt and she shrank from his touch.

It was a troubled marriage, and she grew reckless in her

unhappiness, as rumors soon reached his ears of a lover in another township. Warin's men found them together and dragged them before the clanspeople. He had been publicly humiliated, but she stood defiant. Warin showed her no mercy, hanging her and her lover together. He never married again, setting his heart against the manipulative and untrusting nature of women.

He returned his gaze to Seanna as Stuart crossed the room to greet her, escorting her into the room.

It is clear what his message is and that she has his support! That is no surprise. He is a fool. I think that this young lord's inexperience in the forming of allegiances will leave him alienated from his fellow clansmen and relegated to minor influence in the alliance.

He watched her move gracefully among the men, Lord Edmond's son at her side, as they mingled among the clansmen, making their greetings.

His contempt rose. *A pretty face so easily sways men. Can they not see the hidden nature of her kind?* For him, the Womara represented a type of independent arrogance he would not tolerate in anyone, let alone a woman, and the thought that one of them would serve as an equal on a council seat incensed him.

Seanna sensed Warin's scrutiny as she walked by him, but she bowed her head in a reserved greeting. She whispered with Stuart as they passed him.

"My time with Lord Arden revealed nothing new about Lord Warin's position, but our talk renewed my concerns that Warin and his men have been very vocal in their attempts to discredit any consideration of the Womara's membership in the council, as you informed me. His words have inflamed many deep-seated suspicions about the value of my clan. I fear Arden himself has been viewed unfavorably for his support of us. I suspect that Warin's greater objective is to discredit Arden enough that Warin himself will be elected leader of the council."

"Yes," Stuart replied, "but he is crude and opinionated, ruling his clan with little tolerance for nonconforming attitudes. A comparison against a man like him will not tarnish Lord Arden. I have spent several days cultivating the opinions of the clansmen. I am feeling assured that the alliance will proceed, with Arden as its leader, but I must speak honestly and tell you that the position of the Womara is not so clear."

As Seanna's face reflected her concern, Stuart tried to smile reassuringly. "There is nothing more that can be said this evening to sway perceptions. We must await the outcome tomorrow."

Seanna squeezed Stuart's arm more tightly. "I believe you are right. The formation of the new alliance will happen, but I am not ready to place the fate of my clan only in the hands of these men."

"What do you mean?" Stuart asked.

"I will share something with you after the vote," she said.

In the morning, Seanna paused before the doorway of the meeting hall, taking a few deep breaths before entering. Small groups of men filled the room, engaged in hushed conversations. She nodded to the men as she walked through the center, seeking out Stuart, then standing silently at his side. His sideways glance conveyed his reassurance as they waited for the last of the clan members to arrive.

Lord Arden sat waiting in his chair on an elevated platform; a few steps separated him from the clansmen standing before him. He rose and raised his hand, asking for attention as the room went silent.

"My fellow clansmen, we all know the purpose of this gathering. Today, we will decide to form an alliance that provides for the mutual protection of our lands and begins the process of a creating a new port that will build trading routes to the north. Today, we vote for progress and a new vision of the future."

The men murmured their agreement.

"We can afford to be generous and inclusive in this vision so that everyone who lives within these lands is granted the same protections and treated equally."

Heads shifted pointedly toward Seanna, but she kept her gaze on Arden. Warin and his group of men murmured under their breath.

"Before us is a vote on whether we will move to unify the clans into one body with a governing council. We will then develop the seaport and the trade routes necessary to extend beyond our lands. We will build united forces on land and by sea to defend our coastal areas and to protect those routes and ships. Every clan has a place in this new union."

The men nodded in concurrence as Arden continued, "Before we vote to form the alliance, we have a second consideration, one that is of great consequence to the clan of the Womara. They have petitioned for full clan recognition, and to be included in that council and the new alliance."

Lord Warin stepped forward to interrupt. "How can we take them seriously when their leader sends only a warrior scout to represent them?" he asked.

Arden appeared taken aback at the outburst, and some

clansmen spoke up with yeas, while others nodded in agreement, before he lifted a hand to silence them.

"I have made no secret of where my allegiance lies concerning the Womara's petition, but I will share with you what feelings guide my commitment to their inclusion. I know something of the ways of this female clan, for they have touched my life in a most personal manner."

Warin huffed but stepped back to join his men.

"A future leader of the Womara is not assured that rank by birthright alone. She must be tested not only in skill and courage but also in her ability to govern. The young Womara woman leaves her clan for years to travel the wilds or place herself in service to others. Although many of you never knew my older brother, if the fates had been different, he would be standing before you here today."

Some men whispered among themselves at the mention of Arden's kin.

"Many years ago, my brother and his men were returning home from a journey to the coast, when raiders ambushed them, butchered my brother and his men, and left them where they fell. A small group of Womara warriors, with their young leader, came upon the massacre. They tracked and hunted down the killers before they escaped back to the sea, and slaughtered them all.

"When they passed through the gates of my township, it was a solemn procession. My people had never seen a sight such as these women warriors that day, bearing the bodies of my brother and our kin, and the heads of our enemies for our pikes. They remained our guests for many days, sharing our grief, and together we watched the funeral pyres burn."

Men voiced their approval at the justice the Womara clan had served, before Arden went on.

"I offered Dian, their scout leader, silver for the return of our kinsmen, but she wanted only one thing. She asked for the privilege to live among my people for a time so that we might better understand one another. I honored her request, and in the months that she dwelt among my clan, we learned much about each other and our shared desires for our people.

"The death of my older brother made me clan leader before my time, and a few years later, Dian became the chosen leader of her people. Through the years, I have found her perspective and sound counsel of great value to me. She remains to this day a strong ally and, more important, a friend."

Arden paused, and his eye turned to Seanna.

"Dian has not taken this council meeting lightly, as you suggest, but has sent one who has had to forge her own path—her daughter, Seanna—to serve as the voice of the Womara and their leader one day, when the time comes."

Seanna watched the men's surprised expressions as they turned to look at her.

Arden continued, "Seanna has been more than just a scout for the alliance. She has chosen to build bonds among you based on her service, the merits of her actions, and the value of her word. The combined perspective that she gives us as the future leader of the Womara and as a warrior will add depth to our endeavors."

Warin's voice rose above the din of the men. "These are pleasant sentiments, but their worth is untested."

Arden's steely glare flashed a warning to Warin. "Hold your tongue. Your attitudes are well known and are out of place here."

Warin stood defiant at the rebuke but fell silent.

"I have spoken my convictions, but I am not the only voice to be heard here," Lord Arden continued, as he gestured to Seanna.

She climbed the stairs and faced the clansmen, pausing to make pointed eye contact with the crowd and allowing her gaze to rest on Warin, before speaking.

"My lords, it is an honor to stand before you as the voice of my people. Some of you know me because I served and lived among you in past years. For those of you whom I do not yet know, I have given my oath of service to Lord Arden as a warrior scout for your protection. In the brief time I have to speak before you, I must attempt to convey the essence of what my clan is." She paused. "Will it be enough to tell you that we love our land, our families, and our freedom as dearly as you love yours? That our hopes and desires are not so different, and that we seek acceptance and unity? We share a common past, in which my ancestors stood beside yours to defeat invading enemies. My clanswomen fought fiercely that day long ago, and many of my kin died. Your forebearers granted an ancient treaty to the Womara in honor of that victory, giving us permanent rights to our region."

She paused again to look at the faces of the men. "We are a clan, we have our land, but to this day we have remained separate in the eyes of many men."

The murmurs among the clansmen rose as they glanced at one another.

"It is true that we are women who choose to direct the destiny of our own lives. Is that any different than any man's birthright? We do not ask for special consideration and stand ready to earn your respect for that choice. My leader has sent me because I represent the change that is necessary for the future of my people."

She took a steadying breath.

"I wonder if all leaders feel what I feel today, carrying the weight of the aspirations of their people. I ask that we look not to our differences but to what we have in common and how the unity of our clans makes a stronger whole. Diversity moves us forward. As a clan of women, we may look at the world differently, but we offer the prospect of balance to our progress. I seek the privilege to stand beside you in accord as we pledge our oath to a new kind of future."

The room was still as Seanna descended the stairs and stepped back beside Stuart. He and Arden alone had always known that the leader of the Womara was her mother, but they had vowed their silence of that knowledge to Seanna. She had wanted to be considered for her worth first, not simply because she was the daughter of the clan leader.

Stuart judged her words: *Her declarations were strong. I have never seen this quality in her. She is truly embracing this new role as a leader. Dian should be proud. I think I understand Seanna's wisdom in her choice to face the clansmen alone, but will her status and her words make any difference to the minds of these men?*

The room hummed with discussions. Stuart attempted to gauge, based on the countenances of the surrounding clansmen, whether Seanna had moved them. Some of the men's faces appeared to reflect a new admiration, judging by the nodding heads and approving glances toward her. Stuart watched Warin survey the room, too, and then whisper among his men, shaking his head. He wondered if Warin was considering that the outcome of the vote might have shifted, decreasing the power of his destructive rhetoric.

His face mirrors the resentment of a rigid man facing a possible unwelcome change. The tide may have turned against him, but I would wager that he will not yield, and that his vote will still be no.

11

TURNING TIDES

Seanna wrapped her arms around her knees, pulling them close to ward off the chill of the morning air. She had been sitting quietly on a hillside outside the walls of the encampment in the grasses since well before dawn, watching the sky change colors as the sun crested the rise, illuminating the hills with a soft golden glow.

It is the day after the vote, and here I sit, still in disbelief. I have failed my clan.

She recounted the previous day's events and the clansmen's vote again. The clans present totaled twenty-six, consisting of the five largest clans and the lesser clans granted voting rights. The first show of hands in the vote established the formation of the alliance and its governing council. The second vote before the clansmen was to include the Womara in the alliance and grant them a seat on the alliance council. The consenting votes had not been enough for their inclusion.

The no votes had come from Warin and the lesser clansmen of

his region, sticking together in their opposition like a dark, brooding cloud. Seanna had stood tall at the calling of the vote but had flushed in anger at the outcome. Lord Warin had stood smugly, his arms crossed on his chest. His gloating expression had incensed her. Stuart had remained motionless, rendered speechless by the decision, and Lord Arden had looked crestfallen at the realization that his advocacy had failed to reverse enough opposition to the inclusion of women.

A narrow majority had voted Lord Arden the leader of the new alliance. Seanna knew that his strong guidance would be essential to navigate the long and arduous process of bringing together a group of men unaccustomed to working in unity, particularly facing the adversarial undercurrent of Lord Warin.

Lord Arden had approached her afterward. "This does not mean the end of our quest. In time, we will petition the council for a reconsideration."

"I think that time has passed" had been her only response.

Afterward, she had drawn Stuart to her side. "We must talk now. I have a decision to make."

Stuart had cautioned her, "Yes, but before you do, there is something I must share now." He leaned closer to her. "Do not act in haste. We must think with clearer heads. All eyes watch us. Let's depart."

She had acquiesced, controlling her suppressed anger as she glanced back at Arden, who watched them leave.

Seanna shivered and rubbed warmth back into her arms as she rose slowly.

I am to depart today, but I cannot return to my clan in defeat. I have contemplated for hours my course of action, measuring the scope of the oath that I made to James. I have another path before me, and I will be bold in this gamble.

She walked the length of township to the great hall and stood before its massive, carved oak doors as she finalized her thoughts.

The new council is meeting this morning to begin its preliminary discussions, and I will stand before it to speak, even if I am uninvited.

The hall was filled with the boisterous exchange of men's voices, but the clansmen stopped talking as she passed them.

"What is she doing here?" she heard Lord Warin ask.

She glanced around the room, seeking one man. Lord Arden was standing among a small group, and as she approached, they broke off their conversation and turned to her with questioning expressions.

"Lord Arden, may I have a moment with you?" she asked. The men looked surprised but stepped away, giving them leave to talk in private.

"I wish to address the council before you begin your talks today," she asked.

"What is it that you need to share with the council?" Arden asked sharply. "This is not the place to contest the outcome of the vote."

"That is not my intent, but I ask that you grant me leave to address them nonetheless. I have something of worth to offer to the discussions—something that could be of significance to the progress of the alliance. Let me speak—then judge the value of my words and whether they warranted the council's time," Seanna stated.

"Why have you waited until now?" Arden asked.

"An oath and a vow of secrecy constrained me, as well as a belief that revealing that information would endanger someone. I reasoned I could hold to that vow while securing inclusion in the alliance, but that logic has proven to be at the expense of my clan's future."

Arden knitted his brows as he tried to make sense of her words.

"I mistakenly thought that I could have both: keep the honor of a vow and earn our place on the council. I now believe that enough time has passed that I can risk compromising that oath for the sake of my people."

Arden rubbed his forehead, studying her face for a long moment. Then he turned away from her, cleared his throat, and asked for silence from the gathering.

"I need quiet," he asked again, as all eyes turned to him. "Seanna has requested an audience before the council. I have granted her that time, and I ask that you give her your attention." He gestured to her to begin. The men exchanged surprised glances as she stepped before them, viewing the room of waiting faces.

She caught the eye of Lord Warin, whose expression conveyed his condescension. *He's expecting me to grovel and plead for a place on the council,* she thought.

"What is the meaning of this interruption, Arden?" Warin snapped.

"I do not know the nature of it," Arden answered honestly. "I trust only that Seanna would not make such a request without warrant."

Seanna stepped to the front of the men. "My lords, I have asked Lord Arden to delay your talks this morning for an opportunity to stand before you and share the story of a chance encounter a year ago that could alter the course of the alliance's plans."

Seanna watched the men's curious glances at one another, and then at Lord Arden, searching for some indication of what was to come, but Arden's face showed just as much surprise as their own.

She recounted the discovery of the pass, the ambush, and the chance meeting with James, and when she finished, silence hung in the air. Lord Arden and the council stared at her. Arden had seated himself and, with his hand resting on his chin, had not moved throughout the telling of her entire tale. His face appeared slightly flushed as he stared at her, and Seanna wondered, *Is he feeling betrayed because I did not share such a revelation with him before the vote?*

The council members began to talk among themselves, openly discussing the validity of her words, before Warin stood up, interjecting loudly. "You expect us to believe this preposterous tale to be true? She is desperate to disrupt the direction of the council and grasping at straws with this far-fetched tale."

"On what basis would you discredit it?" Lord Arden snapped. The men whispered among themselves but offered no open disagreement with Warin's comment.

Seanna interrupted, speaking directly to Arden.

"There is more. Before I departed those mountains, I pledged an oath to the prince that I would return and that we would recover the body of his father. That time is near, and I will depart soon to meet him. I wish to go bearing a message of salutation and introduction from this council."

"This is ridiculous," Warin exclaimed. "If we are going to support this supposed evidence, then we must send a company of men with her to prove the existence of such a discovery. You will show us the way through this pass," he demanded.

"No, I will not," Seanna stated, looking defiantly at Warin.

"Then we will find it ourselves," he threatened.

"You can try, but you would not make it through the Womara's defenses." She stood tall, stepping closer to him.

"Stop." Lord Arden stood up. "The pass is on the Womara lands. What are you speaking of, Warin?"

"But such an opportunity as this, if it exists, must be taken," Warin retorted.

"It is not your opportunity to take. It is mine," Seanna answered. She turned to Lord Arden and continued, "I now see how idealistic and naive I have been in this perception that men would see the value of our inclusion in an alliance, but we will no longer wait for this council to grant us its favor. The Womara do not need your permission to advance our cause if we are not in union with the alliance."

The bitterness of her words darkened Arden's expression.

"This is all hearsay anyway," Warin snapped. "You place too much value on a chance meeting a year ago. He has forgotten his pledge to you."

"We will see. I will still go," Seanna answered.

"What are you proposing?" Arden asked.

"If the council has determined that the Womara have nothing to offer, perhaps the value of this reunion will change your minds. It could serve your interests and benefit the greater objective if I went as a member of the council," she answered.

"You offer an empty bargain," Warin said loudly. "You cannot force this council's hand."

"Not force, milord. A political advantage used for persuasion, if you wish to judge it," Seanna answered.

Warin's glare was venomous.

She continued, "Let your hesitation be your guide, but there are others who see the possibility of opportunity. Yesterday, at the conclusion of the vote, after our defeat, I confided in Lord Stuart this same tale I have just disclosed to you. He revealed to me that his father would be receptive to new progress and would want to know the outcome of any meeting, should it occur."

All the men turned sharply toward Stuart in surprise.

"What does she speak of?" Arden asked Stuart.

Stuart stepped forward. "My father and Dian have discussed the possibility of a union if the alliance failed. For our clan, all the opportunities evaluated have always included the Womara. As the future leader of my clan, I believe it is in the best interest of my people to consider such an alliance and the development of trade routes. The possibility of this new route is an opportunity that we cannot squander, as Lord Warin has inferred. It could be the beginning of a discussion of a linked trade to the northern continent that would have taken us years to develop. I think my father would agree with my words."

"You cannot build a port without the support of the alliance," Warin said.

"And why not?" Seanna replied. Warin's face reddened in anger at her challenge.

"I give you leave to talk among yourselves. I depart soon. Think carefully on all that I have shared," she stated, before exiting the room.

Dressed for travel and ready to leave, Seanna stood before Lord Arden in his private chamber, at his summons.

"I have some questions to ask of you," he stated.

"I imagine that you do, my lord," Seanna replied.

"Dian knew of your discovery all this time?" he asked.

"Yes, but I asked her for secrecy, to honor my oath given to the prince. I was overconfident in gaining a place for our clan. She conceded to my insistence to achieve acceptance on our merit alone."

"And you knew of her proposed pact with Lord Edmond?"

"That I did not," she answered truthfully. "Lord Stuart revealed this fact to me only last night, and without his father's counsel. It appears that the opportunity to gain a critical advantage with Lord Edmond, should the alliance fail, was too great for my mother to squander, too. She would lose nothing by allowing me to try to win the vote into the alliance."

"You are angry with her," Lord Arden stated.

"I must bow to her reasons. I wish only that I had been informed," she answered coldly.

"You and Lord Stuart may have created a greater divide with the recklessness of your words, and Lord Stuart viewed with suspicion in future council decisions. I question such a rash move to speak his mind outside the directive of his father, and in open opposition to the council. He risks much," Arden said. "I hope you have an understanding leader when you return home and recount your conditions proposed to the council. I am unfamiliar with this person who stands before me. If you had come to me first, I could have used this knowledge to advance your cause."

"I am not so sure, Lord Arden," Seanna said. "Even when such an advantage was presented to the clansmen, the result might have been the same, and I judged as having manipulated and swayed their views. We have overestimated the willingness of men to change, for they remain bound by the same prejudices that have kept them intolerant for centuries. The Womara can no longer wait for the nature of men to evolve. I have acted for the future of my clan. Would you have done anything differently?"

Arden did not answer her question, but said, "Warin could be right. There could be no reunion. Or if there is, have you considered the possibility that you might not return after you find the body of the dead king? The circumstances may have changed greatly in the year that has passed for this young prince, supposedly now turned king."

"I will return," Seanna said. "But if I am wrong, then it is the sacrifice of only one warrior."

"Not just one warrior," Arden said, as he rose from his chair. "You are the future leader of your clan. There is much to lose."

"There are others who can lead," she challenged. "But what kind of leader would I be if first I did not honor an oath given? No one but I knows of the location of the pass. I may arrive to stand upon that mountain slope alone, but I have given my word, and to break it would be dishonorable. The outcome for my clan or even for the alliance does not hinge completely on that reunion."

"What do you mean?" Arden asked.

"I could venture to lead an envoy of alliance men to travel to the city and request an audience before the king. But, again, that action would also require the inclusion of the Womara in the alliance and the council."

Arden nodded. "The council knows that the direction of any beginning dialogues could change dramatically if an agreement were negotiated between our realms. I disagreed with their reasoning that they believe they can afford to wait for the outcome of your journey. They will not reconsider granting your clan a council seat until after your return, and have decreed that you bring a proposal from this new king."

He paused. "I cannot assure you that even meeting that condition will guarantee the Womara's place in the alliance."

Seanna nodded. "I agree, and I thank you for your candor. I feel it is now the council that takes a risk. My oath is to return a dead king to his son. For now, I cannot speak to more than my word given to a prince. My aspirations for anything beyond that pledge will depend on the seeds of a possible friendship. I will take a personal salutation from you only, but I will bear no message from the council that does not include the Womara in the alliance."

Those were her final words as she departed.

12

A JOURNEY HOME

Within three days of leaving Lord Arden's chamber, Seanna reached the outer borders of the Womara lands. The solitude of the journey had done little to soothe her storming emotions as she gathered her thoughts.

Her mother would know of the clan's defeat by messenger, but not of Seanna's final words to the new council. Approaching the forest perimeter, Seanna longed to slip unnoticed into the quiet of the tall trees but knew it was not possible. Her arrival had already been announced by a series of signals begun miles from the outside boundaries—protocol not broken even for one known to them.

Thea waited beside her horse at the periphery of the forest and waved her greeting. She strode toward Seanna, who dismounted to meet her. They embraced, laughing, stepping back at arm's length to look at each other.

"It is good to see you, my friend. It has been too many months since we parted last," Seanna spoke.

"Yes, too many," Thea smiled. "It is good to have you back. We have much to talk about." Her dark eyes flashed with excitement. Seanna grinned, seeing the reasons Stuart was so smitten with her beauty and the allure of those beautiful eyes, which contained an element of mystery and a glint of mischief.

"You look tired," Thea said.

"It is nothing a few days at home will not cure," Seanna replied, as they began to walk toward the trees.

"Only a few days?" Thea asked.

"My visit must be brief."

Thea stopped on the trail, holding Seanna's arm. "You have only just arrived. I have heard of the outcome of the clan gathering and vote. I am sorry for our clan and also for you. You have worked tirelessly toward this goal, but why must you leave so soon? Are your duties not fulfilled?"

"Not all," Seanna answered.

"What is happening?" Thea asked.

"You are so curious!" Seanna pulled her along the pathway, trying to lighten the mood. "You know I will tell you everything, including about my visit with Stuart. He has a message for you."

They walked toward the village with arms linked. Seanna paused before the township and inhaled the deep, rich aroma of the forest.

"I never tire of the scent of the trees," Seanna said wistfully, turning to her friend. "I must meet with my mother, but afterward, you will hear all my news."

Children's squeals greeted them as approached the center, flocking around the two women, bouncing with energy. Adults waved and called greetings. Seanna turned to make her way to the hall. At this time of day, her mother would be inside, handling the daily business of the clan.

"I will be at the river after sunset, at our favorite place. That will be a good meeting point to begin to share all of your accounts," Thea said.

"Yes." Seanna nodded and kissed her friend's cheek in farewell. "I will join you later at the springs."

Inside the center of the hall, her mother stood within a small cluster of people, her head bent forward as she listened with keen interest to an elder woman urgently conveying a personal request. Seanna paused to observe them at a distance, unwilling to break the intimacy of the moment.

She admired this quality in her mother: Dian listened intently to her people's problems, evoking the feeling that they were her only concern in that moment.

And that very skill of listening has made you very politically astute and cunning, my mother, Seanna added to herself. *I must try to temper my conclusions about this new turn in your plans until we speak.*

Seanna watched Dian for a moment longer, before her mother lifted her head, sensing a presence. She turned to gaze toward her daughter, and a radiant smile transformed her face. Seanna stared into eyes that were the same shade of green as her own. Dian leaned forward and whispered to the older woman, pointing toward Seanna. A toothless grin transformed the woman's face in recognition as Seanna smiled back. The old woman turned to Dian, nodding in agreement, and made her departure.

Seanna advanced and bowed before her. Dian reached for her shoulders, drawing her into an intimate embrace. They touched foreheads, Dian's special greeting for her only child. She stepped back to look at Seanna fully.

"Word has already reached me, my daughter. I know our appeal for inclusion in the alliance has failed."

Seanna did not lower her gaze but nodded as she looked into her mother's eyes.

"Do not forget that you have done us a great honor by standing before the clans," she declared.

Seanna's brow furrowed, but she said nothing more. She reached into her tunic and handed her mother the scroll from Lord Arden. Dian touched the paper to her breast, lingering for a moment. "It must convey his regrets," she guessed.

"I think it will convey more than that," Seanna said. "Why don't you read his words?"

Dian looked puzzled at her daughter's tone. "I will later, not now," she answered.

Her expression softened, and she added, "You are wearied." She placed her arm around Seanna's shoulders. "Go rest a while. We will talk at dinner, and you will tell me everything."

Later, in Dian's private rooms, they shared a meal together. Her mother insisted on hearing every facet of the gathering of clansmen and the vote for the alliance. Seanna watched her mother's expression darken when she told Dian of her stand before the council and Stuart's words.

"You have taken a bold step, my daughter, and you and Stuart have acted impulsively. You should have waited to consult with me."

"Why did you not tell me of such a talk with Lord Edmond?" Seanna asked. "You betrayed my trust."

"The knowledge of those talks with Lord Edmond would have

overshadowed your judgments, and there were other consider-ations," Dian answered. "You would feel different now if the vote had been in our favor. Maybe I was wrong to let you carry the burden of the gathering alone." Seanna kept her face blank, mask-ing her emotions.

"But in the end, it is you who compromised your vow to sway the actions of the council. You have learned a valuable lesson in the difficult decisions that a leader must make and the compro-mises that must be made at times for the sake for your people," Dian concluded.

Seanna continued to sit silently before her. "We will talk more, but not tonight. Go join Thea now."

As Seanna left the room, she paused in the doorway, turning back to look at her mother, sitting before her open window, star-ing out into the night.

By pale moonlight, Seanna and Thea lowered their naked bodies into a pocket of hot mineral water at the river's edge. Seanna sighed with pleasure as they leaned back against the rocks, listening to the rushing water and staring at the stars. Seanna shared the events of the last several weeks as Thea lis-tened intently.

"It was good to see Stuart again, and a great comfort to have his support. He is a true friend," Seanna said. "And he will be visiting soon. He has missed you."

As the moonlight illuminated Thea's face, Seanna saw her friend's joy at her news. It was the same joy she saw in Stuart's eyes when he spoke of Thea.

"What would you do if he asked you to be his wife?" Seanna asked.

"I don't know." Thea paused. "I love him, but I love my way of life here, too. Can I have both?" She laughed.

"Stuart is the only man I know who could balance both your worlds," Seanna answered seriously. She sank lower in the water, feeling something undefined tugging at her heart.

Is this jealousy I feel? I should rejoice in their love for each other. Can I ever hope for the possibility of such a life?

"There is more I have not told you," Seanna said.

"Is it why you are leaving so soon?" Thea asked.

Seanna nodded. "I have found the pass between the mountains."

Thea's eyes widened, and she sat upright. "Why did you not tell me?"

"I could not. The knowledge was held in secret until the vote for the alliance."

"But there is no alliance for the Womara!" Thea answered.

"Yes, but I am going back over the pass," Seanna replied.

"Why? What is there?"

Seanna shared the entire story of James and her oath to return, and the new demand of the council that she had initiated.

"I will go with you," Thea announced.

Seanna only shook her head. "I will not risk the safe return of any clanswoman. The oath is mine to keep, and I must go alone."

"What does your mother say?"

"I have not told her of this decision yet," Seanna answered.

"Who is this man who can exact such an oath from you?" Thea asked.

"A different kind of man, I think," Seanna said, as Thea eyed her questioningly. *I cannot speak the simple truth even to my friend—a truth that there is something deeper that compels me to go, something beyond a duty or an opportunity . . .*

I want to know if he will come.

At midmorning, Seanna made her way to the central hall. Glancing up from her books, Dian looked at Seanna with a smile.

"Come, daughter. It is a beautiful day. Let's walk to the meadow and sit a while."

Linking arms, they walked through the village onto a path that led them past crop fields and into a small meadow dwarfed by an immense oak tree. It had been their favorite since Seanna's childhood, when Dian had sat and watched her spend many hours climbing upon its massive boughs, and later, when Seanna had come alone as a young woman seeking silent refuge under its great limbs.

Dian knew now that the tree was a poignant symbol of Seanna's shift from child to young warrior. As she had begun her training as a bodyguard and scout, their days together had changed. Seanna's natural ability had been evident at a young age, and Dian had directed her into a preparation for service that demanded discipline and fortitude of its young charges, conditioning both the body and the mind.

You were only twelve, my daughter, when you returned from your rite of passage, a half-moon cycle alone in the deepest part of the forest interior, with nothing but a single blade for protection. I breathed a sigh of relief when you staggered back, haggard and hungry but alive. Yet, from that day forward, with the recognition that your youth had passed, you changed. My heart ached when I watched you in the distance, sitting for hours in the great tree, when only Thea's pleas for company would bring you down from your solitude.

Dian placed a wrap at the base of the tree, and they sat together. She opened a small bundle containing a meal of bread, hard cheese, apples, and sweets. They ate in silence, enjoying the warmth of the day and its gentle breeze, the songs of birds, and the sunlight filtering through the branches.

Dian looked at her daughter with a serious expression. "I have something to share with you, and I do not know where to begin," she said, breaking the stillness.

"What is it?" Seanna asked with concern.

Dian hesitated. "Let me just read the words." She watched Seanna's puzzled expression when she opened the same scroll that she had delivered from Lord Arden. She bowed her head and began to read.

My love,

All that I have hoped for through these long years has not come to be, as you now know. The new alliance is a victory, but the council begins the work ahead without the Womara, and for that reality, I feel momentarily vanquished.

Seanna represented your clan admirably, the manifestation of your dedication as a leader and a mother. She held true to the belief in the union of the clans that has been your guiding beacon. Or so I thought.

I could not have predicted a more complicated twist in our plans than Seanna's tale before the council. The meeting of a future king has now altered the considerations of the alliance and has far-reaching implications for all. But you and Lord Edmond could now hold the upper hand in that outcome, and I do not fully understand your reasoning for the concealment of this profound happenstance.

I do believe that the time has come to share our secret with her. I have honored your wishes for all these years and let our daughter grow into her own warrior and woman. As she stood in the council hall, alone before the clansmen, I knew that you had been right to keep her birthright hidden. She commanded the moment through the power of her presence, and I believe she will be an influential leader in her own right one day. But before she departs, I feel that she should now know everything. You alone shall decide whether this is the time to share our love with our daughter.

Arden

Seanna flushed, staring at her mother in disbelief. "M-m-my *father*?" she stammered. "But Arden had a wife for many years."

"Yes, but you were conceived before that time," Dian said. "I stayed with his clan for many months and left with a greater understanding of the outside world of men. I also left with the love of a very special man and a precious secret. He knew I carried our child when I departed.

"Our worlds were very different, and I was always going to return to my mine, but we rejoiced in the daughter we had together. Loving your father and bearing his child was a joy. Your conception was never connected to him, because I had returned home to dance at the fire rites a month earlier, but I had already known that I carried a life in my body. Only your grandmother knew your father's identity, and she respected my wishes in keeping that confidence. In time, yes, Arden took a wife, but she could not bear him children. You are his only heir."

Seanna continued to stare at her mother in shock as Dian took both of Seanna's hands in hers and drew her daughter closer. They touched foreheads, and then Dian kissed Seanna's checks and pulled back to look into her eyes. "I know this is not easy for you and that you may have many questions. I am here to answer them all," Dian answered.

"Why do you say I am his heir?" Seanna asked.

"Because before the time of his plans to build an alliance, we spoke of the unification of our regions, of creating an alliance that would secure the future of our clan," Dian answered.

"And has not Lord Edmond's pledge changed that?" Seanna asked. "I now understand Arden's anger."

"I have never questioned Arden's loyalty, only his optimism about men coming together in a united purpose. In a way, you are very much like him," Dian said. "I hoped for a different outcome, but the Womara would be assured a place in a changing future, no matter which course prevailed."

Seanna said nothing. The sun had moved lower in the sky; it was late afternoon. They walked back in silence. At the path toward the river, Seanna took her leave, asking to be alone.

Dian kissed her forehead and looked into her eyes. "You are a most beloved daughter. Do not judge your father harshly. He has always honored my wishes. He has never been able to hold a most cherished child."

Seanna only nodded weakly as they parted.

At the edge of the water, she lowered herself into a pool and let its warmth wash over her as she tried to sift through her confused thoughts. Then she submerged herself in the water. For the moment, she did not want to think at all.

Later, she sat beside the river with her knees drawn to her chest and her chin resting on her arms as she stared at the sky. Rivulets of water ran from her long, wet hair down her naked body, and she listened to the night sounds in the distance and a chorus of frogs from the meadow ponds.

Everything has changed with those few words written on one small scroll.

Seanna thought back through hundreds of encounters with Lord Arden and saw nuances in many of those actions—namely, his unflinching belief in her value as an alliance warrior.

How could I have been so blind?

At daybreak, Dian sat before the open window of her chamber, breathing in the crisp morning air. She had paced her room the night before, recounting all the events of the last several weeks and pondering Seanna's impending departure.

There is much to consider, in light of what could await her. She has been defiant in her insistence that she go alone. Have I placed too great a burden on my daughter with this revelation of a father? And what of this king?

When Seanna had first returned from the pass, Dian had asked many questions about James himself, trying to gauge his qualities as a man. Seanna had spoken only of what she thought could be a growing friendship. Dian had listened carefully to her guarded words and suspected Seanna had not shared all her real feelings. Dian sensed there was more than just an oath driving her daughter to that mountain.

Seanna arrived in Dian's chamber upon her summons and stood silently before her.

"You are angry with me?" Dian asked.

"I do not know what I am feeling," Seanna replied.

"You judge me harshly for my decisions, and Lord Arden and me for our secret. Do you think anyone would have believed the disclosure of your birth, and Arden judged just as harshly as you for trying to sway the sentiments of the clansmen? It was not the time for this truth to be known," Dian said.

"And this knowledge will not be exploited to our advantage?" Seanna asked.

"It is your secret to keep," Dian added.

"But you now want me to press the benefit of my meeting with James for the Womara?" Seanna asked.

"Yes," Dian answered. "If the alliance had failed, we would have moved forward with our interests. You now know Lord Edmond is receptive to a union to further his interests in a port city."

"And what of Lord Arden?"

"I hope that the possibility of a new union will influence his persuasions with the new council for our inclusion. Had the alliance not been formed, I would have urged him to join forces to develop a powerful coalition of our combined clans. We would control the trading ports."

"You have played both sides skillfully, Mother," Seanna said.

"As any good leader would," Dian retorted. "But we must now take advantage of the first move with your new king."

"He is not my king," Seanna answered.

"And you return to what?" Dian demanded.

"I do not know, but I leave tomorrow. We will see what the future holds when I come back," Seanna replied.

They stood for a moment in silence. Then Dian spoke up: "It pains me that you should leave with this bitterness between us. I hope that, upon reflection, you will come to understand the hard—sometimes impossible—choices a leader must make.

"Take your leave and make your preparations to depart, but this is my final decree: You will leave with several scouts, and you will show them the passage. I will give you one cycle of the moon for your journey." She rose from her chair. "If you do not return, we will come find you."

13

TREACHERY AND DECEIT

L ord Orman forced himself to keep a calm face as James stood
before the king's advisory council, announcing his impending departure, the day after next, back to the mountains to retrieve
the body of his father. His fellow councilmen exchanged startled
glances before the protests began.

"Your Grace, how would that even be possible? How could the
body still be there?" one man asked, rising to his feet.

James raised his hand to deflect such inquiries and halt any
further questions. "I have arranged all the details," he announced.
"You will ready the city for my return and begin the preparation of
the funeral rites for the fallen" were his closing words.

The room buzzed with the speculations of the councilmen
after James left, but Orman sat back in his chair, stroking his
beard.

*And why was I not even informed of this event? As the head of
the council, I should have been the first to know of any plans. Is it
a coincidence that this departure is almost a year to the day since*

the first journey? I think not. I should have known better than to
underestimate this new king.

Orman had always assumed that time was on his side in his
wish to exact his influence over the inexperienced prince, even
after the botched assassination of the king. James had survived,
and, as the chief advisor to the king, Orman was prepared to
take his young charge under his wing as confidant and counselor.
James was not to become the new sovereign for two years, on
his twenty-fifth birthday, and the king's advisory council would
assume the guidance of the prince. More than enough time for
Orman to use his influence to sway the future decisions of this
inexperienced young man.

Orman soon discovered that this undertaking would not be
easy. The carefree youth who had traveled to those peaks had
changed. James had returned hardened and withdrawn, forced
into manhood by terrible circumstances. He viewed the world
differently and conveyed an air of restraint. Orman saw a great
degree of mistrust behind those eyes and underestimated the
young prince's strength of conviction and a passion to avenge his
father.

James would not accept a provisional regent or any other
impediment to his assuming the throne immediately. He petitioned the council to revoke the regent and crown him king without any delay.

He stood before the council with an impassioned plea: "I need
to take my place now as the rightful ruler of our realm. The people
will need the presence of a king to direct the strategies of defense
and reaffirm our loyalties and alliances. I will not risk our lands
to marauding foreign soldiers who could lay waste to our country. The message will be clear to all who oppose me, especially my

cousin, who has fled the country. I am king. Come take the crown if you think you can."

James's coronation followed within a week, and Lord Orman keenly observed James's face as the crown was placed upon his head.

It must be a lonely moment for this young man standing before his subjects, crowned without family at his side. His ordeal has made him stronger. But it appears that my opportunity to impose greater influence upon this young ruler has been lost. His inner circle has narrowed to only a few trusted advisors and his personal guard. My position has not changed, but James's confidence has. That trust died with his father.

Orman was a patient man, though, and an opportunist. His allegiance was always on the side of the strongest contender. When the messenger had arrived from the mountains with the announcement of the ambush, the death of the king, and James's survival, it had forced Orman's hand, and on his advice, Thomas, James's cousin, had fled that very night with his bodyguards.

Orman had assumed he would be the appointed regent to the prince and that James would be his direct responsibility. He had thought he would occupy his time with the grooming of the young prince to be king, buying valuable time for Thomas to build an army. He had taken a great risk to send a message by a trusted emissary months earlier to the exiled cousin.

Much had changed during Thomas's absence, and their plot had not gone as planned. Orman's words of further patience and caution to Thomas had not been well received, his spy reported.

I now can see that controlling Thomas's erratic and petulant nature from abroad could prove to have been a serious error in judgment in manipulating this puppet cousin to control the power behind the throne.

James had shared his thoughts privately with Cedmon, who had sat beside him before the council shortly after his return from the mountains. He had recalled the details of his ordeal to the councilmen but maintained his suspicion that Thomas was a true traitor.

"How is it that a once-beloved cousin has now become a most dangerous enemy?" he had asked of Cedmon.

They had grown up together, and James intimately understood Thomas's limitations as a leader. He was selfish and egotistical, never pondering life much beyond his own immediate needs. He had questioned Thomas's ability to be strategic enough to plan such a sweeping coup to obtain the crown for himself.

"I fear that my cousin is merely a pawn for someone else who is much more ambitious," James said. "Does he think he can forge foreign alliances across the sea? I will learn who shelters him and, more important, who planted the initial notion of his right to the throne. But I must be careful where I place my trust."

Cedmon nodded his agreement.

Lord Orman returned his attention to the impending journey of the king. He concentrated on all the details James had recounted a year earlier, searching his memory for more clues. In the weeks that followed the prince's return, the king's council had searched unsuccessfully for the seeds of the plot and connections to those responsible for the assassination.

Orman, for all appearances, had handled the search aggressively, but all avenues had revealed nothing, even after the appearance of the unknown woman. In the end, based on James's recollections, the council determined that Thomas had acted alone, on a hastily constructed plan, when the opportunity had presented itself.

"We must garner our armies and cut Thomas down now, while he is weak," a councilman said.

"I counsel caution," Orman offered. "We have a new king. We must know who our allies are first." His true thoughts, he kept hidden: *Yes, I must know who our allies are but also, more important, who our enemies may be.*

He had not dismissed the woman he held responsible for foiling his plan by saving the life of the prince. He would find her. Orman had pressed James for every detail of the attack, especially the facts regarding this woman who had been reported directly to him by the king's guard, Malcolm.

She was a mystery, and he had suggested that her unexplained appearance made her complicit in the act of treachery. Orman had implied to the king's council, and to James, that even though she had saved James's life, she was merely a piece of a bigger puzzle. He intended to deflect further inquiries from the dead king's inner circle, especially those directed at him.

"You must tell us everything that you can remember," Orman told James, as he sat before the council days after he returned.

"I have told everything as I remember it," James answered.

"What can you tell us of the woman?" Orman pressed.

"Only what I observed," James answered. "I was in so much pain, my mind was not clear."

Orman had always suspected that James was not sharing all he knew. He had recalled the details of the attack, recounting how a guard in their hunting group had reported back with concerns about the suspicious tracks, but it was too late to avert the ambush. He was sent to hide among the boulders; he had listened in terror to the ensuing fight and then the silence. He had been spared watching the murder of everyone in his party, including the young page who had been disguised as royalty and had died in his place. The killers did not linger, taking all the horses and departing within an hour.

James had remained hidden among the rocks and, after several hours, despaired that no one was coming to find him. Afraid to leave his hiding place, he spent a cold and frightening night huddled among the crevices, the eerie silence of the dark mountain heightening his terror.

In the morning, he crept from his concealment. The rocks were wet from the morning mist, and in his descent, his foot slipped. He plunged several feet, breaking his leg and knocking himself unconscious. When he awoke hours later and shifted his body, he screamed at the excruciating pain of the broken limb. He spent the remainder of the day in agony, dragging his body back to the campsite.

The council had watched the expression of the young prince change as he described his despair and the desolation of the scene of the ambush. All the men, including his father, were dead, but he dragged himself to his father's corpse to feel the rigid, cold body. James was unashamed when he told the council that he had rested his head upon his father's body and cried.

When night descended, he wrapped himself in his father's bloodstained cloak and lay beside his body. Throughout the hours of darkness, and racked with fever, he listened to the whispers of dead men carried on the wind.

For a full day, he lay in a state of delirium among the dead but was shocked into wakefulness when he heard the sound of hooves on rock in the distance. Thinking the robbers had returned, he gazed around frantically, searching for a way to escape. His only recourse was to drag himself to a stand of bushes for concealment. He conveyed his terror as he lay hidden among the undergrowth, unable to quiet the pounding of his heart within his chest.

The appearance of a lone woman stunned James. He wondered whether he was hallucinating but watched her from his concealed vantage point as her eye followed the trail that he had made while dragging his body into the brush. He knew she would find him. The hallucination became real when she spoke and commanded him to reveal himself.

Beyond that, he could remember little, he had stated. The woman was a skilled healer. She tended his wounds and dulled his pain and his mind with her herbs, calming him enough that he could rest and gather his strength. She had agreed to take him down the mountain, where she would leave him to his fate.

"It is an incredible tale, my prince," Orman had said. "But how could you spend several days with her and know nothing of her? What were her origins? Is it possible that she traveled the same route as the attackers?"

Orman had noted James's look, registering his displeasure at being pressed.

"She did not know who I was," James had stated. "I told her I was a rich nobleman on a hunting trip and separated from my escort."

Orman had added, "And she asked nothing of you for this great service?"

Orman's eyes and ears, Malcolm, the guard commander, had watched her that day and saw no offering of valuables. But they had exchanged some final words as the prince had leaned closer to the woman, speaking in whispers, before she turned to travel back up the mountain slopes and disappeared into the trees.

James had flatly refused to implicate Seanna in any conspiracy, frustrating Orman's questioning. Taking Cedmon aside, Orman found him equally uncooperative. "Why would the prince protect her identity?" he asked.

"He is not. He has told you everything that he can remember," Cedmon answered.

"The prince speaks of the possibility that she traveled from the coast by boat and then across the open wasteland to reach the mountain. What could have been her purpose?" Orman asked.

"I do not know," Cedmon answered. "I did not speak with her. I was thinking only of the gratitude I felt for the safe return of the prince," Cedmon chided.

Orman knew this route he proposed was possible, for it was the one taken by the small band of Thomas's men and mercenaries who were to execute the ambush. Had she discovered their tracks back to the landing site on the coast?

The murders done, the killers had returned to the beach and reported to the waiting men that all were dead. Their treachery was rewarded with treachery, as Thomas's men overpowered them and killed them, then weighted their bodies with rocks and cast them into the sea, eliminating all witnesses to the deed.

In the time that had passed since James had taken the throne, Orman had concentrated his efforts in a search to discover the origin of the unknown woman. Thomas appeared contained for the moment, but James had taken the council by surprise when he had announced the trip back to the mountains to retrieve his father's body. The preparations for his departure were made in secrecy, and Orman was furious that Malcolm had not detected any unusual actions.

Idiots surround me. But what is this king doing? he thought.

From atop the stone battlements, Thomas had watched the arrival of Orman's man on horseback across the marsh. He stood bracing himself against the chill wind blowing over the small inlet sea. Wrapping his fur cloak more tightly around his shoulders, he gazed at the bleak landscape. He could smell the rotting reeds of the freshwater marshes that surrounded the castle. *I hate this place*, he thought. *The men are beasts and the women no better. How could I have let Orman convince me that this was where I should seek sanctuary? When I am king, Lord Orman's head will be the first to fall for condemning me to this godforsaken hell.*

It had been many months since he had received any communications, and he paced with impatience until the man joined him on the walkway. "My lord, I bear a message for you from Lord Orman."

He handed Thomas a scroll, which he read quickly.

It came as no surprise to him that he was the accused instigator of the assassinations, deemed guilty of the act of treason by having fled the kingdom even before James had returned, having escaped under the cover of darkness when they had received word that the king was dead and James lived.

Like Orman, Thomas had been shocked to learn that James was the lone survivor and was returning to the city under the protection of his guards. The plot had been foiled by a clever decoy: a pageboy, dressed as James, who had fooled the mercenaries sent to kill him. Orman could not explain how James had survived in the harsh mountains alone, beyond that he had been aided by a woman who had returned him to his men.

"A woman!" Thomas had shouted. "Who was she?"

"I do not know," Orman had answered. "But I will find out. For now, we must make it appear that this was your plot alone while I work covertly toward our objective to place you on the throne. We will find you a refuge and a sympathetic ear. Then you will build a coalition of men who will mount an army to challenge your right to be king. We have spent too many years formulating this plot to abandon our quest now," Orman had counseled.

James is king, he read on. Thomas looked up in surprise at the messenger. "It is true that James is crowned?" he asked.

"Yes, my lord, he is," the man replied.

Thomas sent the man away. *Orman was supposed to have been appointed regent for several years, until James reached the right age to take the throne. Something has changed? It appears that Orman has not been as persuasive as he thought himself to be.*

He gazed out on the desolate marshes again, knowing that James would now move to solidify his forces.

It will take me time to build an army, let alone one with the strength to challenge my cousin outright. I do not have much to offer these barbarians besides the prospect of new land holdings and titles to any conquered territory, but it will not take much convincing. They are a bloodthirsty lot, and greedy. They will relish the prospect of war for such a prize.

14

RETURN TO THE MOUNTAIN

James sat listening to the rhythm of the oars upon the water, momentarily lulling his apprehension. He and his men had been traveling on the river for a day. They had departed at dawn, but the night before he had paced restlessly inside his chamber, awaiting the morning light. Alone in his room, he had felt a rising panic as he struggled to recall the details of the mountain landscape. Although Seanna had asked him to commit them to memory, would he be able to remember the natural landmarks that would lead him back to his father? He secretly doubted his ability to locate the mountain tomb, so well disguised within the rock outcropping.

He had boldly pronounced that his city should ready itself for the burial of its fallen king, and he could not rest until he had fulfilled his promise to his father to bring him home.

I will be disgraced if I come back without him. And once that oath is fulfilled, I will be free to finish the other: to hunt down those responsible for the ambush and avenge my father's death.

The sails hoisted, they sailed smoothly toward the mountains, and as he listened to the melodic flow of the water against the bow, he felt his determination renewed.

He breathed in the musky scent of the water and gazed ahead at the distant outline of the mountain peaks.

My last journey toward these mountains was a year ago, but the memories are still vivid in my mind. I stood in this very place with my father, sharing the excitement of a new adventure together.

James's heart winced at the recollection of his father's smiling face. Cedmon joined his king, and they sat together in the quiet. "I am not the same youth I was the last time I traveled this river," James said.

"Are you remembering your father?" Cedmon asked.

James nodded.

"I am thinking of him also."

James sighed deeply. "There is so much I wish I could ask him."

Cedmon shook his head knowingly. "But I sense more is troubling you. You are thinking that she will not come?"

"Yes. It has been a year, and promises can be forgotten," James said.

"If she does not, you are accompanied by the best soldiers and trackers in the kingdom. We will find him," Cedmon offered reassuringly.

James looked out over the water, his thoughts returning to Seanna.

Yes, I am worried that she will not return. What do I know of her? And our time together was so brief. I have asked myself many times if our experience changed me fundamentally or if it was all a fabrication of my mind. Did our conversations around that nightly fire stir a deeper level of understanding in me? Or have I always possessed these ideals at the core of my being, until a cataclysmic event unleashed what lay dormant within me and set me on this course?

When James had returned to his city from the mountains, he had begun observing his surroundings differently. Previously, the people of his kingdom, especially the women, had been practically invisible to him. He had never considered the possibility that others, no matter how menial their roles, might carry hopes and aspirations such as his.

He had shared his thoughts about Seanna with Cedmon upon their return. When he spoke of her virtues out loud, they seemed like the musings and fantasies of a young man, magnifying her strength, her intellect, and her beauty. Cedmon had listened patiently to James's declaration of his revealing talks with Seanna. In repeating them, he felt as if his reflections sounded trivial, punctuated by the fact that she had departed into the forest like a phantom.

Cedmon looked concerned when he responded, "I wonder if one woman could be all those things, Your Grace," he answered. "I would caution you against placing too much trust in her coming."

"I do not know what to expect," James shared. "I can tell you only that she was unlike any woman I have ever met, and that I have judged against her example all the women I have met since then . . . But time has passed, and I now question my recollections. She is little more than a stranger to me, but when we parted on that mountain, I felt as if I knew a part of her at her very core. I hope that there is some truth to that feeling, and that she will return."

~

Seanna scanned the distant vista from her vantage point in the shadows of the forest. Lying low between the mountain ranges, a green valley stretched as far as she could see. The winding curve of a river bisected the landscape, and the morning mist partially obscured the tops of the mountain. She watched the line of men still miles away, snaking along the valley floor, and counted them.

They number almost fifty, but I cannot distinguish their features. I will not know whether James is among them until they are closer and it is too late for me to escape.

Waiting patiently as they advanced, she judged their arms, knowing that if the encounter turned sinister, she would not survive a fight. The time for her to leave undetected was now, but she suppressed the instinct to flee and remained there, standing and waiting among the trees. It was the agreed-upon time of return, and her strong sense that James would be among the group made her pulse quicken.

A few men broke from the line and climbed over a slight rise. The morning mist began to break, and weak sunlight filtered through the forest canopy. A single rider moved forward, then paused, silhouetted against the sky as he surveyed the tree line. Seanna held her horse back, squinting into the flat light, unable to distinguish the gray figure as the rider advanced. His waiting men and horses shifted nervously, heightening her vigilance. Then the rider moved into a ray of light that illuminated his face.

Seanna exhaled her held breath, recognizing James's face. He shouted a greeting to her, and she raised her hand, smiling in acknowledgment and urging her horse forward, as he dismounted and strode toward her.

James halted before her, staring at her for a long moment, grinning broadly. He placed his hands on her shoulders, and she thought briefly that he might embrace her, but he took a slight step backward, grasping her forearms as he looked into her eyes.

"You have come," he said.

"Yes. I gave you my word," she answered.

"It is good to see you again, Seanna," he said, smiling.

"And you, my lord." She smiled back.

Seanna studied him. In the passing of a year, the youth had changed into a man and stood before her in the fullness of his prime. He was tall and lean, with well-defined muscles. The richness of his tunic denoted nobility, and his bearing was that of a king. His dark hair fell below his shoulders, and his face bore a close-cropped beard. The brilliance of his blue eyes had not changed, and she felt herself flush as he gazed at her.

James examined Seanna in return and judged her as more womanly. Her thick hair was pulled back into a single, long braid that could not contain its loose tendrils, wet from the morning mist. Her cheeks looked flushed with the cool morning air, and her unflinching green eyes, lined with dark lashes, were just as penetrating. He released her arms, breaking the intensity of their exchange, and looked away in a moment of reserve as he shifted his attention to the men staring at them.

James laughed. "What a curious sight we must be."

Her eye followed his to the standing men, and she laughed as well. "Yes, we must."

"I wish to share with you that on my descent, I left the path to inspect the tomb of your father," Seanna informed him. "It is undisturbed and still protected. We hid him well. He is safe and, I sense, waiting for you."

James sighed with relief. "I was worried that I might not be able to find his tomb if you did not come. It has been hard to wait this year to bring him home."

She glanced over his shoulder, viewing his entourage again.

"We are in the company of my most trusted men, and they will help me bring my father back. The rest of my men wait at the river with the boats," James announced.

Seanna nodded.

"But first, let's sit a while by the trees and talk more," James offered. He signaled to an aide. "Bring us some wine," he commanded. The boy moved quickly to the task as James motioned to Cedmon.

"Seanna, this is my man Cedmon. He served my father and is my trusted confidant. He is the only one who has known all the details of this journey and the role you played in saving my life."

Cedmon bowed slightly. "At your service."

Sienna bowed in return, her hand on her heart.

"We will rest here. Send a rider to the river to begin the preparations of the funeral barge. My father is coming home," James ordered with pride.

"Yes, Your Grace," said Cedmon, smiling at his king. He stepped away, giving James and Seanna privacy, and conveyed the orders to the messenger.

When James turned back to Seanna, she was grinning. "I see you are indeed a king now. Has everything that you spoke of come to pass?"

"Not everything . . ." He paused. "But I am most anxious to hear your story," he continued, as they walked toward the trees. "I have many questions. Most important, what of your quest with the alliance?"

"I have failed in that endeavor, Your Grace," Seanna answered, looking away.

James stopped and faced her. "I am sorry. I will want to hear what happened."

They moved into the shade of the trees and stood under their branches. The aide handed Seanna a glass of wine and lingered a moment longer, staring, before James waved him away.

"I can see that you might be a great curiosity to my men."

"Yes, I suppose so," she answered, smiling over the rim of her glass.

They drank together in the stillness of the trees and the brightening morning light as the activity of his men in the distance fell away. James reflected silently on the moments they had spent around a fire on that dark mountain as he observed his thoughts. *It is as if no time has passed between us.*

"I want to hear of all your trials, and there is so much to share that I do not know where to begin," he said.

Seanna turned toward the peaks. "We have a long climb before we reach your father. We should get started. We will have time to share our stories later."

The midmorning sun hung low in the sky when they began their ascent up the mountain trail. A small group of men stayed behind to set up camp at the base of the tree line and wait for their return. For the remaining men, the climb was steep and arduous, impeded by their numbers, animals, and supplies. They ascended the mountain slowly, with Seanna and James in the lead, walking single file and making jagged progress.

When they stopped to rest, Cedmon pulled James aside and said, "I am impressed with the skill of this woman to have traversed down such a difficult trail with even a single horse and a wounded man. Now she moves all these men and beasts up the mountain trail with orderly precision, as well as any military commander could."

"I think that you are beginning to see that my observations of her were not just the projections of a pain-induced mind." James laughed.

Cedmon nodded. "Your words were true, my king."

The sun had moved behind the mountains when they finally reached the location of the ambush, marked by stone hovels covering the bodies of the men lost that day. Returning to the remnants of the camp, James felt his face darken as he stifled his emotions. He relived for a brief moment his initial excitement at the adventure in the mountains with his father and the hunt the next day; his feelings quickly changed to the raw anguish of tragedy and death.

James knew his face conveyed his distress, and he was grateful when Seanna suggested they keep moving. "Let's camp a little higher and closer to your father. We will retrieve your men tomorrow," she ordered.

Does she also want to shed the remembrance of the faces of dead men? he wondered.

The guards would gather the clothing, weapons, and bones of the fallen from the rock tombs and bury the remains with honor when the party returned home. In the meantime, James ordered his men to make camp higher up. They climbed beyond the ambush site and settled among the rocky crags, then busied themselves preparing for the evening as the sun moved lower in the sky. Dark descended over the peaks as all settled in for their dinner; the glow of the men's fires and the low murmur of conversations afforded a degree of comfort, keeping at bay the lingering ghosts of slain men.

Their food served, James watched Seanna grinning at him across the firelight. "I think I know your thoughts right now," he said, chuckling. "This is quite different from the last time we sat here, is it not?"

"Yes very different, but familiar at the same time," Seanna answered. "Let us toast our return and honor the men who lost their lives here." They raised their glasses and drank solemnly.

Over the next couple of hours, they talked. James shared an impassioned story of his ascent to the throne, the escape of his cousin, and the threat of a growing opposition army. He listened with keen interest to Seanna's recounting of the clan gathering, the formation of the alliance, and the failure of the vote. He sensed her hesitation when her words described the new leadership of Lord Arden.

"What happened with your Lord Arden?" he asked. "You spoke so highly of him and with great surety about the success of your appeal."

Seanna nodded. "My opinion of him has not changed." She handed James the written scroll containing the personal salutation from Arden. "I think you might better understand the man when you read his own words."

James read the parchment by the light of the fire. When he had finished, he carefully rolled it up and placed it in his tunic. "He speaks of a new time that is still inclusive of all interests."

"Yes," Seanna replied. "He still holds to the aspiration of real change through the alliance, but he underestimated the deep prejudices of men. I was also overconfident in my assumptions of the value placed on my service to the alliance as a scout. I must be candid with you, Your Grace. I gauged that failure after the alliance was formed and chose to reveal to the council our encounter and my impending journey." Seanna paused. "The existence of the pass was not revealed, and the date of our meeting was unknown, to the councilmen until my departure, but I still used this knowledge to exert influence over the council— and I was still unsuccessful. When we retrieve your father, I hope that you will still grant me the honor of an oath fulfilled."

James searched her face in the firelight, evaluating the burden of her compromise. "It must have been a great disappointment for you, after years of seeking that objective. We have both had to grow into our politics quickly and learn to make difficult choices."

Seanna nodded as he signaled to the aide for more wine.

"It appears that you have a strong ally in Lord Arden, who embraces progress. It is no easy task to transform the minds of men of our world. They hold fast to that which they know and do not welcome change. I speak of my challenges with my own council, for I now envision reforms in place of archaic rules. I often feel disillusioned about my hope to create a realm shaped by greater equality and opportunity."

"It requires a different kind of fortitude to have a vision and to be the catalyst for change in a kingdom, or even one small part of it. That you have aspirations to be such a king is greater than you might know yet," Seanna answered.

James felt his heart swell with her simple truth. *She empowers me with her words in a way that I cannot explain. I want to believe that these are honest sentiments, but, again, what do we know of each other?*

They sat quietly and watched the stars in the black sky. James turned to look at Seanna. "Tomorrow we will recover the body of my father, and you ask that your oath be fulfilled."

"Yes," she answered.

He hesitated. "Yet I have more to ask of you. You believe you have compromised that oath, but I do not judge it so harshly. My request goes beyond the oath that you have given me and will fulfill your obligation."

Seanna looked at him, uncomprehending, but remained silent.

James continued, "I ask that you return with me to my city and walk the funeral procession to my ancestors' tomb to bury my father. In truth, I have no right to request any more of you, as you have already given me my life, but it would be my honor for you to be by my side as I bury my father. I did not do this alone. That honor is yours, too."

He waited for a moment, watching her face, but could not read her thoughts. He added, "The message that you gave me from Lord Arden is also a timely one. It is unfortunate that you bear no message from the alliance council, but fortuitous for your clan that we still might begin a dialogue about what this meeting could mean for the future of both our people."

Seanna could hardly contain her astonishment and shivered as the hairs on her arms stood on end. *I could not have imagined what more he could have asked of me. I never anticipated such a request.*

She sat quietly, thinking, *I have always trusted my instincts to guide my life. Are the threads of fate and duty mystically woven together and testing me in this moment, as I stand upon a precipice? Do I believe I can bend them by the power of my free will and choose my destiny?*

She looked at James across the fire. She had memorized his

features a year earlier, and his face before her now clouded her judgment. She had made the long journey back through the pass knowing that she could have found herself standing on these slopes alone if he had not come. She had even contemplated an escape route, if needed. But she had not envisioned a journey beyond this now-so-familiar mountain.

She forced her expression to remain calm to hide her inner turmoil. *James's offer is the opportunity that I should seek. Fate has offered me a path to benefit my clan, and a means for inclusion in the alliance.*

But her stomach constricted as she realized, *All this opportunity has no bearing on the simple truth that I cannot bring myself to refuse him.*

James waited patiently, watching her face in earnest, before he asked one more time, "Seanna, will you return with me?"

She sat up taller. "It would be a great honor to see your city and accompany you to your ancestors' tomb to lay your father to rest," she replied.

James's face broke into a radiant smile. "I am very glad of that."

She smiled back, knowing that her answer alluded to duty and did not convey any of the bewilderment she felt as she lay down to sleep that night, unable to contain her stirring excitement about the unknown journey ahead.

James also lay awake, examining his thoughts. *So she will return with me! It felt right to ask her to come, but have I used to my advantage her dedication to the alliance and to her quest for progress for her clan? Is my request not born of a sincere desire to further a greater understanding between our different regions?*

He rolled onto his side and breathed deeply, settling into the stillness of the night. A short distance away, Seanna reclined on her side, and he gazed at the tangle of her tawny hair, wishing he could reach out and touch the wild mane.

As a woman, she perplexes me. The hardness of her warrior garb does not mask her femininity, but she mystifies me in the containment of her sentiments. I cannot read her emotions. For now, it is enough that I will return home with her at my side.

The following morning, they rose at first light and moved with a unified purpose, dividing into small groups to carry out their undertakings. Seanna would lead James and a group of men to the king's burial site. When they left, the others broke camp and built small carts that would be attached to the horses pulling the remains of the king and his men.

The rocky outcroppings appeared indistinct from all the others on the slopes. There were no visible traces of human activity; Seanna's tracking skills had ensured that the burial site was virtually undetectable. The men removed the entrance rock, and there was the faded purple cape that wrapped the body of their king. They began to remove the corpse but recoiled for a moment at the faint smell of decay. Composing themselves, they gently removed him, placing him on top of a makeshift carrier lined with the robes of royalty.

James lifted the purple shroud to gaze upon the mummified remains of his father. He placed his hand upon his father's chest, bowing his head for a moment in a silent conversation with him.

I am here, Father. I have come to take you home.

Seanna moved away, giving them time together.

The man who ministered to the burial of the dead stepped

forward and viewed the remains. James stepped aside and allowed him to prepare the body for travel. When he had finished, the men lifted the carrier onto a small cart and secured it with ropes before descending the trail.

With grim faces, all the men stood in hushed silence when they returned to the first campsite with the king, before kneeling to their fallen sovereign.

Cedmon said quietly to James, "This is a momentous day, Your Grace, and Seanna is indeed no ordinary woman to have returned to ensure this extraordinary event."

"I owe her a great debt and have asked her to return with me as my guest," James answered, noting Cedmon's surprised expression.

The group pushed on to reach the base camp. The steep and rugged trail was even more challenging with the extra burden of carriers and small carts, but when they reached a gentler slope, the worst of the descent was over. The men welcomed the sight of the forest and their campsite in the distance, having no desire to spend one more night among the foreboding peaks.

The encampment that evening was a solemn affair as men settled in small groups around the fires. The torches would burn all night while the guards stood vigil, surrounding the body of the king and the remains of their kin.

Cedmon had moved among the campfires, announcing that Seanna would be returning with them. In the still of the evening, there were hushed whispers around the fires. The men discussed the mystery of this woman and her possible origins. Many had believed that the retrieval of the king's body was impossible, that it had been the delusion of a young man in shock and pain. They had indulged their new king on his quest but now understood the magnitude of what had passed in these dark mountains between James and the woman he called Seanna.

The men who had retrieved the body spoke with reluctant esteem of her tracking skills and the fact that she was heavily armed. Where she had come from? they whispered. Those who could read the signs of the land formed their own conclusions. Her horse's tracks had revealed a descent from the mountain. It appeared that she could have come only from some point above, in the higher peaks, and possibly overland.

Cedmon had contained his initial thoughts when James had announced that Seanna would be traveling back with them. Having now journeyed up the peaks himself, he understood better the bond that Seanna and James had forged under such life-and-death conditions. But there was even more to it than that, he sensed. He had guarded over James since his boyhood and observed the subtle changes in the king around Seanna—changes that only Cedmon could have noticed.

He had watched James following Seanna's movements when she was not looking.

She is indeed a handsome woman under her men's clothing, and she does not flaunt her beauty. I have never observed a woman who carries herself with such confidence. There is an element of danger about her, though, for she moves among us without fear, and I have little doubt that she could use that sword at her side if provoked.

He wondered if James's fascination with her would diminish once they left these mountains. For the sake of his young king, he hoped not. He wanted James's judgment of her sound character to be valid, and hoped there was merit in their continued friendship. In the end, he concluded, the question did not need an answer right away, for she was coming with them, and he owed her his duty of protection.

The men moved hastily the following morning, eager to reach the boats waiting upriver and start the journey home. Moving away from the mountains, they began to shake off their sense of foreboding. Superstitious by nature, they believed the peaks were now cursed and harboring the ghosts of men murdered before their time.

Seanna embraced no such superstitions, but as they began to travel along the lower valley, watching the mountains recede in the distance, she questioned herself. *I must continue to trust my feelings, but have I judged wisely, when James and I know so little about each other? Will this untested friendship change as we move away from these familiar surroundings?*

She watched James and evaluated the group of men who rode beside him. *The scrutiny of his men is certainly no different than what I already know, but soon I will be among them in a foreign land, and entirely alone.*

She set aside her concerns and returned her thoughts to the advantages that James's invitation presented her. *I will be the first representative from the other side of the mountains in this new land, and I will not lose this chance to discuss new alliances.*

The landscape they traveled transformed into a gentle, lush valley with willow trees that lined the long river. James pointed out the geography along the way as the men pushed hard to make it to the boats by midday.

Shouts of welcome greeted them as they approached the

remaining men and waiting boats at the camp. They planned to travel upriver for several hours before mooring for the night. Seanna looked in the direction from which they had come. She had a practiced eye for distance and landmarks that would lead her back, if needed. She knew that if there was a time to turn back, it was now.

She saw James pause on the gangplank.

He is watching me and waiting to see whether I have changed my mind. Seanna turned toward him, looked upriver, and stepped onto the boat. The men moved in haste as they secured the king's body and settled the horses in their stalls, beginning to relax as the return journey was underway.

When they moored several hours later, it was dusk. A small group of men and horses disembarked from the boat, forming a hunting party for the chance of some fresh game for the evening meal. Seanna turned to James. "I would like to go with the men, if I may."

"Of course. I will join you," he answered.

"Would you mind if I went alone?"

James could not hide his surprise. "Are you sure?"

"Yes. It will be an opportunity for your men to know me better, or at least get used to me," she replied with a grin.

James called Cedmon to his side. "Tell the men that Seanna is coming on the hunt."

Cedmon raised his eyebrows but made the announcement. The men looked taken back and then a little deflated.

Seanna laughed. "Well, that is a common reaction when a men's hunting group has the inclusion of a stranger, especially a woman."

James did not see her mirth; he looked at her with only trepidation.

"It will be fine. How much trouble can I get into?" she asked, as she disembarked from the boat.

Cedmon returned to James's side as they watched the hunting party move toward the meadows in the distance. "She looks like a lamb moving among a pack of wolves," he noted.

James relaxed into a smile. "Yes, but I think this lamb would bite back." They both laughed.

Seanna had no desire to hunt outside the need for food and would never have killed a creature in sport, but she thought, *If they can observe me in closer quarters, they might form some more tolerant perceptions of me. When we return to the city, they could add an element of candor to the stories that I know will come.*

She and the men moved single file toward the grasses, searching for game grazing in the meadow at sundown. They sighted two deer in the distance. Dismounting, they crouched low, moving carefully through the long grass, silencing the chirps of crickets. A few men with bows moved forward, signaling silently for Seanna to join them.

The deer continued to forage as the men judged their distance. Their leader indicated in a sweeping gesture that Seanna should attempt the shot.

Yes, I'll take the shot, but I am sure you hope that I will miss, she mused.

The leader's sidelong glance at the men and his smirk conveyed his skepticism. She would miss the mark, and they would return empty-handed, ending any more impromptu hunting trips with her along.

The men continued to glance at each other in amusement

as she moved in front of them, staying low, her bow ready and the first arrow nocked. She moved cautiously, so as not to alert the deer to her presence. When in range, she stood up and released the arrow, killing the first deer. When the second deer startled and turned to run, she struck it down with her next shot. The men looked at one another in amazement at her deadly accuracy.

The leader laughed out loud. "Well, there's our dinner, lads!"

The other men laughed in turn, slapping one another on the backs and grinning at Seanna as they moved to examine the kills.

"They are good clean shots. Well done," the leader said, giving her a respectful nod. They dressed out the animals, tied them to the packhorse, and headed to camp. When they arrived at the moored boats, the men cheered at the anticipation of fresh venison for dinner.

Seanna dismounted and stood among the hunting party. As she admired the deer, she overheard a guard ask the hunt leader, "Did the woman get in the way?"

"On the contrary—she made the kills!" he answered, and she saw him raise one bushy eyebrow.

Seanna secured her horse and thought, *Well, for the time being, this appears to be one small victory.*

She glanced at James, who was grinning and laughing among his men. She smiled herself.

It is good to see some gaiety replacing the men's solemn moods, and to have a respite from James's renewed grief over the last several days. He deserves to celebrate his triumph.

When James invited her to dine on the boat with him, she suggested they eat at the fire among the men, reasoning, *Let me use this goodwill to my advantage. I vowed to myself that once I stepped upon the deck of this boat to return with James, I would be committed to a course of action that promotes a better understanding between our peoples.*

"As you wish," James answered, leading her down the plank.

Seanna nodded. *This endeavor is no different than my undertakings of the last several years, slowly building a coalition between clans. Now, the task of bridging the divide between different realms is even greater.*

Sitting among the group at the evening fire, Seanna drank from the tankard of ale that the men passed around. The leader of the hunting party raised his cup. "I offer a toast to the provider of this feast, Seanna!"

She bowed her head graciously. It was the first time that any of the men besides James had called her by name.

As the venison haunches roasted on the spits, Cedmon spoke up. "You have some skill with a bow. Where did you get your training?"

All the men turned to her in anticipation of her answer. James glanced at her and nodded for her to begin.

"I am a warrior scout for my clan and trained in those skills," she began. "I come from the lands to the south of the great mountains." She watched the expressions of surprise on the men's faces.

James added, "The clans of that region have formed a new alliance, and they hope to create new trade routes to the north from their lands. Seanna ventured here to scout the coastlines for that purpose."

Seanna glanced at James. His information was factual, but he did not disclose the actual route through the pass, leading the men to assume that coastal access had brought her here.

She continued, "Our coastlines have always been vulnerable,

especially the points to the north. To this day, the scouts of the Womara and other clans keep vigil along the boundary."

"For protection?" Cedmon asked.

"Yes. In the time of a great invasion to our coast, we almost lost our lands to the invaders. Our past will not let us forget how close we came to being overrun."

"I have heard many stories of a great war. Your clan fought in this battle?" Cedmon asked.

Seanna nodded. "It changed our history."

"Can you tell us the tale?" a young page blurted, speaking out of turn, his eyes sparkling with excitement. His face turned red at his outburst, producing laughter from the men. Seanna looked at James, who tipped his head and raised his glass for her to begin.

"Yes, I will tell you a story of my people," she answered.

She watched James relax and settle back. The ale and the warmth of the fire had taken the strain out of his face, and he looked like an eager youth at the prospect of her account. She glanced around and saw similar excitement on the other men's faces.

"This is a story of my great, great, grandmother's time. It began with fire," Seanna started.

15

THE GREAT INVASION

The sentry standing on the bluff at the farthest northern outpost stood frozen in disbelief as he viewed the outline of twenty ships taking form, emerging through the coastal fog. He stumbled before running to sound the first alarm that would set off a chain of warnings to the villages along the coast. A solitary Womara scout traveling along the coastal range had heard the warning bells chiming in the distance, signaling that some type of invasion by sea was imminent. She galloped ahead to examine the upper cliffs of the deserted northern coastline.

She would later report that she had lain hidden on her belly among the long grasses as she counted the raiders' ships anchored in a small bay. A band of the raiders stood upon the deserted beach below, gazing up at the rocky barrier of the cliffs while two of their men climbed slowly up the face. The Womara scout's heart stopped as she watched the first solitary raider pull his body up and over the cliff edge. Standing, he signaled to the waiting men below and threw down the first rope. She did not wait to watch as the remaining raiders began their slow ascent, gathering in number at the top of the bluffs. She crawled away, retrieved her horse, and rode through the night to reach her clan.

Rowan listened intently as the scout recounted all she had seen, swallowing long breaths to steady her speech. "The entire coastline is under attack, and raiders are massing along the upper coastal cliffs. They must be traveling by foot into the interior, traversing the base of the mountain range and across the lower valleys. I estimate that they will arrive within a two-day march to launch a surprise attack."

The woman who stood gathered around the scout gasped.

"If they secured the northern coastline and interior, they could continue to press west and south until they closed the loop of a great net, while distracting the coastline clans with the attack by sea," Rowan spoke to the anxious women.

"The clans in the interior know nothing of this advancing attack," Rowan stated, gripped with fear at the realization that the valley of the Womara lay directly in the raiders' path. Her thoughts raced. *Eight boats carrying about fifty men each means an estimated force of four hundred men. My warriors number fewer than two hundred and are untested in battle.*

Rowan signaled for Asha to join her at her side. "There are too many. We cannot hold them back. We need the fighting men of the surrounding clans."

"The nearest township is a full day's ride away!" Asha replied, unable to disguise the panic in her voice.

Rowan wasted no time in dispatching a fresh rider to the township to spread the alarm of the impending assault, and an urgent plea for fighting men.

She placed her hand on the messenger's shoulder. "You must

ride hard. Warn the clan of Lord Alfred. We will move to meet the marching invaders and will hold them for as long as possible. All will be lost if they do not come."

The rider nodded solemnly, mounted, and spurred her horse forward, leaving Rowan and Asha standing alone. "We are the only clan standing between these invaders and the lands to the west. Can we impede the raiders' advance long enough for the arrival of the other clansmen?" Asha asked.

"I do not know," Rowan replied. "But we must march to meet whatever awaits us."

Rowan took a deep breath. A chill ran down her spine, not from fear of the battle but from the thought of enslavement.

She composed herself, before commanding, "Organize the warriors. I will join you shortly."

Rowan ran to the village center and ordered the evacuation. The elderly and youngest children splintered into small groups. Moving quickly, they gathered food and weapons, intending to disperse into the deep forest, gorges, and caves. The women exchanged rushed goodbyes. A few of the smaller children began to cry, sensing the anxiety of their mothers, but were quickly hushed. Rowan directed some warriors to follow the groups, seeking strategic places throughout the forest to kill as many invading men as possible. The remaining children, too young for battle, stood before her.

"Take your bows and flee deeper into the forests. Climb the tall trees and wait. If the invaders penetrate the interior, pick off as many as possible from the high canopies," Rowan ordered.

She tried to smile reassuringly at the young faces, each struggling to show bravery. "Go now. Have courage."

Rowan sought out her daughter, Landra. "You will lead the women into the forest and protect the children," she ordered.

"No, Mother, I am going with you. I am the best archer," Landra challenged. "You will need me at the battle," she replied, showing no fear.

Rowan winced. Her daughter was seventeen and barely a woman. Turning away so that Landra could not see her face, Rowan wiped away the tears stinging her cheeks.

The remaining clanswomen, who formed the core of the Womara's defense, gathered in the clearing, moving swiftly to ready their horses and their arms. Rowan paused to watch her child as Landra silently prepared her bow and weapons, moving with the precision of a well-trained soldier. The warriors formed their lines and silently departed into the forest. Rowan glanced back once to view the deserted and silent village that was their home, knowing that they might never return.

At dawn on the following day, the Womara scout galloped back with the warning that the raiders were close. She jumped from her horse, announcing, "They are less than a mile away and just beyond that rise."

The women moved to the edge of the forest line and waited, viewing the vast, open meadow that lay ahead and the mountain range silhouetted in the distance. When the raiders gathered at the crest of the rise, Rowan silently counted the growing forces on the hill, then looked at Asha, indicating with a grimace how badly outnumbered they were.

Asha grabbed her forearm. "I know your thoughts, my friend. Do not think that you have condemned these women to death. They stand here with you because that is their choice. You are our leader, and we follow you. And if this is to be the day of my death, then I will die as a free woman, and I thank you for that."

Rowan reached out and squeezed her friend's hand tightly.

The Womara warriors stood ready, staring across the expanse. Many had painted their faces in the battle colors of their previous clans, but Rowan saw fear beneath their war masks.

When taken from my home, I was no older than some of these youngest warriors, and now there is my daughter, standing bravely among them.

Rowan's heart ached with renewed anguish. *She was born into freedom, with a warrior spirit. She does not question the battle, but I know that we fight to the death, and as a mother, I would give my own life if I could save her.*

Rowan scanned the faces before her, searching for words of courage, and felt her heart filling with pride. *These are the very women who would once have cowered in their homes, watching their men killed and their villages burned, waiting to accept whatever fate was decreed by an invading force. Today, we determine our own destiny.*

Rowan rose high in her saddle to speak. "Women of the Womara! Warriors! We hoped this day would never come. But there they are." She pointed across the meadow to the rise. "Those are the men who will burn your homes and rape your daughters before your very eyes."

The women shifted uncomfortably at her words as she continued, "Those are the men who will kill or enslave everyone you hold dear in this world. We have lived together as family and friends, but today we are warriors, and we must fight to protect what is ours!"

The women cheered, raising their shields and swords in the air.

"I do not invite death, but I will not let any man take my freedom! Will we let them violate our bodies or enslave our children?" Rowan shouted.

"No!" the women yelled.

"Will we let them break our spirits?"

"No!" the women chanted.

"What is our pledge to those who will try to take this from us?"

"Death!" the women yelled, beating their shields. "Death! Death!" The chant grew louder.

The women watched the dark line of men moving down the hills and into the meadow as Rowan continued to rally their courage. "We are called the Womara because we live without men. We are also the Womara because we live free!" she shouted. "Who are we?"

"The Womara!" the women cried, hitting their shields. "The Womaraaaaa!"

The raiders gathered at the base of the hills as the women repeated their war cry, continuing to beat out their defiance.

"Leaders, take your places," Rowan ordered.

The women on horseback, Asha among them, rode out to the sides and in front of the women.

"Bow warriors, take your positions!" Rowan commanded.

Sixty women archers, Landra among them, massed in groups of tens, forming lines behind each other.

"Make your arrows count! Take down as many men as possible in the first charge," Rowan yelled. "Aim for the strongest fighters;

pick off any men with long spears. Support our warriors from both sides."

Rowan's eyes fixed on her daughter, and their gaze lingered for a moment, but she turned sharply when she heard the raiders yell the order to attack. The men began their charge across the open meadow, shouting their own war cries as the women braced themselves.

The men ran faster, swords and spears held high, as they closed the distance.

The archers waited, and, instead of unleashing a high volley of arrows, each woman picked out a charging man, taking deadly aim.

"Loose the arrows!" Rowan yelled.

The first arrows flew, taking down many of the running men in front and causing those behind to trip on the fallen bodies, breaking the momentum of the charge. The first line of archers moved back as the next line advanced and loosed their arrows. Each line kept moving forward to replace those who had already shot their quiver. Within minutes, close to a hundred men were down and dying, before the remaining raiders closed the distance. When the men were midway across the meadow, the warrior women charged to meet the onslaught.

"Death!" the women yelled in unison.

Almost at the point of contact, the center of the Womara charge dropped to the ground and rolled through the running men, slashing legs. The women running behind the line of charging women warriors struck down the fallen men with fatal sword blows before they could rise to their feet. The element of surprise in their assault momentarily confused the raiders, and the remaining women diverged into two streams, moving to either side of the mass of men.

The women fought in small clusters of three or four with their backs together, facing outward, protecting each other. They thrust and slashed as the men moved within range. The archers picked off fighters from the side, and Rowan and her leaders fought on horseback, slicing down upon the men below them.

Landra watched as women fell, but she never stopped shooting her arrows. The women fought fiercely but were no match for the men, who struck with brute force and began to penetrate the small, protected groups of fighters. The men cut through the mass, intent on taking down the archers. She kept shooting until she was out of arrows.

A lone raider broke through the line, intent on her. Landra threw down her bow and pulled her sword. She rushed to meet his charge but feigned a move to his right side, pulling his sword thrust off balance. She spun full circle, turned into her attacker, and slashed him high across the top of his abdomen. He screamed as he dropped his sword and gripped his stomach. She choked down the taste of bile in her mouth at the sight of his spilling entrails and the metallic smell of blood.

Landra recovered quickly but was stricken with horror as she saw her mother's horse, at the center of the battle, cut down from beneath her. Landra slashed viciously through the fighting men, her sight fixed upon Rowan, as her mother stood, facing the raiders' leader. The air was filled with the cries of men and women as they fought and with the groans of the wounded and dying.

When Rowan's horse fell, she rolled clear. Rising quickly, she found herself alone, staring into the blood-streaked face of the enemy. He charged, and Rowan blocked his blow from above with her shield, but she did not hear Landra's warning call as another man approached from the rear. It was his blade that ran her through from behind.

Rowan sank to her knees and placed her hand over the fatal wound, trying to contain her lifeblood. She gasped, spitting up blood as the shouts of the battle faded and her vision blurred. She could see Landra's stricken face as she tried to close the distance between them. Her daughter's visage transmuted into Landon's ghostly form, standing in the clearing beyond the fighting, in the last remnants of the morning mist. His eyes implored her to follow him as he beckoned with his outstretched hand, before she slumped to her side and died.

Landra saw her mother struck down and screamed in rage as she cut her way into the center to face the leader. He turned to meet her charge, his sword ready.

"You bitch of a whore," he snarled.

She dropped to one knee, using the momentum of her attack to slide in before him, kicking his feet from under him. He fell to the ground and struggled to rise as Landra jumped up and kicked him backward. She rushed to stand above him and, gripping her sword with both hands, drove it into his heart. The man's eyes were opened wide, then frozen in death. She placed her foot upon his torso to free her blade and jumped over his prone form.

Landra readied herself as more men surged forward, but the raiders stopped short when the sounds of horns in the distance resonated through the forest. Hundreds of Lord Alfred's men emerged on horseback from the shadows of the trees into the clearing. Momentarily confused, the raiders stood rooted in place. Then, outnumbered, they turned to run. The clansmen on horseback charged across the meadow, beating down the remaining raiders trying to flee in the chaos.

Lord Arden's ancestor Alfred had arrived too late to save many of the women but was in time to finish the battle as they surrounded and slaughtered the enemy to the last man. Alfred's men surveyed the fallen and the great numbers of dead among the small groups of women.

The remaining women warriors, Asha among them, numbered fewer than fifty and stood splattered in blood, still gripping their swords and bows. Landra had dropped to her knees beside her mother's dead body and gazed down at her face. Rowan's eyes were wide open, staring into the beyond. There was a slight smile upon her face.

Landra grasped her hand. "We are saved!" she cried, fighting back her tears. "You have delivered us, and your sacrifice has not been in vain."

She brought her mother's hand to her lips and kissed it, before gently setting it back down on her chest. She closed Rowan's open eyes.

Landra rose to face Alfred and his men. "She was my mother," she spoke proudly. "I am Landra, clan leader of the Womara."

16

A FALLEN KING RETURNS

Upon the river the following day, Seanna watched James busy himself with his men as the boats moved steadily under a wind that filled their sails, blowing them farther from the mountains. She sat quietly, looking out over the water breaking on the bow, watching the willow trees and tall reeds on the banks.

She was enjoying a sense of goodwill forged among the men around the fire the night before, and as she observed the passing landscape, her mind drifted. *I understand the excitement of being an adventurer who knows that her eyes are the first to see a new land.* She smiled to herself. *But I am certainly far from home and my quiet forest.*

Inhaling deeply, she sat back to enjoy the feel of the warm breeze, listening to the warning cries of wild birds as they rose from the banks and took flight, disturbed by the approaching boats. As her thoughts turned back to James, she tingled at the reminder of the good fortune his invitation had bestowed upon her.

He is an interesting man. I find him difficult to place in a category of men that I can easily define. My instincts tell me he is a person who is tolerant and open to new beginnings. Most men are beyond my comprehension, but I wish him to be different.

She thought back to a conversation with her mother just after she had returned from the trials of admission to become an alliance scout. "How can we ever make progress with the likes of men?" she had asked with frustration, after recounting the deliberate berating of many of the men present that day.

Dian listened and nodded knowingly, "I think you may change your sentiments one day, my daughter. But I agree that trying to talk to a man who does not care to listen is like rowing against a strong river current," she shared. "Only when a man has a sincere desire to know a woman can she reveal her true self. A strong woman needs a confident man, for their true bond is based on equality. This union calls for a changing nature of that man."

"I am not sure I know what you mean," Seanna replied.

Dian smiled. "When you meet such a man, you will know."

The remembrance of her mother's words made Seanna look to James again. She smiled when he glanced over to see her watching him, then joined her at the bow. "I am too preoccupied with my duties, and I have neglected you," he said.

"On the contrary, I am enjoying sitting here and marveling at the beauty of your passing country," she answered.

James signaled his servant for some drink, and they sat silently for a few moments, savoring the taste of their wine. "The river is very soothing to me," he shared. "I find that the sounds of the moving water free my mind, if only briefly, from thoughts of my duties."

"I love the water, too," Seanna answered. "There are hot mineral springs along my river where I spend many an hour," she shared. She looked away, surprised at the expression of her sentiment.

"Something we share besides a love of adventure," James said, smiling.

For the next several hours, they sat together as James recounted the history of his people and details of the land they passed. He watched Seanna relax into the rhythm of the journey, and in a lull of his narrative, he thought, *With each passing mile, I begin to think that the difference between our people and culture does not seem so great.*

The scenery slowly changed, becoming populated with human inhabitants, small huts, patchworks of cultivated fields, and grazing cattle. News of the funeral boats traveled quickly ahead of them, and citizens lined the banks, kneeling to honor the shrouded casket of their fallen king. James waved as they passed.

"The homage of your people is moving. Your father must have been a most beloved king," Seanna said.

"He was," James replied sadly.

The river widened and forked as a tributary merged in from the west. The bustle of the river commerce quickened as more ships and barges moved toward the great city. Men ferried the large barges and ships carrying timber and livestock that moved along the banks by ropes or by rowing against the current. The sun was moving behind the hills when they glimpsed the outline of the stone city's turrets looming in the distance. The castle stood high upon the hill over the river, against the sunset sky.

"My home," James stated proudly, his eyes shining with pride.

"It is magnificent," Seanna said, beaming back at him.

"We should prepare to dock soon," James suggested.

The sails were ordered lowered, and the men manned the rows as they approached the city. James pointed out to Seanna a portion of the river that diverted into a large canal and encircled the metropolis, allowing the passage of ships and barges between ramparts.

Then he directed her sight to the outer walls. "That section of the river mouth opens to the sea, providing a natural barrier to the front portion of the city. The outlying structures were built for the accommodation of commerce and ships but are still protected by the stone wall, reinforcing the defensive strengths of the lower portion of the port."

"I have never seen anything like this," Seanna answered, as the boats moved closer to the docks and she gazed up at the scale of the wall. "The sheer size and architecture are impressive," she added.

James nodded. "In our early history, this was a quiet coastal village built around the inlet. It developed into a port a hundred years ago. The river canal was a natural fortification, and the inner and outer rock walls were built for defense." He pointed out the divisions of well-fortified stone structures and impregnable sections. "Our design, on a smaller scale, may well be considered for your ports," he stated.

"I agree," Seanna answered.

James continued, "The commerce of trade grew from the flourishing town and surrounding villages. The large harbor was developed into a primary trading site, able to accommodate goods from the northern continents and beyond. We have dominated the commerce of this region for many decades. But I see an even greater advancement in more expansion. There are places beyond this realm that have remained closed to trade. I intend to extend our reach. My vision could be a point where we might begin our talks," he offered.

"It is my hope, Your Grace," Seanna answered.

James's words gave Seanna pause. Staring up at the enormous walls of stone again, she envisioned the first of group of emissaries from the clans of her region arriving at this new city, marveling again at the expanse of the docks busy with the activity of the day.

My mother was right to have pressed for the prospect to culti-vate such a powerful partner and a possible future political ally. The opportunity is immense, and my responsibility to develop such a possibility is a worthy challenge of any future leader.

Their boats approached a series of stone ramparts, which were busy with the movement of men. Large wooden docks accommo-dated the ships and barges. Warehouses stood ready to be loaded with the docked ships' merchandise as the middlemen who traded for profit secured their wares. On top of the warehouses were built living quarters, and from some of the windows faces observed the movement of the boats below.

"Hold here for a moment as we get prepared," James said.

Seanna waited, observing the bustle of the docks. The fisher-men sold their fresh catch right from their boats, and game and fowl were traded in abundance as people carried on the business of selling goods. Servants scurried behind their masters, holding the day's purchases. Cooking stalls operated along the ramparts as the cooks called out to the people strolling by, announcing their delicacies. The smells of prepared food permeated the air, com-bined with the scent of the sea, the odors of animals, and the sweat of men.

Beyond the docks, Seanna could see that access to the rear

of the city was over a wide bridge that crossed the river, leading to the massive, carved wooden doors that secured the entrance. Within the walls she glimpsed some of the interior houses and buildings, which rose in levels through long and steep streets. At the very top of the plateau stood the castle. Purple flags, a tribute to the returning king and fallen warriors, fluttered in the wind.

Cedmon approached. "Your Grace, the carriage is waiting to carry your father. We will move the procession through the city, but I wish to secure him in the palace as quickly as possible."

James nodded as men shouted directions in anticipation of the approaching royal ship, while others along the rock rampart walls hurried to action. The ship moved alongside the wooden dock, and men stopped to stare and point at the tall woman dressed in men's clothes standing beside their king. Seanna became aware of their observations and watched James take notice of the gestures, too. He turned to her with a frown and commented, "I imagine that you will be an object of curiosity for a while. I hope it will not be too distracting to your visit."

"I am not concerned," she replied. "I understand I will be a distraction for a time, but I do not want my presence to overshadow the importance of this moment."

The king's men disembarked with the horses. "Where should I ride?" she asked Cedmon.

He turned to James for direction. "She rides with me at the head of the procession," James said, and Cedmon nodded.

"That is an honor, Your Grace," Seanna said.

"An honor you deserve," James replied.

Cedmon signaled the dockmen to act. They jumped to fix the ropes and set the landing ramp while Seanna prepared to leave the boat. He helped her walk her horse off the ramp as his attention focused on the commotion of the crowds as they gathered to watch the woman and the removal of the king's body.

"Come secure the casket," Cedmon ordered the waiting king's guards.

They lifted the casket of the fallen king gently onto a pallet and moved it to a waiting carriage. Men shouted more orders as horses and supplies were unloaded. Several mounted guards stood at the rear of the carriage, ready to escort the king's body. Seanna stood for a moment, affectionately patting the mare's nose. Glancing up, one guard among the king's escort caught her eye and stared at her.

"Move out." Cedmon's orders rose above the commotion.

Seanna mounted her horse and joined James as the procession began to move from the rear ramparts of the city toward the entrance. Passing through the massive gates, the carriage continued its slow journey through the main street of the city, as citizens, kneeling in tribute, lined the way. The activity of the marketplace was waning at the day's end and went silent as the king's coffin and procession crossed the open space, making its way toward the palace.

Seanna viewed the sea of faces in the crowd before her. There were many distinctly different races of men and women; it was a cultural melting pot, just as James had described it in his stories. Some people stared openly and whispered among themselves.

I can see that I am a curiosity to those standing before me. I expect that, but I hope that the rest of James's people will be as gracious and accepting as he and his men have tried to be. These will be interesting days ahead, she mused.

~

The arrival of the king's procession at the palace spurred to action the guards and servants, with James at the center of the activity, directing their tasks.

"Take the king to the viewing hall," he ordered. "Cedmon, follow my father and make sure all the preparations are complete. He will lie in state for three days."

Cedmon bowed. "Yes, Your Grace." He smiled broadly, then turned to Seanna and added, "And you, my lady, are most welcome in our city."

Seanna smiled back. "Thank you, Cedmon."

James turned to her. "You must be tired. I know I am."

Seanna nodded. "I think the excitement of the day is catching up with me," she admitted.

"Prepare a chamber for my guest," he ordered his head servant.

"Where would you like her accommodated, Your Grace?"

"Place her close to my private rooms. Come, Seanna. Let me see my father's resting place before we retire."

They walked together down a long hall to the antechamber that held the king's body. The room was already illuminated by evening lanterns. The casket had been placed upon a long marble table draped in magnificent purple cloth with gold-threaded embroidery bearing the crest of the king's ancestors.

James gently placed his hand upon the casket. "I can hardly believe that he is here."

"Yes," she said. "Your father is finally home."

James personally escorted Seanna to her rooms, talking briefly about the pleasantries of the following day. "We have had a long journey, and I hope you find your rooms pleasing," he said, pausing outside her door. "I must go attend to some final details for my father, but I will call on you in the morning. You have attendants who will provide food and any other items you may request. I wish you a good night's rest."

Seanna placed her hand upon her heart, bowing her head, and said her good night as she entered her room.

James stood alone in the hallway after she had closed the door to her chamber, leaning his head against the door frame. *I feel exhaustion and exhilaration distilled into this single moment. Nothing in my reunion with Seanna has disappointed me so far. I do not know what the next day will bring—who can say any such thing with certainty?—but for now, I know that I am content.*

Seanna closed the door behind her, leaning against it. She took a deep breath, grateful for the privacy of her chamber after the long journey and the close company of so many men. She glanced around the room, marveling at its lavishness. She could no longer refute her exhaustion as she eyed the large bed at its center. Ready to drop onto it fully clothed, she stopped short, eyeing the two female attendants awaiting her direction shyly at the side of the room. Unsure what to say, she stood silently.

One woman stepped forward. "Milady, we have brought you some cheese and bread with wine. Would you like something different to eat?"

"No, that is fine," Seanna replied, as she proceeded to remove her weapons and her filthy outer clothing.

"May I prepare you a bath?" the younger servant asked in a timid voice.

"Yes, I would like that," she answered.

She undressed, and her soiled clothes were picked up by the other attendant, who departed the room. Standing naked before the drawn bath, she thought, *I am sure that I am being examined, no matter how discreetly, for any extra appendages or worse. It is a comfort to know that at least it will be recounted that for all outward appearances, I do appear to be a normal woman.*

She lowered herself into an elegant marble bathtub, filled with scented water, and smiled at the young servant who emptied another bucket of hot water into the basin, sighing with pleasure as she sank lower into the tub.

The servant left her to enjoy the fragrant water in privacy. Lying back, she recounted all the day's happenings and marveled again at the course of events that had brought her to this moment. Her thoughts turned serious when she remembered the guard leader and his keen observations of her.

It was more than just curiosity. I must be mindful to remain vigilant, no matter how welcoming appearances are. Some men might not be pleased with my arrival, or with the fact that I aided in the rescue of the king. James and his man might be my only allies.

Lord Orman sat quietly at his desk in his private chambers, when a servant knocked on his door to announce the arrival of a visitor. He let out an exasperated sigh, throwing down his quill on the paper he was writing.

I don't need any more distractions today, besides my duties of dealing with the arrival of the king.

"What is it?" he answered with annoyance.

The door opened, and the servant was pushed aside roughly

before he could announce the guest, as Malcolm rushed into the room.

"What are you doing here? I am about to leave to greet the king," Orman snapped.

"It is she!" Malcolm exclaimed.

"Who?"

"The woman who came down the mountain last year. She has returned with the king."

"What?" Orman stood up, stepping toward him. "Are you sure?"

"Of course I am. There is no mistaking her."

Orman paused, needing a moment for his thoughts to stop spinning. "Where did she come from?"

"The men who returned with the king told me that she was waiting for them on the mountain," Malcolm answered. "They learned that she is from the continent to the south," Malcolm replied.

Orman felt his stomach lurch. "Then their meeting was planned?"

"It appears so," Malcolm answered.

Oman struggled to keep his face calm and his thoughts to himself.

So, the king has not told me everything he knows, as I've always suspected. He has gone to great lengths to protect her identity—but for what purpose?

17

THE KING'S COUNCIL

Seanna awoke with the first light of dawn, lifting herself up in her bed to rest on her elbows; she looked down at the nightgown she was wearing, remembering where she was. The night before, she had not protested when the servant had placed the gown on her after the bath and led her to the bed. She remembered nothing after having laid her head down upon the pillow.

She sat upright, raised her arms above her head, and stretched. Looking around the chamber, she felt a tinge of excitement. *My first new day in the city. What awaits me?*

The morning light filtered through the curtains of her windows, and she walked across the room to open two doors that led out onto a small balcony. Standing in the sunlight, she turned her face upward to feel the warm rays on her skin and took in several deep breaths of fresh air. She heard running water from a distant fountain and smelled the faint scent of flowers. Her gaze followed the stone stairway descending from her balcony into a lush garden. *What beautiful grounds. I think I will explore.*

James found her later, walking along the garden path. He observed her as she paused to smell the blossoms. She wore a light-colored tunic that fell below her knees, and soft, matching boots. Her unbound hair cascaded down her back, blond and light brown strands highlighted in the morning sunlight.

He stood quietly, admiring her appearance from a distance, realizing, *I have never seen her out of her scout's clothes.*

When he joined her on the path, he said, "Good morning. You look well-rested."

Seanna looked up, smiling. "I am, and well-attended."

James caught himself staring at her a moment too long, captivated by her warm smile.

"Thank you for your gracious hospitality," she added.

He bowed low in an overdone gesture of chivalry, and Seanna laughed.

They continued their stroll through the garden. "There are many places I would like to show you over the next several days," James said. "It will be a pleasant diversion from the funeral arrangements for me to acquaint you with my city and its people."

"I look forward to it," Seanna replied.

"There is one obligation I must conduct today, and that will be to present you to the king's council. I think it best they meet you as soon as possible. This meeting may quell any speculations or rumors that could be formed about your presence here. I am sure that after your introduction, the council will be most welcoming."

"I hope so," Seanna answered.

I have arranged an informal meeting in the council chambers later this morning," James added, but privately his thoughts were not so optimistic.

Seanna's arrival at the palace has already launched a stream of gossip, and I intend to counter the speculation with facts. The men who returned with us have already dispelled some of the rumors by speaking well of her character and offering some facts about her origin. But the knowledge of her all-woman clan has seemed only to enhance the mystery that surrounds her.

Seanna interrupted his thoughts: "Of course I should meet them. I feel that is part of my duty as your guest. I imagine they will have many questions for me. My desire is for them to get to know me better."

James nodded and said, "That is my wish also," but he thought, *In truth, I find no pleasure in the duty of meeting with a group of difficult men, no matter how informal. I expect my lack of candor will not sit well with them.*

Leaving the gardens, James and Seanna walked through the palace and made their way toward the council room and the waiting council members. In the large hallways, Seanna paused, gazing up at the ceilings, admiring the splendid structural design and the beautiful craftsmanship of the wooden beams. The artistry of the space was evident down to the intricate ironwork of the hinges, locks, and bolts on the doors.

Imposing stone columns lined the hall, and the walls were ornamented with magnificent paintings and hanging tapestries depicting scenes of nature, water, and animals on the hunt. Sunlight diffused by panels of multicolored glass windows cast rainbows on the walls.

James smiled patiently as she stopped again, to marvel at a carved statue. "Everything is beautiful. There is so much for me to see," she said.

"Yes," he said, "and my descriptions only touch on some the most notable features within the palace. As you can see, we are fortunate to benefit from architectural and artistic influences of the cultural diversity among us."

"I agree, Your Grace. It is most impressive," Seanna answered.

James stopped walking. "I think it's time you started calling me James."

"Yes, Your Gra—James," she replied, and they both laughed.

Seanna listened to his animated voice as he continued his orations. *His eyes sparkle with pride for his home. I am fortunate to get to know this part of him. We have the foundation of a true friendship, and I find my admiration for this man is growing, too.*

When they arrived at the council chambers, James touched her upper arm lightly as he guided her through the open door. She looked down at his hand, startled by his touch, and noted the sensation of warmth that lingered afterward.

An immense, ornately carved wooden table dominated the center of the room, around which the council members sat. The men stood to acknowledge their king but eyed her warily. She glanced around at the stone-faced group, their scrutiny all too familiar, with expressions that reflected a mixture of curiosity, disdain, and disapproval. *How many times, and on how many different occasions, have I stood in front of countenances such as these, their judgments cast before I have uttered a single word?* she wondered, as the irritation she experienced whenever she was subjected to such an inspection stirred within her.

James addressed the council. "Gentlemen, I wish to introduce Seanna, of the Womara clan," he stated.

All eyes remained fixed on her. She kept her gaze steady as she made eye contact with many of them. Standing tall before them, she bowed her head slightly and placed her hand over her heart. "My lords, it is an honor to meet you."

"Will you not come forward to welcome my guest?" James asked sharply to one man; the impasse broke when the man stepped toward them.

"Allow me to be the first to welcome you," he offered.

"Seanna, this is Lord Orman, the principal advisor and head of the king's council."

Orman bowed his head in formal acknowledgment. Seanna returned his gaze with a nod as she judged him. *He has the impressive look of a statesman, with his silver hair and beard, but there is no real warmth or welcome behind those piercing gray eyes.*

James invited her to be seated next to him at the head of the table. "You have already heard much speculation surrounding Seanna's return with me, details of the retrieval of my father's remains and my rescue. But today I am here to introduce to you the woman who is responsible for saving my life," James said.

The councilmen spoke to each other in hushed words, behind raised hands. Seanna watched their exchanges and noted that Orman, sitting opposite, was the one who studied her most closely.

James continued, "She is from the region that lies to the south of our kingdom, below the great mountain range."

The councilmen exchanged surprised looks as they whispered among themselves again.

Orman said, "If I may first speak for the council and express our gratitude for the safe return of our king . . . It was a fortunate coincidence that you stumbled upon such a tragic scene, averting an even greater tragedy if we had lost our prince."

Seanna nodded in acknowledgment.

Lord Orman continued, "How is it that you came to find him in such a remote place?"

Something in his cold manner of questioning put Seanna on her guard. James stiffened in his chair, eyeing Orman, but nodded his head for her to respond.

"I traveled over the mountain range that separates our regions and traversed a pass that I discovered," she answered truthfully.

The men around the table exchanged startled looks and began to talk openly, before James signaled for silence. Seanna sat calmly, observing their reactions, knowing that her words would be provocative. In their walk earlier that day, she and James had discussed disclosing this piece of information.

"It serves no purpose to withhold the truth of the pass any longer; its location will be surmised in a matter of time," Seanna had said. "Your trackers who accompanied us up the mountain have probably already deduced that I came down from somewhere in the high peaks."

"Are you sure you wish to disclose it?" James had asked.

"I have no concerns about revealing the pass to your council now," she had continued. "Only I and a few Womara scouts know its exact location. Anyone who discovered the route would have a long and dangerous descent on the other side and would find himself at the base of the Womara valley as an uninvited guest. Withholding this truth would be judged as not forthright, and I would prefer that your council hear it from my lips."

James had reflected on her words and ultimately agreed with her logic.

Orman continued, "It was this pass between our lands that you found and then traversed alone, into unknown territories?"

He posed the question as more of a challenge than an expression of curiosity.

"I am a scout for my people and well accustomed to the wild," she replied. "I have explored those ranges for many years."

"You were traveling alone through the wilderness, and a scout, no less?" a councilman asked, as the men shook their heads questioningly.

He continued, "How is it that no one has ever found this pass before?"

"Its existence was described among my clan in tales generations old, but no one had ever searched for it," Seanna declared. "My ancestors spoke of its discovery by someone from the other side. He had explored your territories to the north, traversed the mountain peaks, and discovered the pass. Navigating the opening, he crossed through the mountains but in his descent was gravely injured in a fall. Our scouts discovered him near death and took him to our healers, where he spent a season among us."

Orman studied Seanna closely during her discourse, unable to read her face as he tried to gauge the truth of her words. She seemed well-spoken and poised.

And now indeed we know that this is the same woman who saved the king's life, but what do we know of her and this proposed truth?

He prided himself on his ability to detect the subtle deceptions of the body that unskilled liars often revealed; therefore, he thought, she must be very skilled.

The night before, Lord Orman had sought out Cedmon upon their return with the fallen king and pressed him for every detail of the journey, seeking any discrepancy in Cedmon's and the men's observations about Seanna. Cedmon had been uncooperative, answering Orman's inquiries with caution and measured words, openly suspicious.

Finally, Orman had lashed out: "Are you not concerned about the intention of this woman? The safety of your king is at stake, and whether she poses a threat to him and our region. You should be more vigilant for the man you have been entrusted to protect."

Orman recognized he had gone too far with his words as Cedmon's face reddened at his insinuation. Cedmon stepped forward, forcing Orman to take an involuntary step backward.

"Maybe you should have traveled to that mountain with us," Cedmon answered sharply. "You would then understand the great difficulty this woman overcame to bring us all down from that godforsaken place with our fallen kin. If malice had been her intent, why would she have risked journeying into our land with no one to help her and no way of escape?"

Orman glared at him.

"Be careful what you suggest," Cedmon warned, "for she has the king's favor and you do not." With that, he turned and walked away.

Orman watched him go, enraged at his impertinence.

It appears she has your favor, too. But how could she have swayed the king's man in such a short amount of time? I do not need any additional distractions, on top of the containment of Thomas's overseas rants, with the appearance of this unknown woman. She could be a dangerous challenge, and as a scout, might she have found Thomas's landing site for the ambush?

"I have heard of the women warriors to the south of our regions. Are you of that clan?" Orman returned to his queries.

"Yes," Seanna answered. "I am from that clan."

The question evoked mild gasps and surprised looks from the council, but James's expression darkened at his words. Orman had kept this knowledge secret, never revealing to anyone any of the facts he knew about the Womara. James's face flushed as he leaned forward, staring at Orman, while the men talked among themselves.

Orman asked for quiet. "It is my duty to the king to be well-informed of the things outside the boundaries of this realm. We are not so isolated that accounts of women warriors have not reached my ears."

The councilmen glanced at each other with questioning looks. When the prince had returned from the peaks a year earlier, Orman had felt justified in sending out spies to seek out information about the female scout, traveling alone, who had departed that day from the mountain. He had not found her, but he had learned of the Womara's existence.

James continued to glare as he chided the council members, "This meeting is not about questioning the validity of my guest's words. I have asked Seanna to return with me not only in gratitude but to begin a discussion of building diplomatic bridges between two great regions. There is a newly formed alliance in her southern realm that I now have knowledge of, and the opportunity to explore new possibilities."

Aware that Seanna was watching him across the table, Orman attempted to control his astonishment before saying, "Your Grace, you have caught the council at a disadvantage with this new communication."

He looked at Seanna and asked her directly, "What is this alliance?" She spoke openly of the recently formed union, the council, and its purpose. She added her own opinion that she viewed the discovery of the pass as an auspicious new beginning between their realms.

Orman judged Seanna even more suspiciously. *More than auspicious! You are either a brilliant strategist or blessed with a momentous gift of fate in the discovery of the king. Either way, you would be a fool to allow such an opportunity to pass.*

His eyes narrowed as he continued to observe her. *A diplomatic bridge that combined the interests of these distinct lands would indeed be a significant development, promoting a major alliance between the two realms. Such a union would present a formidable barrier along the entire coastline and would greatly challenge James's cousin's chances for a future invasion along a largely unprotected coastline.*

"Is the purpose of your visit to our city to act as an envoy for your alliance and to secure permission to trade in our port?" Orman asked pointedly.

"That has not been formally discussed yet!" James snapped.

"I understand, Your Grace. I am merely wondering whether the council should prepare for such talks," Orman added.

It was Seanna who responded, unflustered by his tone. "That was not the first purpose of my journey. I returned to honor my oath. The alliance and its council was not a union when I first met your king. I am here without their directive and bear only a message of salutation from Lord Arden, its newly elected leader. At the time of my reunion with your king, I did not know that I would be traveling to your city. To be invited as a guest was an unexpected honor."

Heads nodded in acceptance of her explanation, but Orman wanted to press more. James stopped him short, standing up abruptly and announcing, "That is enough questions for today."

All the councilmen rose quickly, as James signaled to Seanna that they were leaving. She bowed to the councilmen, making pointed eye contact with Orman.

Is she challenging me? he wondered. He sat down as the murmurs of the councilmen faded into the background. *This woman is unsettling, with her steadfast gaze and unapologetic demeanor. She does not look away in submission, like most women I encounter. There is a potency to her character that I cannot define and that makes her very difficult to judge.* He stroked his beard. *What is it about the unapologetic nature of unfettered women exacting sovereignty over their lives that unleashes a desire in men, including me, to repress them?*

Was he challenged, no matter how subtle her actions? He was unsure, but he still felt a strong urge to break her spirit like a wild horse.

I do not believe in the premise of a community of women who can prosper without the presence of men, but my spies report the contrary. How do they not pose a threat to an ordered society? Why have they been tolerated? James's men have verified her scouting skills. But a warrior? How good a fighter could she possibly be? No woman could be the equal of a well-trained male soldier! What would be the outcome if she were subjected to such a test?

Orman had listened to the council members' many theories. All agreed that the tale of rescue was compelling, but several men had voiced their concerns about the king's obvious regard for the woman and talk of an alliance. How could they take seriously any proposals of an alliance without an envoy? Why had her clan not earned the alliance's support?

It pleased him to hear the dissent among them, and he noted with particular interest the words of suspicion regarding the premise of a warrior class of women and their fighting prowess. Some men stated that it was unfortunate they could not observe her supposed abilities firsthand. He did not add his voice to the debate but paused at the question.

If there is a way to expose her skills—or her lack thereof—to do so in front of the king could be a worthwhile gamble. If she is exposed as a fraud, any talks of the growing alliance would crumble.

James was visibly irritated when they left the room but regained his composure. "Let's get away from here. I want to go for a ride," he announced. "Change your garments and have the attendant bring you to the stables. I will meet you there."

"Yes, I think a ride would be good," Seanna agreed.

They departed the city over the moat bridge, spurring their horses to a full gallop into the surrounding meadows with a detachment of guards following at a distance. Riding with abandon, James attempted to shake off the residue of the unpleasant morning.

"Follow me, Seanna," he challenged, laughing out loud and urging his horse to leap a small hedge. They rode for several miles before reining their horses to a stop beside a small stream. James felt his annoyance dissipating amid the exertion of the ride. He took a deep breath, listening to the birds in the distance as the afternoon sun waned.

He turned to Seanna with a look of exasperation. "Is this how it is for you every time you stand before a group of men such as the council today?"

"What do you mean?" she asked.

"I mean, how do you abide such arrogance and keep a civil head?" James asked. "Such an air of disrespect and so much effort expended just to find a starting place for conversation. I think I can begin to understand your clan's exclusion and the difficulty you have faced with the clansmen of the alliance and their council."

Seanna nodded at his words.

"I cannot force their acceptance," James spoke truthfully.

"There are always varying degrees of acceptance from men," Seanna replied. "At first introduction, I and the reality of our clan can be difficult to accept. With time, men's perceptions can change, and I would hope that the rancor of your council will diminish once they know me better."

James was not as optimistic as he answered, "I must admit that I did not expect so much resistance from the council today. I was naive in my assumptions that when the time came to meet you, they would be more accepting."

He paused, thinking for a moment. "They are also cautious, and probably rightly so. I must protect my people, and there is a looming threat in the distance. An alliance among realms is no simple thing. I should have picked my moment better. The councilmen are within their rights to ask for a formal envoy," he concluded.

"It is an ambitious proposal, and I understand your council's restraint," Seanna offered.

James nodded. "Let's return. The sun will be setting soon." He turned his horse in the direction of the castle, and they rode back in silence.

~

Later that evening, James invited Seanna for dinner in his private chambers. Standing on his balcony overlooking the gardens below, they watched the sun sink into the sea on the distant horizon. James was quiet as he gazed at the sky's change from rose to purple. "Beautiful, is it not?" he asked.

"Indeed," Seanna answered. "I hope the beauty of this evening is lifting your spirits."

James continued to gaze at the horizon. He turned to Seanna. "I hope you do not mind that we dine alone tonight. I find myself wishing to extend the peacefulness of our ride this afternoon and, in truth, to have some time away from the stares of the curious. My failure to appear in court tonight is a message of my displeasure," he added.

"The day was more challenging than I anticipated, but it did not take away from my wonderment at this opportunity to see your amazing city." Seanna smiled.

The attendants served dinner to them at a small table within the chamber, and after the first glass of wine was poured, James began to speak. "I do understand rancor. When I first proposed some changes to the council for the betterment of the people's condition, I encountered the same opposition you experienced in the council rooms today."

"What kind of changes?" she asked, leaning toward him, sipping her wine.

"Simple things at first," he answered. "Small pensions were given to the widows of men in service to the king, especially those who had died with my father in those mountains. It was appalling to me that I had to argue with the council to preserve the quality of life of the widows and their children."

James paused to savor a taste of his wine. "But when I returned from the mountains, I observed with a keener eye the plight of my people and their struggle to maintain a basic existence, with a sharp division between prosperity and destitution. I viewed women in the streets, widowed or abandoned, begging or selling themselves and struggling to survive. I watched small girls playing, full of life and laughter, but saw that the light in the faces of their older sisters was gone. It is an unfulfilled and reduced existence, as you told me before."

"Those are remarkable observations," Seanna exclaimed.

James leaned toward her across the table. "I attempted to balance the inequity when I decreed that the vendors' stalls in the marketplace would be made available to women who sought a place to trade or sell their wares. This change was difficult to enact; I had to face the council's argument that women would have no head for the world of commerce and would disrupt the flow of normal business."

He smiled at her. "I remember you speaking of the prosperity of women in the trades. I am proud to say that the women in the marketplace here have thrived and prospered too."

Seanna beamed. "That is a remarkable accomplishment."

"Indeed," James answered proudly. "The council began to grudgingly give way to my ideas, but to break down resistance, and to bend the wills of men to gain their cooperation, requires more than just a decree from the king. Today was no exception."

"It can be challenging for some faced with differences. We did present quite a tale this morning," Seanna said, attempting to lighten his mood.

"You are very generous in your views, especially with those who were not so gracious in their welcome," he added, thinking of Lord Orman.

He watched the burning logs in the fireplace settle, and his tone was serious when he looked back at Seanna. "I think our time together in those mountains changed me beyond just surviving the ordeal. Since then, I have looked at the world—my world—differently. The council—or, should I say, mainly Lord Orman—has questioned the source of my changing views."

"Why, when you have brought such positive changes?" Seanna asked. "Did this trouble you?"

"Yes," James answered, "it did disturb me. I felt like a blind man who wakes one morning to see his world for the first time. I now see with different eyes." He searched Seanna's face. "Yet how could I describe such a thing to these men? Even more, I believe these ideals took seed after the time we spent together and the influence of our conversations. It was a powerful awakening for me—one that changed my perceptions for the better. When the council knows you more, they will understand the source of my insights."

He lifted his glass of wine in an informal toast to her.

Seanna lifted her glass in return and said, "You honor me if you believe that our time together awakened this new awareness, but you give me too much credit. I believe that your willingness to envision a better world for your people has always been within you. I spoke a truth to you on that mountain when I told you that I sensed a special quality within you, that I viewed you as a man of purpose. Nothing about that opinion has changed for me," she said.

James stared deep into her eyes, smiling at her words and encouraged by the passion of her sentiments. He found himself wanting to linger on those eyes, alive with the flickering firelight, as he searched her face for something more, something that he could not define. Then he remembered himself and broke away from her gaze, drinking his wine and gathering his senses.

"Tomorrow we will forgo any formal encounters. I will show you more of the city and the marketplace, and we can take another ride in the afternoon if you would like," he said.

"I look forward to it," Seanna replied.

James escorted Seanna to her room after dinner. He lingered for a moment at her chamber door, hesitating as if he wanted to say something more, but then simply wished her a good night.

Inside her chamber, Seanna walked out onto her balcony, feeling the cool air against her skin and listening to the night sounds of insects in the garden.

It has been a most challenging and interesting day. I have a deepening respect for the ambition of James's endeavors, but I have been naive in thinking that this growing new relationship with him alone was enough to build a bond between lands. My lack of diplomatic skill with his council might have been evident today. The intricacies of building bridges of this magnitude are humbling.

When she lay down to sleep, she remained unable to quiet her thoughts. *I am still astounded at James's recognition of the possibilities of real change for his people. He is standing on the threshold of something profound as a leader.*

She rolled onto her back, staring at the ceiling. *I cannot seem to separate my emotions from what I feel when he looks at me a certain way. He is a grateful and attentive host, but I must remember my duty. I serve as a diplomat now, no matter how unseasoned I may be. I cannot confuse my excitement about these new experiences with misread feelings.*

18

A CHALLENGE OF SWORDS

Seanna masked her disappointment when James announced that Lord Orman would be accompanying them on their excursion around the city's market square that morning. James shared that Orman had approached him in a conciliatory gesture, offering to acquaint her with the city and professing that he and the council needed to do more to make Seanna feel like a welcomed guest.

"It was difficult to disguise my displeasure about the inclusion of his company," James informed her, "but I agreed for the sake of diplomacy. I am not sure what prompted the council's sudden change of heart, but I am hoping they have sincerely rethought their previous conduct."

Seanna could not help but think Orman's change of attitude was more than a mere opportunity to be an accommodating host. *Something about him is not to be trusted. I have not forgotten that he has always known about my clan. Why would he have withheld that information, especially from the king?*

James added, "Lord Orman has also announced that the council is arranging an evening banquet in your honor. It will be an opportunity to introduce you to the prominent citizens of the city."

"I am honored," she replied, disguising her true thoughts: *A banquet. How tedious!*

In the center square, Orman's grand narrative about the large, open-air marketplace was not necessary for Seanna to be impressed by the quantity and variety of the wares on display. The square was stirring with the sounds and activity of early-morning commerce. A noisy crowd, goats, sheep, pigs, cows, clucking chickens and ducks, and the occasional call of an exotic bird added to the chorus.

Butcher shops displayed cuts of meats and poultry, and fish vendors touted the fresh- and seawater catches of the morning. The scent of just-baked bread that lingered in the air made Seanna's mouth water. The stalls sold rounds of cheeses and a variety of vegetables, herbs, and fruits, some of which Seanna had never seen before.

"It is most impressive," she expressed to her hosts. She glanced at James, smiling, enjoying the feeling of a familiar connection with the people who bustled through the market, just like at home, everyone stopping to judge the wares or haggle over prices.

She bent low at the spice stall to take in the exotic aromas of pepper, cinnamon, and cloves that permeated the air. Some vendors sold precious metals, porcelains, bronze cooking vessels, and textiles of every variety. Craftsmen, such as tanners, blacksmiths, shoemakers, and wool and cloth dyers, worked from within their shops, which lined the side streets leading into the square.

These wares are in such great quantity here, but mostly a very rare commodity in my lands. Any clan that acquired trading rights in this region would surely become wealthy! It was a valuable reminder to her of her duty to develop this tremendous opportunity.

The presence of the king with Seanna, the head of the king's council, and a bevy of personal guards created an additional flurry in the marketplace as the entourage paused to talk with the vendors and shopkeepers. Seanna was enjoying herself, stopping to chat or admire wares. She lingered at the stall of a blacksmith to admire the workmanship of a weapon he was crafting.

"Your work is beautiful," she told him.

"Please, milady," he offered, as he extended the sword to her to hold, allowing her to gauge its weight and balance.

Lord Orman watched her interaction with curiosity. "She appears to know her weapons," he commented.

"And you question it?" James interjected.

"Oh, no, Your Grace! It just such an extraordinary concept, is it not? Women warriors!" Orman added, smiling at James.

Seanna continued to examine the weapon closely, pretending that she had not overheard Orman's comment to James.

So, there is *something to his change of heart,* she thought. *And all this graciousness could have a hidden meaning.*

Their attention was diverted before James could reply to Orman's remark, when a young girl shyly approached the group with a tray holding cups of wine from a local merchant. James sipped it, savoring the taste, then tipped his glass to the merchant in appreciation of the refreshment, and to the delight of the young girl standing before him.

Seanna crouched low before the child, talking to her at her eye level. "Is your mother the seller of this wine?"

The young girl nodded, staring at Seanna with wide eyes as her mother beamed with pride from the stall. Seanna was humbled for a moment as she looked into the smiling face of the young girl, knowing that this woman and her child were a direct result of the changes that James had implemented. She turned to look at James, holding back a swelling of emotion as he sent his servant over to the woman to purchase the wine.

Orman watched the exchange between Seanna and the young girl with fascination as a prideful James beamed at a visibly moved Seanna.

Here could be the very association between the reforms implemented and the changes in this young king. It is possible that Seanna has exerted more influence on him than I have perceived. That she is a woman who appears not to rely on the lure of the feminine wiles but rather speaks to his intellect makes her more threatening than I previously thought.

Leaving the market square, they climbed the stairs to the stone walkways and guard towers that surrounded the city, giving onto a bird's-eye view of the town, the surrounding townships, and the port. James provided detailed descriptions of the town's architecture and its original defensive strategy. Orman silently questioned James's judgment in so openly sharing the details of their city's defenses.

He and James watched as Seanna walked the length of the wall, leaning over occasionally to look to the sea below. "She is very observant, is she not?" Orman commented.

"What do you mean?" James replied irritably. "Speak plainly."

"Nothing, Your Grace. It is just that I would advise caution. We still do not know much of her or her clan."

"It appears that you know a great more than I," James retorted. "I have not had time to address this lack of disclosure with you yet."

"Do not judge me harshly, Your Grace. In time, I would have needed to present such information to the council and you, as we measured the full scope of our vulnerabilities, if war is on our horizon. We would have been judging what kind of combined force this southern realm could present if their loyalties were with our enemies. I ask only for clear thinking until we know what we are dealing with."

James turned away to stare silently ahead to the sea, his brows knitted in thought, and Orman sensed that the questions had disturbed him.

Descending the walkway back to the town's streets, James turned to Seanna and said, "I am ready for a different diversion. We will take our leave now."

"Yes, as you wish," she answered. She turned to Orman and added, "This has been very informative, and I thank you for your time this morning."

"It has been my pleasure, but I have arranged one more stop," Orman replied quickly. "I planned a visit to our guards' quarters so you could observe some training practice before you depart for the day. I thought it might be of interest to you, as a soldier yourself."

Seanna judged him coolly as she glanced at James.

"It is at the discretion of my guest," James answered him.

"Of course. That would be interesting," Seanna answered, with muted enthusiasm and some suspicion, wondering, *What is his true intention?*

The arrival of the king and his guest at the arena put an immediate halt to the training activities. The men had been practicing with swords, standing in twos in front of tall wooden posts, engaging in various thrusting and slicing strokes against the wood. James signaled with a wave of his hand that everyone should continue as they stood observing. Seanna watched the men executing their basic drills, comparing their movements with her clan's own style. *Many stances are the same, but we are slightly unconventional in that we incorporate more body movement into the basic weapon positions.*

She commented to James and Orman, "Your men appear very skilled and well-trained."

James acknowledged the compliment, and Orman gestured for the guard's commander, Malcolm, to join them. "Our guest has praised the proficiency of your guards," Orman stated.

Malcolm bowed at the accolade.

Seanna recognized him as the guard on the dock the day of her arrival, the one who had watched her so closely. "I think I know you," she remarked.

Malcolm hesitated, before answering, "I was on the mountain a year ago. I had the privilege of escorting our prince home after your rescue."

Seanna nodded back to him. She had not remembered him from the mountain, but he had now revealed the connection. She caught Malcolm's side glance to Orman.

"I am curious about the respective comparisons to the training practices of your clan," Orman said, diverting the conversation.

"The basic moves are similar," she answered. "Your men are practicing a leverage thrust?" she asked Malcolm.

"Yes," Malcolm answered succinctly, offering no other

comments, his manner dismissing the question a little too tersely as he glanced at Orman again. His abrupt answer received a stern glance from James.

Seanna watched the exchange of looks between the men and thought, *Well, I see that there is no point in asking any further questions, as any comment I might offer will not be taken seriously.*

Orman interjected. "My apologies. I think it will take some time for the men to adjust to such queries coming from a woman."

Malcolm offered empty words: "I did not mean to offend."

Orman added, "They are a narrow-minded lot. I am fortunate enough to have known the prowess of your clan's fighting ability. I hope you can understand the men's skepticism over the idea of a woman's ability to defend herself in a real confrontation."

"I do not like your insinuation," James remarked. "Seanna has nothing to prove."

Orman feigned surprise, stepping back. "My king, I meant no offense. All of this is merely conjecture, isn't it, without anyone seeing her skills in action?"

Seanna understood the baiting. "Of course. No offense taken," she replied, half-honestly. *Orman is not to be trusted if my instincts are true, but I wonder just how far he is willing to press the matter.*

James's expression was filled with irritation as he moved closer to Orman to speak, but Seanna gestured for him to pause. "It is a common cynicism I often face. I think a small demonstration of my skills might lessen some of the skepticism," she offered.

James continued to stare at Orman, but Malcolm and the guards exchanged eager looks.

"I see no harm in it. We will meet back in your training arena this afternoon, and I will do my best to entertain you and your men," she said, glancing at James reassuringly.

I wondered if I might be challenged at some point. Now I know it is Orman who is the divider, and Malcolm his puppet.

The news that the woman calling herself a warrior scout would demonstrate her fighting skills to the king's guard spread rapidly. When she and James arrived back at the arena in the late afternoon, it was filled with as many of the town's inhabitants as could squeeze into the space.

James stared, horrified at the crush of people jostling for position. "This is outrageous," he murmured under his breath. "I apologize." His face flushed with annoyance. "You do not have to perform in this circus."

Lord Orman crossed the arena with arms open, feigning innocence. "Your Grace, I did not anticipate such a crowd."

Seanna said nothing, but James pulled Orman aside, speaking angrily under his breath. "I don't know what you hope to gain from this performance, but any outcome that humiliates my guest will not be viewed favorably in my eyes."

He walked away with Seanna at his side, vowing to deal with Orman later for this affront. He turned his attention back to Seanna, who seemed unfazed. "Let's get this over with," he told her. "Where shall we begin?"

"Such a crowd," Seanna commented. "I think we need more than a mere display of the bow. A demonstration of swords with one of your men should suffice, do you not think?" Seanna replied.

James nodded reluctantly in agreement but kept his thoughts private. *I think that my hesitation has more to do with my personal concerns. I feel as if I am betraying her, because, I must admit, I am just as curious as these other men.*

"Bring over the guard's trainer." James turned to Orman, who motioned to a man on the side of the arena to step forward.

"You will judge a contest of swords," James ordered. The trainer was surprised at the command, but the seriousness of James's tone indicated that his request was an earnest one.

Seanna stepped into the center of the training ring. The crowd hushed as she bowed her head, her hand on her heart. "I am Seanna, of the Womara clan. I come from a region to the south. I am a scout for my clan and a guest of your king in this great city, and I have been invited to give you a demonstration of my fighting skills."

Some of the people in the crowd clapped politely, as the guards standing around the center of the arena smirked to one another. James watched her closely; she seemed entirely composed. He seated himself in the king's viewing stand, feeling slightly uneasy, questioning his judgment for having permitted such an exhibition. Orman seated himself beside James, watching the crowd.

"I challenge one of the king's guard to a swordfight," Seanna announced. The audience whispered among themselves, and Orman exchanged glances with the men.

"Will the commander of the king's guard accept my challenge?"

The crowd roared its approval, shouting for Malcolm, who hesitated for a moment before stepping into the center ring, bowing to the spectators.

James glanced at Orman, who was looking intently at Seanna. "Do you think Malcolm is uncomfortable at the prospect of having to fight a woman?" James asked, wanting to assess whether Orman had any reaction to Seanna's having singled out Malcolm.

"I don't think any of our guards enjoys the anticipation of having to put someone in her place," Orman replied coldly.

Lord Orman's words put James on his guard as he scanned the faces of the crowd, gauging their temperament, his stomach lurching. *Am I guilty of misplaced judgment here? Could some among them wish to do her harm?*

The crowd began to murmur with excitement, and a bookmaker took wagers as quickly as he could record them. The betting did not go unnoticed by Seanna, and she beckoned to James to speak with her.

"I did not think that this day would end in such a spectacle," he apologized again.

Seanna removed her outer vest and checked her sword. "I think that you should place some wagers," she stated matter-of-factly.

"Of course," he replied, puzzled. "I should bet in your favor." Seanna nodded, as he realized she was deadly serious. "And will I win?"

"Yes, I do believe you will," Seanna replied, with a coy smile.

James returned to his seat, smiling to himself as he hailed the bookmaker. He watched Seanna step to the center, facing Malcolm, with the guard's trainer between them.

I cannot fault her confidence, James thought.

"Shall we agree to the terms of the contest?" the trainer asked.

"You will decide whether a strike counts as a kill, or we shall fight until someone concedes," Seanna answered. Malcolm bowed his acknowledgment, grinning in amusement. James watched Seanna's expression remain blank at the subtle mockery.

Malcolm quickly lost his grin as Seanna turned to address the crowd again. "I wish to make this contest more challenging for your enjoyment. Will you double your wagers if I take on another fighter?" she asked.

The crowd yelled, amplifying the excitement in the arena as people began another round of betting. James looked questioningly at Lord Orman.

Orman's expression tightened under the king's gaze, his confidence wavering at Seanna's bravado. He shifted uncomfortably in his seat.

"I will ask your champion to pick four more men to join him in the challenge," Seanna spoke again to the crowd.

"All at once?" the trainer asked. Seanna nodded.

Orman winced, and the stands of people fell silent. He glanced at James, who had not moved, sitting with his hand resting on his chin, watching the drama unfolding before him.

"Pick your men," she ordered Malcolm, and the murmur of the crowd resumed. The trainer of the guard hesitated momentarily and turned to look in the direction of the king. James nodded to proceed.

What is her game? Orman wondered. He watched Malcolm point to four of his men, signaling them to stand beside him in the center.

Facing Seanna, they exchanged wary glances as the guard's trainer told them to take their final places and draw their swords. Orman, leaning forward in his chair, watched intently. Malcolm's glance toward him flashed a look of concern that something was not right. When he watched Seanna give Malcolm a slight smile, a chill ran down his spine.

The arena went silent; the crowd barely breathed. Orman realized he was holding his own breath as the trainer's hand dropped, signaling the start of the fight. Not hesitating, Seanna charged forward, dropped, and rolled between the two men to Malcolm's left. As she did so, she knocked one man down with a blow to the shins. He fell to his knees, grunting, before receiving a full strike across his chest. She stood up behind the second man, delivering what would have been the death blow to the back of his neck, controlling the blade, and driving him to the ground as he held his hand over the point of contact.

"Two kills for the challenger!" shouted the trainer, looking at the stunned men crouched in the dirt.

Seanna turned to face the remaining three men, who stared at their fallen comrades. Orman leaned toward James, scowling at her theatrics. "These acrobatic tricks would be no challenge for real fighting."

James raised his hand to silence him as Malcolm signaled his men to spread out and begin circling, keeping their attention upon Seanna.

Seanna watched as Malcolm stood fixed in the middle of the arena but signaled his two men to circle her. She shifted her body, turning slowly, keeping her eye on Malcolm in her center and the other men in her peripheral view, as she waited patiently for one to make a move. The man on the far right telegraphed his intent, and Seanna was ready, meeting him full force with a blocking blow. As he dropped his sword hand, she struck him across the throat with the flat of the blade. He staggered at the force, dropping his sword and grimacing as he grabbed his neck, expecting blood.

The trainer stepped forward to yell for the kill, but Malcolm and the remaining man did not wait, rushing forward simultaneously. Seanna had picked up the fallen man's sword and now held a weapon in each hand. The men charged in, but she was able to keep them at bay with blocks from both weapons. Seanna blocked the outside man's thrust as she dodged his next blow, spinning away and striking with the opposite sword.

"Kill!" shouted the trainer.

The crowd gasped as Malcolm, now standing alone, faced her. Malcolm's glare conveyed his frustration and contempt, but Seanna was unfazed, her focus fixed. *I will not be finished with you so easily. A defeat in front of your men will be enough of a price paid for your disrespect, and a strong message to your Lord Orman not to underestimate me.*

Seanna tossed away the second sword to face him on equal terms. As Malcolm watched it fall to the ground, his face flushed with anger at the gesture. He bellowed as he charged toward her, trying to drive her to her knees with brute force. Seanna deflected his blow and moved out of range as Malcolm stood before her, glaring. She could wait, holding him back, conserving her energy by using her agility the way she did against any larger or stronger opponent. She watched for a weakness and waited for an unguarded action, observing Malcolm with detached indifference as the crowd yelled encouragement to their champion.

Malcolm continued to move in a circle, breathing deeply. Seanna glanced in the direction of Lord Orman, heeding his intense stares, but her body stiffened when she noted James's controlled expression, unable to judge his emotion.

Seanna returned her focus to Malcolm just as he charged forward, this time giving her the opportunity that she had been waiting for. He delivered his driving thrust while he was slightly off balance on the front leg, allowing Seanna to catch his sword at the hilt and drive upward. Malcolm fell to one knee, and the sword left his grasp. The crowd cried out as Seanna picked up the fallen sword and immediately crossed both blades over Malcolm's throat, preventing him from rising to his feet as the spectators went silent.

She stared down at Malcolm as she forced his head up to prevent his throat from being cut, then applied slight pressure to the blade angled against the vein, indicating her deadly intent. Malcolm, unable to move, drew deep breaths, scowling up at her.

The trainer stepped forward. "Do you concede?" he asked.

Seanna lowered the bottom sword but continued to press the upper blade against his jugular, never releasing control. She applied pressure under his jawbone, making a slight cut. Blood trickled down his neck.

The trainer repeated, "Do you concede?"

She pressed harder.

"Yes," mumbled Malcolm. "Yes, I concede."

Seanna immediately released the sword, and Malcolm stumbled forward, placing his hand over the wound. The trainer signaled that the victory was hers.

The crowd was stunned. James looked at Orman, who had paled and was gripping the arms of his chair at the conclusion of the fight. James, utterly engrossed, was not sure of what he had just witnessed. It seemed like an eternity before he broke the silence, rose from his chair, and began clapping. As he walked toward Seanna, he continued to applaud loudly.

Orman rose and followed suit. The crowd, roused from their silence, began cheering wildly and calling Seanna by name. James and Orman stood before Malcolm, who still knelt in the dirt.

Orman looked down at Malcolm with disdain. "Get up, you idiot!" he snapped. "Remove yourself from our presence."

"How so, Lord Orman?" James said. "Yes, he was outfought and has been humiliated, but I think the error of judgment was yours. Did you not know of these women's fighting abilities?"

Malcolm stood up slowly, venomously eyeing Orman. James walked away to join Seanna as she recovered her garments, and they waved to the spectators before exiting the arena.

Orman watched Malcolm walk away as he stood alone in the center of the arena, gathering his thoughts.

I am chastened by what I have just witnessed. Her skills were astounding. I was foolhardy to discount the reports from my spies. The combination of weapons training from an early age and the acrobatics she incorporates into her techniques makes her an impressive fighter.

Orman felt his chest constrict as he realized, *And there are hundreds of these women with these same fighting skills?*

When Seanna had stood at the center of the arena, accepting the adulations of the crowd, her bearing had incensed him.

She has beaten me at my own game, and Malcolm, at my direction, has paid a high price for his disrespect to her. Now any speculations about her fighting skills will be dismissed and her esteem duly earned, even solidified, in the eyes of the king.

His chest tightened again.

It enrages me! This woman, and her clan, I suspect, back down to no man and demand equal treatment, secured by force, if necessary.

This demand was no less than any man might have made in response to a similar insult, but to have seen a woman answer such a challenge disturbed him. Orman had watched James's face closely during the contest; such a display of prowess might have repelled other men, challenging their masculinity, but James at times had appeared mesmerized.

Orman conceded. *The old ways of thinking have certainly died with the passing of James's father. I saw this when James took the throne: a herald of a new age. This woman's arrival is a harbinger of change, and there will be no holding back the tide of reform.*

He had watched James and Seanna depart together and understood that their bond came from more than the king's close brush with death; it was a strong union sealed in mutual respect.

With her victory, Orman knew, Seanna had quelled any doubts that James might have had. His gamble to humiliate her had failed miserably. He could not wait long to see what price he would pay for this great miscalculation.

19

A VICTORY AND A BURIAL

Seanna and James left the arena for the palace, followed by his guards. Behind them, the crowd was still cheering. She glanced sideways, studying James' expression, trying to read his temperament. James kept his sights focused straight ahead, the nuances of his face revealing nothing, and she began to wonder whether his enthusiasm had been genuine or merely a display for the crowd.

As they continued to walk in silence, Seanna feared the worst as she glanced at James again.

I would have thought little about men's opinions concerning the outcome of such a challenge in my land, but here I am in unfamiliar territory. Should I have tempered such an exhibition with diplomacy?

She had witnessed more than once how the display of her clan's fighting abilities could change relationships; men were slow to alter their view and to accept an equal dynamic between men and women as a strength.

I may have squandered James's good graces by threatening the foundations of a belief system in which men, and men alone, are dominant.

She caught herself as she realized that it mattered greatly to her what he thought. *If I see that familiar look of division on his face, then the burial of the king tomorrow evening cannot come quickly enough.*

But when they reached the palace entrance, James dismissed his guards and turned to face her, breaking into a wide grin. "That was the most amazing show of swordsmanship I have ever witnessed! I have so many questions I would like to ask. Can we talk more, or do you need to rest?"

Seanna expelled a sigh of relief, grinning in return, grateful to dispel the tension. "Let me remove my weapons and change my garments. It is my pleasure to answer all the questions that I can."

For the next several hours, they sat cross-legged in the grass under the shade trees in the private gardens.

"Can all the women in your clan fight like you?" James asked.

"Not all," she answered. "It is not so much about the ability to fight like me as it is about the spirit behind it. Every woman is prepared to defend herself in some manner."

Over the course of their conversation, James's inquiries were not all about the women's fighting techniques, but also about the clan itself and the other women who comprised it. Seanna shared her thoughts with an openness that she had not experienced with many men. She reclined in the grass on her elbows, savoring the warmth of the afternoon and the king's smiling face.

At times the conversation lulled as they paused to glance around the lovely garden, comfortable in these moments of quiet. Seanna watched James's gaze follow the fluttering vibration of a humming-bird's wing, observing the beautiful little creature dart from flower to flower. She studied him closely in profile, appreciating the contours of his face. He turned back to her, smiling, as their eyes met, and he let his gaze linger upon her, making Seanna catch her breath.

Her pulse quickened, and she glanced away. *There is so much more to this man than I could ever have imagined.*

A servant made his way toward them on the path, arriving to escort them to their rooms to prepare for the evening banquet. Standing up, James offered her his hand. "Let's get ready. I, for one, have worked up quite an appetite with all our talking." He laughed. "I shall come to accompany you at sunset."

Seanna grinned back, extending her hand as she allowed him to help her to her feet.

Before her door, Seanna froze. *A banquet. What in the world will I wear?*

But as she entered her chamber, she found her attendants standing with ready smiles, and, as if reading her thoughts, they glanced at her bed. Upon it lay a beautiful gray gown embroidered with delicate silver leaves around the neckline. She looked up with surprise at the women.

"Upon the announcement of the banquet, I took the liberty of finding something for you to wear tonight, milady," the older servant said. "The king directed the court's tailor to make you a funeral dress on the first day of your arrival. I asked the king for permission to have something extra made. I hope you like it."

Seanna ran her fingers over the lovely fabric and smiled at the woman. "You are most thoughtful. It is more beautiful than I would have selected for myself, and I thank you. Now, let's get ready," she said, and the women beamed.

After she bathed, she sat quietly while her attendants attempted to tame her wild hair into an uplifted coiffure. The women laughed when she scowled good-naturedly at their declaration that the style was all the fashion in court. Eventually, they transformed her thick mane into a beautiful coil upon her head, fastened with combs of white mother-of-pearl and silver. The wisps of curled tendrils that escaped the combs drew the eye enticingly to her throat. Studying her reflection in the glass, she viewed a woman she hardly recognized.

Her belly tingled with anticipation at the soft knock on the chamber door, and she turned from the mirror as James entered the room. He stood for a moment before her. "You look beautiful, Seanna."

She flushed at the compliment and his eyes upon her but was too reserved to express her appreciation for how handsome and splendid he looked. His tunic was a dark blue velvet that enhanced the color of his eyes, and was embroidered with the same silver leaves and clasped at his waist with an engraved belt.

The servants stood watching, and James dismissed them with an appreciative nod. She began to stand, but James gently touched her shoulder, indicating for her to remain seated. He cleared his throat. "I think you need something else . . ." He paused as he pulled a cloth pouch from his tunic and opened the bundle.

Inside was an ornate silver medallion enclosing an iridescent moonstone, which hung from a delicate silver chain. "It is a gift. I did not know what I could ever give you that could express the depth of my gratitude, but I designed it myself and had it made for you," he added proudly.

Seanna stared at the beautiful necklace in amazement, then looked up at James's face. *How did he remember?*

She recalled a moment when they had sat around the fire together on the mountain. James had commented on the silver bead with the small white stone that clasped the braid hanging at her temple, admiring the design and the gem. She had shared, in a rare candid moment, the personal details of the clasp, which was a gift from her mother, and the gem, which was her favorite. She stared at the necklace, speechless that he had recalled the exact stone.

"It would honor me if you would wear it this evening," he said.

She trembled slightly as she turned to the mirror. James gently placed the necklace around her throat and fastened the clasp. The momentary touch of his fingertips upon the bare skin of her shoulders sent a tingle through her body. She stared at her reflection with the necklace upon her breast.

James stood behind her, admiring her image. "I can see why this jewel is your favorite. The changing hue of the stone and the woman are a perfect blend of beauty and mystery."

James's eyes sparkled, and their glances lingered on each other before she rose, turning to him. "It is a magnificent gift, James. I shall treasure it always. Thank you."

"Shall we go?" he asked, bowing gallantly as Seanna took his arm.

Their entrance into the banquet room stopped all conversation. James squeezed her arm as they stood for a moment in the open doorway. The guests bowed and curtsied as they walked the length of the hall, and James stopped to introduce her to the prominent guests as they mingled among the attendees. They paused to greet the members of the council, their hosts for the evening.

Seanna was gracious to accept the many accolades of those who had witnessed the event at the arena, Lord Orman among them, but she eventually diverted all the flattery with a simple statement. "Gentlemen, you do me a great honor with your compliments, but after all, I am just a mere woman, am I not?" she asked. Her quick smile and coy countenance brought a roar of laughter from the men.

"Well, that was a clever diversion." James laughed as they moved to the banquet tables. Standing before the guests, he addressed them: "Please raise your glasses with me to toast Seanna of the Womara clan, a woman of honor and truth. I owe her my life, and I am proud to call her my friend."

Seanna smiled and nodded to James as they seated themselves.

Lord Orman offered the next toast on behalf of the king's council. "My toast must express sentiments similar to those of our king," he said, as he lifted his glass. "I will extend my gratitude to Seanna for the return of our sovereign and the unique opportunity she presents to expand our understanding of the peoples and clans outside our regions."

Seanna accepted the praise, graciously bowing her head to the council, doubting that such a change of attitude would have come so easily from Orman.

He may have retreated for a while, but only to lick his wounds.

Seanna rose in return, glass in hand. "I offer my toast to praise the generosity of your king, my council hosts, and the people of this great city. It has been my honor to return with your fallen king and fulfill a sacred oath. I hope that we have embarked upon a journey that will be the foundation of goodwill between our peoples."

Important sentiments, thought Orman, *linking the emotions of duty and honor to the power of this moment. And upon the fulfillment of that duty, how long might she remain here? Is that shining necklace upon her throat a gift from the king? I wonder.*

Orman recounted his words before the banquet, when he had sought out James to speak privately with him, contrite and attempting to recover from the afternoon's debacle, and humbling himself by changing his strategy. He had offered a preliminary discussion with the council about the possible diplomatic exchange between them and the alliance, on behalf of Seanna, emphasizing that they must work for the Womara's inclusion in this ambitious vision, in gratitude for the life of their king.

James had eyed him with suspicion, but in the end had nodded his approval, knowing it was a thinly disguised olive branch. Orman had walked away relieved, knowing he had temporarily forestalled any further criticism of his actions.

The acceptance of Seanna and her clan into the alliance would make them a powerful adversary if I do not cultivate this situation carefully, and I cannot risk any further alienation of James's confidence.

At the end of the evening, alone in her room, Seanna stood upon her balcony, breathing in the night air, listening to the stillness of the palace. Rubbing her arms for warmth, she realized, *I am longing for the sounds of my forest. There, I could calm my thoughts.*

The outcome of the banquet made the day's events a triumph. The council's shift in attitude, spearheaded by Lord Orman, opened the door for a diplomatic discussion. She had judged Lord Orman to be a wily fox, ultimately not to be trusted, but he had conceded a degree of victory to her for the moment. She had also solidified the king's favor, and that would prove to be a great advantage in any discussion she chose to pursue, but still she was conflicted.

I will return to stand before the alliance council having accomplished more than I could ever have envisioned, but why does the victory feel empty? Little is served by staying any longer if I am to act on the achievements that I have gained.

The call of an owl in the distance distracted her thoughts for a moment.

The burial of James's father tomorrow night brings an urgency to the impending decision about my departure. My clan expects my return soon, but I find myself caring less for a victory and more for what I will leave behind.

Sitting on the edge of her bed, she felt tired. Her heart ached at the thought of speaking to James of leaving as her thoughts turned to preparing for her journey home. His personal supervision of all the details of the funeral the next day gave her time alone, and she welcomed the solitude. She lay back on her bed for a long while, troubled by her thoughts, before she finally fell asleep.

At midmorning, and compelled to action, Seanna sought out James. "Could I have the leave of Cedmon to discuss some details of my return trip?" Seanna asked. James looked taken aback by the abruptness of her request. Seanna added quickly, "I wish only to inquire about some of the necessities of the journey."

"You are arranging a boat by river? I can handle those details for you," James replied.

"Thank you, but I do not want to distract you from the funeral," she answered.

James nodded, but he sighed before speaking. "I was still hoping for time after the burial to show you more of my country,"

"Yes, we will see," she offered, irritated with herself for having picked such an inopportune moment to discuss this matter with him.

"I will send Cedmon to you," James offered. Seanna watched him hesitate, and he seemed on the verge of saying more, but he looked away.

Orman watched as Seanna and Cedmon walked together along the palace path toward the waterfront. *What are they discussing? Her departure?*

They returned within the hour, and she left Cedmon's company. Orman had waited patiently and appeared to casually cross her path as she walked back toward her chambers. He stopped her and asked, "May I have a word?"

She eyed him with reticence.

"I presume that you might be making arrangements for a boat soon?" he asked.

Seanna nodded, but her expression conveyed her surprise. "There seems to be nothing that you are not aware of, Lord Orman," she noted with irritation.

"Forgive my prying, but, as I discussed last night at the banquet, the council has agreed to present a formal proposal to your alliance. I need only to know the anticipated timing of your departure."

"Yes, I see," Seanna replied. "It could be soon. My clan is expecting my return, and I have started to make those arrangements for the trip home within a day or two."

"Oh, then I have predicted correctly that a departure is imminent." Orman smiled. "I must prepare my formal salutations from our council, as I have promised."

"I will graciously accept any message that you wish me to convey," Seanna answered cautiously.

Orman feigned a slight smile. "Yes, I know that your clan and the alliance await you, and you will have earned their well-deserved praise for this momentous achievement, but I am sure that the king will miss your presence."

Seanna stiffened as she eyed him warily.

"It is just my observation, but it seems that you and the king have grown very close. Perhaps you will act as the envoy for your alliance in the future?" Orman remarked.

"I have no aspirations to be appointed as the formal envoy. There are others more qualified than I to handle the diplomacy of that role," she answered honestly.

"Yes, such things can be challenging and require a certain set of skills," Orman said. "You are probably ready to return to your simpler duties as a scout."

Seanna looked away as she answered, "Yes, maybe so."

"The king has also been distracted from his duties. After the burial of his father, he will no doubt return to his objective of building the alliances we need for the strong protection of our kingdom. The council has not pressed our concerns for the time being, but building some of those alliances with one of our powerful regions through marriage is necessary." Orman smiled.

"What do you mean?" Seanna asked sharply.

"Only that the king knows his duty to the security of the kingdom. A marriage that forges that alliance must be made, to help deter future threats. We have many possible choices from some of our distant allies across the sea."

He continued watching her expression closely. "I realize that your clan is, shall I say, unconventional in its views of marriage. And such informal arrangements must have their purposes among your local clans, but a sovereignty such as ours requires diplomatic unions."

Orman paused. "A king may have his dalliances, but not when he must choose the person who will reign beside him. Don't you agree?"

He saw Seanna flush. "I cannot answer what is appropriate for your king," she answered, before turning abruptly to take her leave.

He smiled as he watched her go. *I have speculated correctly and found that you might have a possible vulnerability, Seanna. You care for him, even more than I think you know, but you two must ultimately be divided.*

Orman's spies had learned much more about the Womara than he had revealed before the king's council. The information he savored most was that not all clans had welcomed the presence of the Womara among the discourses of a union of clans. If there were others who would continue to stand in opposition, as there appeared to be, he would find them and build different alliances.

As for any of your clan's future aspirations, you have not seen the last of me. I intend to present a compelling argument to the council that I am the obvious choice to represent their interests as the envoy to your new region.

He smiled, sensing a greater quest was about to unfold.

Seanna walked quickly toward her rooms, clenching her jaw.

What a fool I am! Orman, with his silver tongue, reminding me of my place, which I have chosen so willfully to overlook. We may not voice our hidden sentiments out loud, but James is bound to a greater duty, and I am guilty of allowing the lure of my emotions get the better of me.

She straightened her shoulders with determination. *I will fulfill my oath and depart soon.*

Within her room, Seanna could hear the funeral bells tolling from the towers. Her mood was sullen, but not for the somberness of the occasion, as she stood in silence, allowing her attendants to dress her in a black silk mourning gown. Her unbound hair hung loosely down her back. She placed the necklace that James had given her around her neck, touching the stone thoughtfully, feeling her chest tighten at the remembrance of his face when he gave it to her.

At twilight, a gentle knock on the door indicated that it was time, and she followed the attendant down the hallway into an anteroom. James stood waiting, surrounded by the council members and the palace court. Lord Orman, with his silver hair and beard, stood out in sharp contrast with the subdued group of mourners, all dressed in black. James was an imposing figure, standing solemnly, wearing a long black tunic edged with silver, his hair darker against his black clothes, his eyes now a stormy, inky blue.

Eight bearers lifted the draped casket holding the body of the king and placed it upon the horse-drawn carriage. The gathered mourners took positions behind their king, followed by the royal guards. James extended his hand to Seanna, inviting her to join him at his side, directly behind the procession. Lord Orman and Cedmon followed behind with the remaining council and court members.

The procession began the slow descent from the palace to the streets below. The women of the court were shrouded in long veils of opaque black that moved with the breeze, billowing behind them like sails. The city was silent as they passed by slowly, moving toward the tomb; citizens lined the streets, holding small candles that reflected light upon their dark countenances.

As the procession approached the edge of the city, Seanna spotted the large stone mausoleum, its exterior lit brightly by burning torches. The elaborate doors opened into a cavernous vault with stone stairs that descended into the crypt. The casket was lifted from the carriage and carried into the tomb. Following his father, James silently led them inside. The air changed, and Seanna shivered with the damp chill of the darkened tomb; the walls were eerily illuminated by flickering torches, and a faint smell of death lingered in the air.

·

James glanced at Seanna at his side. She had been quiet on their walk through the city, as decorum required, but he sensed something more to her aloofness. He was unable to keep his thoughts in focus in her proximity. Her hair shone like a halo in the dim light; the clear stone at her throat captured the radiance of the surrounding torches, a fiery reflection against her bare skin. She embodied life to him, and a sharp contrast with the death all around them.

James looked toward the tomb of his mother. *You are waiting for your king?* he wondered.

The torches cast elongated shadows of the people standing near the stone walls as the bearers placed the king's casket inside his final resting place, a large stone sarcophagus. James approached his father's coffin and gently placed his hand against the cold stone. Each person bowed his or her head in a final gesture of farewell.

James's first words penetrated the silence, echoing off the walls. "Father, my king, I have brought you home to rest among our ancestors, as I promised. I shall never forget the life lessons you taught me, and I will strive to be a man and a king who will make you proud. You will never leave my heart. Farewell."

A palpable sadness hung heavily in the air as James gestured to Seanna to step forward. She knelt, placing one of her hands on her heart, the other touching the cold stone coffin wall.

She spoke with her head slightly bowed. "Great lord, it has been my honor to return you to your home. I have fulfilled the oath I gave you and your son upon that mountain. May you find peace resting in the company of your loved ones."

She rose and rejoined James. Cedmon stood rigid near the sarcophagus. James saw the deep grief etched upon his face, and his eyes glistened with tears. A great stone lid was placed upon the coffin, and the procession of people moved slowly past, setting flowers on top of the sealed lid. As the last person exited the tomb, James remained inside, lingering beside the casket in the waning torchlight.

He placed his hand upon the stone one more time. *My heart aches to let you go, Father. In this moment, I feel so alone. My only comfort is that now you rest with my mother.*

Bowing his head, he shuddered, severing his last physical

contact with the departed. He took a single flower and placed it upon his mother's crypt before leaving.

The moon had risen and cast a pallor over the town. The mourners stood in silence as the great doors were closed and sealed, and then they turned away from the reminder of the finality of death.

At the funeral supper, Seanna watched James push his uneaten food away. He turned to her and sighed. "I have no appetite. I thought I might have a greater sense of fulfillment after my father's final burial, but I am empty of feelings."

She had spoken little through the evening but reached out now to touch his arm in a gesture of comfort. "You have carried a heavy burden of the vow to your father, and now it has been achieved. I think that you will feel different with time," she offered.

James looked down at her hand upon his arm and nodded weakly. She sat back against her chair, holding the unspoken answer to his coming question, which she did not want to broach, as the silence became more strained.

James broke the quiet. "You are leaving soon?"

"Yes," she answered. "I will start preparing tomorrow to depart the following day."

"I thought you would remain here for a few more days. There is haste in your plans."

She hesitated, knowing she disguised the truth in her answer. "I feel it is time." She turned away from James's hurt expression and was grateful that he did not challenge her.

"So we will both return to our separate worlds and life will continue as normal," James added flatly.

"Yes, our duties await us," she answered, her words lacking conviction.

She rose to bid him good night, disturbed by his last statement and her thoughts. Turning from him, she was struck with a feeling of physical emptiness. She placed her hands upon her abdomen as she walked away.

I have known great men in my life, several of whom I have grown to admire, but never have I known one whose daily presence I yearn for.

Orman had watched them with their heads bowed low in a shared confidence. Seanna had placed a hand upon James's arm—a gesture of comfort, Orman assumed. It was the only time he had ever noted a physical exchange between them. He had watched James's expression as she had departed the room. The king had followed her movements long after she had passed. Orman could not be sure if the anguish upon James's face was for his father or for her.

It is well that she leaves soon!

In the darkened tomb that evening, Orman had been struck by a moment of remorse at the burial of a great man whom he had served most of his life. The sentiment had surprised him. For a brief moment, he had questioned all that he had set in motion and considered that he might bring them all to ruin, driven by his blind ambition.

Surrounded by death, he had felt a chill of premonition run through his body as he had envisioned his demise at the end of an executioner's sword. Could he change the path before him, at first so clear but now clouded by a greater opportunity to subvert the union of James's region with the alliance?

Death might prevail, possibly in the guise of a silent assassin to the king's cousin. Orman could eliminate the threat of Thomas entirely, and all his connections to him. He could foster new alliances. But he would need time to plan.

The guests departed, and James dismissed all the servants but continued to sit in the dim light of the banquet hall. He was deep in thought when Cedmon entered.

"Your Grace, I have come to escort you to your chambers." When James did not move, Cedmon added, "You seem troubled. Are you saddened by the burial of your father?"

James looked up. "That should be the only source of my heartache, but it is another matter that troubles me."

Cedmon waited silently before James spoke again, asking him, "Have you ever been in love?"

Cedmon stepped back in surprise, pausing for a moment, before he answered, "Yes. I was married once and had a son."

James leaned forward. "You have never spoken of them, and I am ashamed to say I do not know much about your life before your service to my father."

"Your father and I were boyhood friends." Cedmon smiled at the memory. "I was the son of a wealthy nobleman who served on the council, and I grew up in court with your father. We spent our youth in the pastimes of most young men. Many an hour we devoted to bow and sword training, hunting, riding, and imagining ourselves as warriors." His eyes twinkled, making James smile, too, remembering how much his father had loved all those things and shared those passions with his son.

Cedmon continued, "I fell in love with a girl from the local village who sold her vegetables in the city market. My father felt that marrying her was beneath my station and refused to give his blessing. Your father was the only one who advised me to follow my heart, but my father disowned me for marrying against his wishes."

James said, "I did not know."

Cedmon laughed softly. "I fancied myself a farmer and left the city to build a life with my wife in the country. I was graced with the love of a good woman and soon blessed with the birth of a son. Your mother won your father's own heart, and he married soon after."

Cedmon watched James's face brighten at the mention of his parents. "Those were happy times. Your father was always a true friend and never abandoned our comradeship, even though our circumstances had changed greatly. We spent time together on the occasional hunting trip when he could persuade me away from the fields.

"We were away on such a trip when a marauding ship landed. The men raided the village and the surrounding countryside, pillaging and burning everything. I returned to find my home destroyed, my fields burned, and my wife and son dead."

Cedmon turned his gaze away for a moment from James's stricken face. He continued quietly, "I thought I would go mad from guilt and grief, wanting to throw myself upon my sword in my desolation, but your father restrained me from harming myself. He would not abandon me, and forced me to return to the city with him. I was not myself for a long time and was kept under his watchful eye as I slowly healed.

"Your sweet mother tended to me in my grief, distracting my

thoughts with her stories. She kept me company in the gardens for hours, so patient and kind. Your birth was a time for celebration, and I finally felt myself able to feel some joy again. I knelt before your father, our future king, and pledged my life in service to him and his newborn son."

"And in that vow, you have never failed me," James replied, looking into Cedmon's steadfast gaze. "Do you regret having loved your wife?"

"Never." Cedmon stood tall. "Her love was the greatest gift of my life."

"But you lost her and have lived with so much pain," James added.

"That is true, and the pain of such a loss has never really left me. But it has dulled with time and is soothed by the memory of her, and I am comforted that she and my son are together, waiting for me."

James said, "You followed your heart."

Cedmon nodded in reply.

"I have never felt so conflicted, and I need your counsel, my old friend."

Cedmon placed his hand over his heart as he spoke. "I am at your service, Your Grace. What troubles you?"

James unraveled the emotions that he had kept repressed for so long and no longer wished to conceal, pressed by his sense of the urgency of time. Cedmon listened patiently as the king shared all of his thoughts and the uncertainty of the course he contemplated.

At the end of his tale, James sat back in his chair, smiling weakly, and asked, "Do you think that a king would not be so conflicted, and instead would be emboldened to action?"

Cedmon answered thoughtfully, "It has been my experience that the words that hold us back cause us more harm than simply speaking our truths. These unspoken words you bear within you are a regret that you should not carry, and the burden of what goes unsaid may haunt you for all your years."

"In this moment, the right path eludes me," James answered.

"You are tired, my king, and it has been a trying day. Rest now. The answer may be clearer in the morning, and I shall be ready for your command," Cedmon offered.

James nodded in agreement, rising slowly from his chair. "Thank you for your counsel." He gestured for Cedmon to remain and returned to his room alone.

20

AN ENDING JOURNEY

Seanna busied herself in the court stables, saddling her horse for an early-morning run. *I will take her out for a little while. We both need a diversion this morning, and I will welcome the time alone. I wish to escape these somber feelings from last night, which linger with me this morning.*

The long journey ahead and the details of her departure added to her burdened thoughts.

I hope that once I am in the solitude of the high mountains, this weight will lift and I might begin to feel like myself again.

Cedmon had been able to secure passage for her journey down the river by barge sooner than planned. Now that those were in place, she could leave. Cedmon had not asked whether James would accompany her on the return river journey; he seemed to sense her urgency to leave. She had not shared her thoughts. *It is best that James and I part here.*

She was rubbing the mare's nose, speaking softly to her, when her horse lifted her head at someone's approach. Seanna looked up in surprise to see James advancing toward her.

"You are going for a ride?" he asked.

"Yes, a short one. She needs some exercise." She thought James looked tired; his eyes were dull, lacking their usual sparkle.

James reached out to stroke the mare's mane. "She does seems ready for a new adventure," he said, affectionately scratching the horse's ear.

"I think so," Seanna answered. An awkward moment of silence passed between them, before James spoke again.

"Seeing you in your scout clothes again reminds me of the very first time I saw you," he noted, looking at her. "It seems like a lifetime ago, that day upon the mountain."

James's brow furrowed. He spoke a little abruptly when he announced, "I have decided on some of the details of your departure."

"Which details?" Seanna asked.

"I have made some changes to the arrangements for your journey home," he replied.

"But I have acquired a place on a boat with Cedmon's help," Seanna informed him.

"I know. Cedmon told me, but I took the liberty of altering those plans. I hope you will not mind. I am arranging for your return to your home by sea, along the coastline. I will be comforted to know that you have reached your lands safely."

Seanna's eyes widened with surprise at his words.

"Also, there will be men along the way who will accompany you and chart the passage. You will be able to report to the alliance the beginning of a new trade route between our ports. An envoy is under consideration before the council; he will convey my wishes to begin discussions of a proposed treaty with the alliance council."

Seanna stepped away from her horse, astonished. "Your Grace . . ."

James admonished, "If our overtures to the alliance are not inclusive of the Womara, then maybe Lord Edmond and his son, Stuart, whom you mentioned to me, will be more receptive? I have met with my own council this morning and formalized all the details. Lord Orman is working with particular zeal on your behalf. I feel heartened at his commitment to my directive."

Seanna's stomach churned at the reminder of Lord Orman's words the day before. She took a moment to recover her senses. "I . . . I do not know what to say. It is beyond what I could have hoped for our people. We have never spoken of any such formal arrangements."

James nodded. "Yes, I know, but it is what I want for you: to return with a victory and a path of progress for your clan."

"I am honored and grateful," Seanna stammered.

He swallowed, stepping closer to her. "But . . . I have something to ask. I hope that I may delay your journey for a day."

"Is more time needed for the preparations?" Seanna asked.

"No, preparations are being made. This delay is my request. There is something I want to show you."

Seanna stroked her horse's nose so that James could not see the conflict on her face. She had started the day resolved to leave, but his announcement changed everything.

He continued, "I want to take you somewhere sacred to me, a couple of hours on horseback from here. Your journey will be delayed by a day at the most."

Seanna stood quietly, trying to gather her thoughts. *What is so urgent about his request?*

"This place you wish for me to see—can you tell me more?"

"I would rather show you. We can leave soon," James offered.

Seanna searched his face. "Yes, we will go, then, if you wish," she answered.

"I will find Cedmon to inform him that we will depart within the hour." James bowed his head, before turning to leave.

James and Seanna rode their horses along a familiar path, leaving the boundaries of the palace and traveling into the open country-side. There were miles of green, open land and blooming flowers that blanketed the hills in yellow as far as the eye could see.

Seanna's mood was guarded and did not match the enthusiasm of her horse, who was snorting at the new smells, prancing, and express-ing her delight to be exploring again. Seanna's uneasiness about her delayed departure began to lessen as she relaxed into the beauty of the landscape before her. Her eyes could linger on James's form unob-served as he rode ahead of her, but she could not repress her regret that they did not have more time to explore this countryside together.

They approached a vast marsh filled with wild fowl and watched as the birds rose, taking flight by the hundreds. James turned to Seanna in delight at the sight, and her heart ached at his smiling face. The ride appeared to be a welcome respite for him as well. He had seemed lost in thought, and they had spoken little since they had left the palace.

Could this be the purpose of this journey? she wondered. *A final remembrance of the things we appreciate most and the bond between us?*

They traveled toward the fringes of the forest in the distance, before diverting from the path into a small meadow. A herd of deer, startled by their approach, bounded into the trees. Across the meadow, Seanna saw a well-worn trail leading to a rustic cottage nestled among the pines.

James turned and smiled, pointing to their destination. They crossed the clearing, dismounted in front of the cottage, and tied up their horses inside a simple wooden pen. Seanna looked around at the tranquil scene, enjoying the scent of the trees, and turned toward the sound of a stream in the distance that reminded her of her own home. She glanced at James with a question on her lips: *Why are we here?*

"This was a place where my parents and I spent time together away from court life," James said. He opened the door, and they stepped into a single, open room with a low, beamed ceiling, oak floorboards, and a stone fireplace at its center. A large bed rested in the corner on a slightly raised platform, covered with a colorful quilt. On the other side of the room were a smaller bed and a bookshelf, which held several books. In the center of the room sat a small table and three chairs, a counter for preparing food, and sideboards for storage. The small-paned windows over the counter opened outward to the window boxes, now empty of flowers.

"It has been several years since I visited here. It was difficult for my father to come after my mother passed, but as a family we spent many wonderful hours here."

Seanna smiled as she glanced around the room, but turned back with a questioning look at her face.

James paused. "I have never told you much about my mother. This place was her favorite, too. She would sit for hours, sewing or wandering to gather flowers, waiting for my father and me to return from our hunt. We would bring a few rabbits," he added with a laugh, "but she would always praise our catch and make us a stew for our dinner that evening."

Seanna ran her fingertips over the wooden counter, imagining the happy scene, listening.

"I never realized how skillfully she wove the lessons of life and manhood for me into her simple stories and conversations while we walked through the forest, searching for mushrooms or just sitting by a stream. She taught me to listen and express my feelings, and her standard determined everything that I came to regard as worthy in a woman."

"I would have liked to know her, for I see her influence in her son," Seanna replied, swallowing back her emotion.

James looked around the room again with an expression of sadness. "I have so many memories here."

"This is a place of good memories," Seanna spoke. "I can see you here with your family. Is this what you wanted to share with me?"

"Yes, in part," he answered. "So that you might know a deeper part of who I am."

"I know the man you are, James." Seanna stopped herself from saying more and quickly looked away.

They stepped outside, and James gestured her to look up into the limbs of a large tree. High in the boughs was a wooden platform, with a ladder on the ground ascending into the limbs. "My childhood fortress," James announced proudly. "My father and I built it together. If its branches could speak, they would share some of my grandest proclamations."

He smiled but seemed nervous. He cleared his throat and said, "I brought something to eat. There is a small meadow over there where we can sit."

Seanna looked up into the tree boughs and said, "Let's climb into your fort and eat there."

James laughed, making Seanna laugh, too, relieving their tension as they ascended the ladder and sat on the landing. The shade of the tree was cool as she looked out through the leaves to the meadow beyond, and the only sounds she heard were those of the stream and the distant cry of a crow.

Seanna gazed up into the canopy and turned to James. "I like your fort. I have a favorite tree such as this at my own home, a sanctuary where I have spent many hours sitting, too."

"So you and I, worlds apart, sat very much the same way," James answered, as Seanna looked into his eyes, considering his words.

"I have done some of my most serious thinking up here," he said. "From this humble platform, I envisioned myself ruling the world." He paused for a moment, "And what did you think about in your tree, Seanna?"

Seanna glanced around at her surroundings. "My thoughts were not so grand, and certainly not that I would rule the world." She laughed. "But maybe I thought I would change a small piece of it," she added.

James's expression turned serious. "I would like to see your world sometime," he replied, looking back into her eyes.

"Of course," she stammered. "I am remiss in not having extended an invitation to you sooner. You are most welcome anytime. It would be my honor to have you as my guest."

"You are not remiss. We have had little time to discuss such things. Maybe I will come someday," James replied, "and I will sit with you in your favorite tree."

Seanna's smile faded at the reminder of her departure. *In this moment, I do not want to think of the obligations that await my return. James and I have lives that are bound by duty. But will I ever be able to return to the way my life was before? Something has changed in me. There are things I have not shared with him, parts of my life that I want to tell him. But now I think that time has run out for both of us.*

They finished their food in silence as the afternoon sun waned. James knew that the time to leave was soon if they were to return to the palace before dark. They climbed down out of the tree, and he stood before his horse, fiddling with the saddlebag, unable to summon his courage as he stared in the direction of the meadow.

He swallowed hard, before turning to Seanna, saying, "I have one final thing I would like to show you before we go."

Seanna look at him questioningly.

"This way." James spoke quickly, before he could change his mind, and led the way along a path to the meadow. He was breathing quickly, aware of Seanna's presence behind him, as he slowed down and stepped from the path.

In the clearing was a circle of spiraling stones, and within the center stood a large stack of logs. The structure that he had built was a replica of the sacred fire Seanna had described to him a year earlier.

Seanna froze in her steps. "Is this a jest?" She turned to him, her eyes flashing in anger.

"No! No, it is not," James answered, chastened by the harshness of her voice. "Let me explain."

Seanna's face was flushed as she stood facing him, her eyes searching his, demanding an explanation. James reached out to touch her, but she stepped away from his reach.

"After our last parting, did you return to the ritual fires?" he asked.

Seanna stepped farther back, her face shocked by his question. "What is this? Why must you know?"

"It is important to me," James pleaded.

Seanna clenched her jaw. "Yes, I did," she answered coldly.

He lowered his eyes and did not speak. *Then I have meant nothing to her.*

No words passed between them for a moment, as his panic intensified. Then he implored, "Please hear my words," and he stepped closer.

Seanna had turned from him, staring at the unlit bonfire, fighting back her tears. Her head pounded, and her heart was beating so loudly, she was sure James could hear it as she continued to stare at the inert logs, feeling her blood rise.

James placed his hand cautiously on her shoulder, and she allowed him to turn her slowly to face him. She could not hide the tears that had welled in her eyes. *How could you toy with me? Is this a seduction and your final conquest?* She stood rigid before him, the tears clouding her vision.

"Seanna, please . . . I have not known how to tell you what I am feeling . . . what I have been feeling since the moment we first met, although those emotions sustained me throughout the time we spent apart."

His voice faltered, but he resumed: "At times, I was so unsure of myself that I thought my recollections of what had occurred on those rocky slopes must be mine alone. I knew when I had returned from those mountaintops that I had met the most amazing woman—a woman I could never forget."

Seanna held her breath as she listened.

"I thought that in my remembrances I had conjured a great fantasy of you, but the moment we reunited, I knew it was all true," he continued. "We have shared many aspirations and thoughts together, but I have found myself struggling to express even the simplest of sentiments to you."

He searched her face. "And now you are leaving, and there still seems to be so much left to say. I have squandered my time and lacked the courage to tell you my truth. Your return home will leave an empty place in my very being, and my life will never be the same."

He moved closer to her. "This fire represents my hopes, my desire, to honor your sacred rituals. I did not know how else to show you my heart. It is my proposal of love."

Seanna choked back her emotion as the tears welled up in her eyes again, and she could not calm the pounding in her chest. Her awareness slowed as her entire life seemed to distill into a single instant; thoughts of duty and obligation, the faces of Lord Arden, her mother, and her clanswomen, all seemed to pass before her eyes. The back of her neck tingled, the fine hairs standing on end at the knowledge that something was happening to her beyond her sensory perception.

James stood before her, his brow etched with concern, waiting.

She released her held breath as calm flowed through her body like water moving over rocks in a river. All thoughts passed away as she felt herself surrender. She lifted her face to look him in the eyes. "I did return to the fires, but not for what you are thinking."

James looked puzzled.

"It was an act of seeking," she continued. "I did not recognize my feelings or understand what I was looking for at the time, but now I know that I searched for a familiar likeness across the flames."

"I don't understand," James said.

"I always turned away from the fires, disappointed, never finding the one resemblance, the one face, I wished to see more than any other," Seanna answered, her face illuminated with the understanding.

"Whose face did you seek?" James asked, his eyes alive with hope.

"Yours," she answered. "It was your face I wanted to see across the firelight more than any other."

James took one stride forward and gathered her to him. She placed her hands upon his chest, feeling his beating heart. He gently touched her face, wiping her tears away with his fingertips, drawing her closer still. Never taking his eyes from hers, he kissed her, softly at first and then more deeply. He drew her arms up to encircle his shoulders. He kissed her face and neck with passionate longing, and she yielded to his embrace.

James released his grasp on her, catching his breath and stepping back slightly, steadying himself. Seanna's eyes beckoned, silently asking why he had stopped.

James was beaming. "It will be dark soon, and the moon is rising." As he glanced at the logs, he took her hands in his, kissing them softly. "I have thought of this moment for so long, and of how I want our beginning to be. Shall I light the fire, my love?"

"Yes. Yes," she said.

As night descended, Cedmon sat waiting with the king's guards at the boundary of the forest in their makeshift camp. In the distance, he saw a swirl of smoke rising into the sky and smiled. Turning to the guards, he ordered, "Settle in, men. We'll make camp here for the night."

James had lit the fire and waited. The flames began to blaze and rose in contrast with the dark blue night sky and the sprinkling of pale stars across its vast canvas. The moon was rising, low on the horizon. He thought he had never seen such a beautiful night or anything more exquisite than the vision of Seanna emerging from the path.

Her body was wrapped in a single cloth, her shoulders and arms bare, and her hair, unbound, flowed around her shoulders.

Look at her . . . She moves like an untamed wild animal, but she comes to me freely. I think I now understand the great mystery my father spoke of, the essence of what a man and woman can be— what they are meant to be to each other. My heart is hers.

Seanna's own heart beat wildly as she stepped from the path into the clearing. The cool air caressed her almost-naked skin. James stood waiting for her, and she looked into his eyes across the dancing light of the flames.

This is my destiny. He is my destiny.

THE STORY CONTINUES . . .

Coming Soon!

WARRIOR RISING

Visit JLNicely.com and sign up for updates and news.

ACKNOWLEDGMENTS

To my brother, Douglas, who was my first reader and has been one of the biggest supporters of "the story": without your encouragement from the onset, I am not sure that I would have had the courage to continue writing.

To my dear friend Linda Ketenjian, who allowed me to read an entire early draft of the book to her over the course of several evenings: reading the story aloud as you listened was magical.

To Donna Aikins, you were a constant source of encouragement. Your regular check-ins, combined with your enthusiasm, kept me going.

To my family and special friends who were my readers: Pam Darling, Tina Zmack, Lisa Hill, Angela Rast, Craig Spencer, and Claire Nicely, your constructive comments and at times tough feedback helped shaped this book.

Special thanks to my fellow writers Tina Zmack, author of the *Dark Surf* series, and Anita Kaltenbaugh (A. K. Smith), author of *A Deep Thing*, two authors who have gone before me and who generously gave their support and guidance.

Annie Tucker, my editor, never let me off the hook and pushed for more in my writing. Check her out at www.annietuckerpublishing.com.

Brooke Warner, publisher for She Writes Press and the president of Warner Coaching Inc., whose patience with my early stumbling of authorship and whose invaluable network of referrals have contributed to this book's completion.

Thanks to my support team: Katelynn Finnie, who worked on design, photography, and general production, and Lisa Hill, my assistant, who kept me on track and sane.

ABOUT THE AUTHOR

J.L. Nicely was born in the United Kingdom to an English mother and an American father. In early years she lived on military air bases and also spent time at her grandparents house on the outskirts of London. It was there, roaming the surrounding woods, parks, streams, and ponds—quiet places, mystical and old—that the seeds of her imaginative stories took hold. In her musings, she conjured magical ports to other worlds, where fairies, water babies, and enchanted creatures lived. The forest-dwelling of the Womara is a reflection of her deep love of all things green.

She now lives on the California Monterey Peninsula and is currently writing the second book of The Womara series.

32927883R00165

Printed in Great Britain
by Amazon